THE SNARL OF THE BEAST

Books by Carroll John Daly:

THE HIDDEN HAND

THE SNARL OF THE BEAST

THE SNARL OF
THE BEAST

CARROLL JOHN DALY

HarperPerennial

A Division of HarperCollins*Publishers*

First HarperPerennial edition published 1992.

LIBRARY OF CONGRESS CATALOG CARD NUMBER 91-58475

ISBN 0-06-097435-4

92 93 94 95 96 MB 10 9 8 7 6 5 4 3 2 1

To
My Boy
JACK DALY

Contents

THE SNARL OF THE BEAST

1

The Attack

It's the point of view in life that counts. For an ordinary man to get a bullet through his hat as he walked home at night would be something to talk about for years. Now, with me; just the price of a new hat—nothing more. The only surprise would be for the lad who fired the gun. He and his relatives would come in for a slow ride, with a shovelful of dirt at the end of it. I can take a joke, of course, but my sense of humor isn't fully enough developed along those lines. I have brains, I suppose. We all have. But a sharp eye, a quick draw, and a steady trigger finger drove me into the game. Also you might add to that an aptitude for getting out of trouble almost as quickly as I get into it.

Under the laws I'm labeled on the books and licensed as a private detective. Not that I'm proud of that license but I need it, and I've had considerable trouble hanging onto it. My position is not exactly a healthy one. The police don't like me. The crooks don't like me. I'm just a halfway house between the law and crime; sort of working both ends against the middle. Right and wrong are not written on the statutes for me, nor do I find my code of morals in the essays of long-winded professors. My ethics are my own. I'm not saying they're good and I'm not admitting they're bad, and what's more I'm not interested in the opinions of others on that subject. When the time comes for some quick-drawing gunman to jump me over the hurdles I'll ride to the Pearly Gates on my own ticket. It won't be a pass written on the back of another man's thoughts. I stand on my own legs and I'll shoot it out with any gun in the city—any time, any place. Thirty-fourth street and Broadway, in the five o'clock rush hour, isn't barred either. Race Williams—Private Investigator—tells the whole story. Right! Let's go.

It's dark and the street lamps on the dirty little street of the lower East Side do no more than throw a dull shadow about a small splash of light. I'm not looking for trouble but that don't mean that I'm not expecting it. I always am. I get as many death threats as a movie star gets mash notes. The rats of the underworld are my natural enemies, and there I am in the very heart of the criminal hangout. So I play close to the curb and throw a swagger into my walk. Outward confidence always registers with the unsavory gentlemen of the night.

There are few people pounding the pavements; some loitering in ill-smelling doorways beneath the street level. Nothing suspicious about any of them; that is, a personal suspicion—yet I know that some one is getting my smoke. Some one is playing the lamb to my little Mary. Nothing tangible, you understand, and no way to explain it. Just instinct warns me that I am followed. It may be the police or a crook with a guilty conscience, or just one of the boys who recognizes me and stalks along in the hope of settling a private vengeance by a bit of murder. Then another figure, running along the sidewalk across the street, beating his hands against the cold, is swallowed up in the darkness.

I shrug my shoulders and plod on. I'm well known in that section of the city; a lad won't chance a shot unless he's so close he can't miss. And the man following me knows that he'll get only one shot. While he holds his distance there is no complaint. When he gets too close I'll have to lead him down a back alley and kiss him goodnight. Nothing alarming. It's an old story to me.

As I move nearer to the East River and a distant clock drones one, the lurking shadows of human forms disappear from the street. It's not the hour so much as the bitter cold. Somewhere below the level of the street the tin-pan notes of a piano drift faintly into the night. A man curses and a window slams. Far distant an ash can clatters on stone and the almost human screech of a cat pierces, shrilling through the zero night.

Then silence, but for the soft tramp of my rubber heels and the hardly audible echo of heels behind me. I don't have to turn to know that my shadow has quickened his pace and now takes two steps to my one; fast, short strides of a heavy body that swings from side to side. Things were getting interesting. I slipped off my thick gloves and wound my fingers about the heavy forty-four in my coat pocket. Then I shot a glance back over my shoulder and caught the dull outline of the swinging figure who was unconsciously hurrying toward a yawning grave. Big, almost massive hunched shoulders, brown cap, and hands sunk in the pockets of a great coat that was wrapped tightly about his body.

And that was all I saw of him. I turned back sharply again, for other feet sounded upon stone steps, then pounded over the pavement toward me. Just a derelict of the night he appeared, shuffling toward me—his right hand outstretched, his left hanging by his side with the palm toward me. He carried no weapon, there was no threat in his approach and his manner was cringing, his body stooped, his voice with a whine in it.

"Two bits for a flop, Mister." The voice was low and shook slightly. He didn't like the part he was playing. And I didn't blame him. The temptation to lift my gun and smack him one was strong but I didn't. It wasn't a big heart or a sensitive conscience that made me hesitate. Just common sense and the hope of a long life. So I resisted temptation, put business before pleasure and saved this bird a ride in an ambulance.

I never had a doubt; wasn't fooled for a moment by the eager hand, the whining voice and the sunken hungry eyes.

His hunger wasn't of the stomach. This was the slouching, running figure that had passed down the street at the last corner, and ducking across had waited my approach in a convenient alleyway. Well planned perhaps. It probably had worked hundreds of times before. But this time they were going to come a cropper. You couldn't pocket Race Williams between two enemies like that; leastwise, you couldn't and get away with it. The thing was too simple. The panhandler was to hold my attention while my shadow was to spring me from behind. Believe me, I threw a monkey wrench into the works. I gave these birds a surprise.

The shabby lad's hand was hardly out before the man behind changed his jerky walk to a run. But if he acted quickly, I was just a bit ahead of him. My left hand shot out and clutched the extended arm before me. My right pulled a rod, and before my whining friend was sure just what had happened I was behind him, my gun playing a tattoo up and down his spine as he stood silently trembling between me and my rushing shadow.

There was a curse as the big boy who had been shadowing me hurled himself forward—skidded to a stop before he crashed his friend and stood still; a shadowy, mountainous mass in the darkness. But the hand that he still held in the air was clearly visible—so was the short section of iron pipe that white, knotted fist held.

"Easy does it." I tried to peer over the shabby man's shoulder and get a look at the face beneath the brown cap. It was an ugly, evil map—what I could see of it. Gleaming, shining animal-like eyes; thick lips above heavy jowls, that were lost in the collar of the great coat which was buttoned tightly about his neck. But his arm was the thing. He had a reach on him like a gorilla. The lead pipe was high enough in the air, but that arm was slightly bent. It was the other that I noted—imagination, I thought at first. Just a trick of the darkness, as I made out the whiteness of thick twitching fingers reaching to the man's knees.

But it wasn't imagination; for as I watched, those fingers

4

closed into a fist—a fist that slowly began to rise and stretch out beside the man whose back I tickled with my gun. Uncanny, it was there in the darkness. You couldn't really distinguish the arm that led from the hand to the shoulder; that was lost in the background of the dark coat. Just a knotted fist seemed to be floating through the air; slowly, but surely and steadily, toward me. The raised hand too was sweeping down by inches.

Uncanny certainly—odd that a human being should have such a reach. But there was nothing to fear really. An embarrassing time perhaps, if I had to explain the shooting to the police. I've explained so often that it's getting monotonous to me—to the law too, for that matter. Judges were looking at me with suspicion. Never anything to hang on me, you understand. But one learned jurist had told me grimly that if I made it a steady practice to appear before him to explain any more little shootings in the night he'd give me a stretch on the principle of the thing. That he would was certain enough. That he could was another matter. But besides the annoyance, there was the expense of a high class lawyer. Good mouthpieces may be worth the money all right—and earn it too—but they put an awful dig in the bank account just the same. And at present my balance at the bank was about as low as the mercury in the thermometer. But back to that hand!

"Young man," I shoved my gun deeper into the generous back before me, "advise your friend that if he isn't more careful of those itching fingers of his I'll lay a row of lead buttons up and down your spine. Come—speak up!" Those hands were still doing their stuff—one of them out by the derelict's shoulder as the head of the awkward, waving creature shoved slightly forward and his feet shuffled on the sidewalk.

"Lay off that stuff." The shabby man shot the words toward his companion. Was it a command or a request? I couldn't tell at first. The hand stopped for a moment; hung so by the other's shoulder. Then the fingers opened slightly and it came on again; the huge carcass moving slightly so that it

5

was partly protected from me by the lad between us.

"Back, you!" The panhandler jerked out the words. And there was no doubt of their meaning. Neither a request nor a command, but a plea in his voice—and then again. "You fool—stop it—drop those hands. Drop them—I say." And this time the whine in his voice was real. But there was more than just reality—fear, horror were all in his screech; his words echoing down the street. He had lost his head altogether. Now he appealed to me.

"Don't shoot me," he cried, his words trembling and rattling in his throat. "I can't stop him—I can't stop him. Look at his eyes."

And I did. They were shining like an animal's; like a cat's—clearly the green stood out in them. For the first time in my life I got a shudder. It was almost as if I could see things behind those eyes, as if I looked down into a reeking mass of rottenness. No way to describe it. I shuddered, yes—with revulsion, not fear. I'm not made to fear a man. It just don't come natural to me, I guess. But more than the eyes I watched the hand, the heavy shoulders, the protruding head—the sudden outward thrust of a great chin.

I swung my gun up and over the shoulder of the whiner.

"Listen, big boy," and there was no question nor pleading in my voice, "if you don't control that laudable desire to fasten your hands on my neck and won't listen to the kindly, fatherly advice of your dirty friend—and don't think anything of your life—why—" and I cut my speech, for the man was swinging slowly from side to side—crouching slightly and getting ready to hurl that huge body forward.

"One more move and I'll plug the two of you," I said sharply—and I meant it.

"He don't understand—don't care," the other man bellowed. "Lead won't stop him—when he's like that, nothing can stop him. Run for it, Race Williams—RUN." And this time his shout was fit to wake the dead.

There may be men with charmed lives; men that lead won't stop, but I have yet to meet them. The dirty lad may

6

have been right, but if I were a betting man I'd lay pretty good odds that at the first bark of my gun a useless mass of flesh would lie on the sidewalk. It was his party, not mine. As for running—well, the bullet-proof man who can pump lead into my dust isn't born yet.

The giant didn't stop; didn't fade back as I poked my rod forward, and what's more he didn't care much for his friend's life. He bent low, protecting his own body—shot his raised hand down, grasped his friend with it and thrust that other hand out toward my neck. I could have given ground and avoided it but I didn't. When I jump I jump forward, not backward. I raised the muzzle of my gun slightly and pressed the trigger. A bullet tore up that flapping coat sleeve. Only a scratch it would give him, but it was the warning of certain and sudden death to follow.

His body may have been bullet-proof. I didn't know about that. But his arm certainly wasn't, and his brain was susceptible to pain. For the moment I thought he wasn't a man at all. There was a grunt, an animal-like snarl, and an ear-splitting agonized screech of rage.

We just stood so—the three of us. The dirty lad, uncertain—his hands half raised in the air. The Terror was bent double, nursing his injured arm and giving queer groans and snarls. And I—I just swung my gun from one to the other, waiting. The show was on—would they continue with the play or ring down the curtain? As for me—I just wanted a good look at that evil face that was buried in great arms. Would I get that look? I thought not. This was New York, and gun shots were no novelty—they were expected and— We all three came erect.

2

A Dead Police Officer

A whistle cut the silence—a low sharp note from far down the block. But it sounded like a great ship's blast to the three of us. Somewhere above us a window shot up and a voice called hoarsely. There was another and another—an answering whistle—running feet—the pounding of clubs, and the play broke up.

I let Dirty-Boy go first. He sort of dashed out into the middle of the street, saw a door open at the top of a few steps before him, and came back again. He called to his friend; cursed when the man just stood there, his head raised as if he sniffed the air. And I was off—down the block—close to the light near the corner when the wagon swung around. There was no clang of bells to warn me, no toot of a screeching siren—just the sudden chug of a motor, the grinding of brakes, and a cry for me to halt.

And I did. Was the game up? I had a good story to tell. I didn't like it of course—this being dragged in by the cops; but most of all my appointment in the night. I couldn't keep that now, and I always make a point of keeping my engagements.

And the game wasn't up. A door opened close beside me; a figure looked out—the frightened, white face of a disturbed householder. They would all be disturbed in that neighborhood, I guess. There was hardly a house you couldn't search and grab yourself off evidence of one kind or another. If there wasn't something criminal involved—why, you could find a still, or at least a few bottles of liquor.

It wasn't exactly the open door that decided me, nor it wasn't the man who looked up that made me hesitate. My friend of the snarl; the lad with the supposedly bullet-proof body had run after me, willing to finish out our little misunderstanding. Mad with pain and rage, he came pounding over the sidewalk. His breath hissed like escaping steam; the moan on his lips was like the snarl of a wounded beast.

He brought up sharply too when the police ducked around the corner, and now he skidded slightly; made the turn; lit straight for the doorway and the figure who stood paralyzed with fear in the dim light.

The man in the doorway recovered slightly, but too late. The door that he frantically tried to close was crashed in upon him. He was knocked to the floor, and the hurtling giant tramped over his body. As for me, I had a little more respect for the honest and curious citizen. I jumped his prostrate form. For I too suddenly decided to seek liberty in flight. There would be a pretty story if I were caught. I was only doing my duty in pursuing the man who had held me up and threatened my life.

The cops were on the job; fearless men followed us into the narrow hall; feet beat close to mine, and mine beat close on the running man ahead. He knew his way, I thought; at least, those pounding feet never hesitated.

There was a cry from the pursuing police, a warning to halt, and a shot; then an answering one from the man ahead as he turned and fired. Nice little place I had picked; the spitting streaks of orange blue flame seemed to meet right beside me. If the boys kept this up I'd be lucky if I only stopped a bullet coming one way. I ducked low as I ran now, hugging close to the wall.

There was the crash of glass, the splintering of wood, the dimness of a winter sky and the towering dirty tops of blurred tenements—and I crashed out into the night. Crashed, was right. The broken, twisted door tripped me and I landed flat up against the railing of the frail back steps that led to the stone yard below. The railing groaned, cracked, then swayed slightly as I clutched for support an "upright." It held as the railing itself gave from the force of another body. The pursuing policeman had done as I had done; dashed blindly over the door, caught his foot and shot forward.

But he was not as fortunate as I. For he pitched headlong to the stones several feet below. I could hear the thud of his body and hear too the dull, unmistakable ring as his head struck the hard stone. Feet pounded against wood there across the court. I didn't see the figure of the giant, but I knew that he sought the fence behind and freedom in the block beyond.

As for me! In a dazed way I struggled to my feet, slightly shaken up—too much so to pursue my foe. Yet I must—for in that lay safety. My head cleared, the blood rushed from it back into my body, and stepping over the débris on the little stoop I stopped dead and shot my hands into the air. Fool! I might have known. More than one policeman had followed us.

A bright light struck upon my face—there was a gruff order to throw up my hands, and behind the flash I caught the reflection of the brass buttons of a New York cop. Bad men to fool with—them. I didn't need to see the gun, for I felt it digging into my chest. My hands just shot above my head before the gruff order to throw up my hands was given. Then his voice—and this time I knew the man; and what was more, he knew me.

"Race Williams." I could feel rather than see the lips curl, and I knew too that his body stretched forward and that his flash for a second lit upon the crumpled heap of his brother officer below.

"You'll pay for this." I knew that his lips curled. Sergeant Rafferty was not one of my friends. But there was real feeling and not just vengeance in his voice as he continued. "I've always known that you ran contrary to the law. But I never could prove it. To-night—" The flash trembled as it swayed from me to the man on the stones below. "You'll have trouble explaining that, and—"

I heard the shot, perhaps even felt the purr of the bullet but of that one can never be certain. Another sound too that might just as well have been imagination. I thought that I heard a laugh; a gurgling, distant sort of a laugh, that seemed to have a growl in it—like an animal—like the snarl of a beast. Sergeant Rafferty broke off suddenly in his speech. His lips smacked, followed by a queer sound deep down in his chest. The light slipped from his fingers, and striking my foot rolled to the stoop. Then he slumped, crumpled up and slid slowly down upon the broken glass and the twisted wood.

I never liked the sergeant, but he went out as a man should. The gun was still clutched in lifeless, useless fingers. Even in death he didn't drop that gun. Death? Yes, he was dead all right. His head lay close to the flash and the rays shone full upon his face. But it was his eyes that told the story, more so than the trickle of red from beneath the collar of his uniform. Unseeing, glassy orbs looked unblinkingly into the glare.

I didn't lose my head, and it wasn't the stirring of the man on the pavement below that decided me, nor the hoarse calling voices in the yard next door. In the fraction of a second I weighed the possibility of flight and the wisdom of staying to face the music. Sergeant Rafferty was known as my enemy. Sergeant Rafferty was dead. What would be the caliber of the bullet found in his head? A forty-four? Maybe! There would be but one bullet missing from my gun and the man who carried that bullet had disappeared into the night. Oh, I know that there are experts who can tell from just what make and caliber of gun a bullet has been fired. But experts are known to favor the prosecution, and scientific statements of denial also are known to lull jurors into deep slumber. The police

11

and I don't fit in together. I didn't wish a trial; a man's freedom often hangs on his past record, and my past was a beaut and no mistake.

Strange, you think, that I should figure all this out in the "panic" of finding a dead police officer at my feet. But there wasn't any panic. There never is with me at such a time. A man needs a clear head then. No one had seen my face—that is, no one but the dead police officer, and no one else was likely to if I played the game now. It was simply a question of finding the hole in the police lines before they discovered their dead brother and spread a net that even an alley cat couldn't get through. This was a question of minutes—perhaps seconds, if you figure closely.

People were shouting; lights were bobbing up—a few fear-crazed foreigners ventured from their rooms. There was enough running around to confuse any one. It was like a meeting of the League of Nations. Questions were shouted in one tongue to be answered in another. Half a dozen languages filled the air like a cheap radio set. Heavy feet trod on old boards. A deep Irish voice called a command. Another answered with a curse as his knees crashed a bannister.

There was only one way of escape—to follow the gigantic figure who had killed the cop. If his passage was blocked he might clear a way for me, but it was hardly possible that the street behind was already covered by the police.

With me the thought is the act. Crouching low, I ducked down those back steps and shot across the stone yard in the rear, toward the wooden fence. A woman screamed; a window crashed up; a voice called—and looking over my shoulder I saw the burly figure of a policeman framed in a lighted window of the second story. One hand was placed on the sill, the other clutched an automatic. His white face stretched out as he tried to pierce the darkness.

There was the crash of wood as another reached the back stoop—a cry of horror that turned almost at once to one of rage. Rafferty had been found! The message snapped quickly from him on the porch to him in the window. Distant

12

voices echoed the cry within the building.

The white hand left the sill, a dart of light flashed through the darkness and splashed upon the wooden fence before me. There was a thud of heavy feet and I knew that the giant's head had just dropped from the fence where he had crouched, watching the play—watching me perhaps. A desperate man that. He had waited to get me if the police failed. Even after murdering the sergeant, he still sought my life. A paid murderer or one who sought private vengeance? But it didn't matter then—I had other things to think about.

The darting flash light shot frantically about the little court; swept over my face on to the fence—hesitated and came back again. I was smack in the light.

I heard the man in the window call; saw his gun raise too—and I fired. I didn't try to hit him. I'm not a murderer. But my shot was close enough to let him know that a man in a lighted window, bent on gun play, doesn't hold an enviable position. The glass smashed above him, fell upon his head and came tumbling down into the court. He fired once—wildly, I guess, for his head ducked back from the window and I did not hear the bullet strike; simply the crack of his gun—nothing more. Then his head disappeared from the window and the light went out.

Five seconds—perhaps ten—before that flash would go into play again. That would be enough, I thought—at least, I hoped. There was the fence just before me, dark and foreboding, with the dull outline of the top of it stretching along the blackness like the horizon across the distant ocean. A bad moment then. I'd need two hands for that fence. In the time it would take to jump, grasp the fence and swing over I would be at the mercy of the police behind and the killer ahead, if he waited in the rear yard of the house on the next block. Get the idea! When I made my leap I'd have to pocket my gun. I'm strong, husky, agile, and all that—but I'm no circus performer and I'd need both hands to hop that fence. Oh, I've heard of guns being temporarily parked between the teeth and I'm not denying that there may be men who can do it, even outside the motion pictures. But for me—I just pocketed that gun, reached the fence, made the leap, grasped the top and swung up on it.

Just the fraction of a second I hung there, but that fraction of a second was too much. The police had played the game well—well or cautiously, I don't know which. At least, they didn't dash blindly into the yard after me. They got to work with their flashes. The one flash was back at the window now and another shot from the rear porch where Rafferty lay dead. Luck! Yes, they had it, for both flashes seemed to light on me at the same time. They just made one mistake—over-cautious that they get the right man. People were screaming and running about now; a shrieking woman dashed into the yard and the police hesitated. And that was my cue.

Then they fired; three shots came almost as one—funny how they all made up their minds together. Two of the shots hit the fence. One seemed to nick the top of it where I had been the split second before—the other tore through the thick boards and pinged against the house. But I—I was dashing across the yard beyond; into the little alleyway toward the next street.

There were running feet ahead of me, I thought—heavy feet, yet feet that struck lightly on the pavement. Hard to explain, that? Perhaps. But it struck me as if the man ahead had removed his shoes, and now the weight of his great body was softened by the even tread of stockinged feet. He panted too, I thought, and once I caught the hiss of his breath—a whining, snarling sort of hiss. Then silence, as I passed through the alley and reached the next block.

The street was deserted. No lumbering form ran up or down it. Not a sound on that block, but behind me came the sharp blast of a whistle and the distant shrill notes of voices. I breathed easier. There is no forest more impenetrable, no place as easy for a man to hide in, as the teeming tenements of New York's East Side. I was safe!

14

3

The Police Are Curious

It would be too much to hope for a cruising taxi in that neighborhood, even at that time of night. So I only gave a glance for one. And I didn't walk easily down the block, like an honest citizen. Not me—I know the ropes too well; the police methods too, for that matter. There would be a call sent in and a dozen men on that block in another minute or two. They'd comb that neighborhood with a fine tooth comb. About the other lad I didn't know, but that they wouldn't find me there was certain.

I loped easily across the street, entered the alleyway opposite, and keeping in the shadows passed to the back of another tenement, through the yard behind and so on to the next block. This process I repeated for three more blocks. Unnecessary so much caution, you think. Perhaps. But then, I'm a cautious man. Since I had fled the scene of Sergeant Rafferty's murder I'd have a lot of explaining to do, and I much preferred that another than I explained that little bit of killing. Gigantic figures that waylay people on the street and kill policemen in mistake for you are not the sort of bed time stories that are swallowed by the police. Lord knows they're gullible enough, without trying to feed them that sort of stuff.

Through the last alley, dodging the last ash can, I came out upon the open street and walked leisurely down it toward the East River. I wasn't over four blocks from my destination—a disreputable neighborhood down by the docks. The letter in my pocket was explicit enough—there was the street and number, and also a description of the house—though that description might fit half a dozen of the shabby holes along the water front.

As I walked along I gave considerable thought to that letter. Was it a trap? Had the attack on me followed quickly upon the letter? Had they been laying for me on the deserted block? But hardly that. The panhandler or the giant could not have guessed I'd come that way, a good half dozen blocks above my destination. No—I had been followed. The boy that tried to shake me down for a "flop" had crossed the street and ducking back waited for me.

Many wanted my life but most of them have taken it out in feeble, half-hearted attempts at ambush. This time things were different. I shrugged my shoulders, broke open my gun, ejected the two empty shells and slipped in fresh bullets. I'd clean her up when I got home. It looked like it was going to be open season for Race Williams. All the yeggs who made threats against my life must have passed New Year's resolutions to finish the job at once.

I dismissed the idea that the letter writer had attempted to trap me—that I was now booked to enter a darkened hallway and be shot down. The letter wasn't clever enough for that—and besides, there wasn't a penny sent in it. My enemies have single-track brains. Race Williams was hard boiled, out for the almighty dollar—it would never enter their heads that I'd hunt up a case in that neighborhood without first getting the feel of a few century notes. I didn't think I would myself, for that matter. But business was dull. We do strange things—and there I was.

When a thing is done it's done. So I dismissed the incident from my mind. It wasn't the first time my life had been attempted and I'm not stupid enough to think it will be the last. It was simply in the course of business. I was a bit more

16

cautious about being followed, that was all. And I took my time too—sauntered along. If I should happen to be questioned I wouldn't gasp out my answers. After a chase like that, a breathless man would be a suspected man.

My business is like the weather. It clears up if you wait long enough. It's surprising what a lot of trouble there is in the world, and it's generally people with money who have the time to find the pitfalls of life and drop into them. It's up to me to get the rope and haul them out. And to-night I carried a letter—a queer, terse sort of note; but to me there was an air of reality—sincerity—in it. I slipped the letter from my pocket again and peered at it under the street lamp. I knew the address all right—but a harness bull had suddenly popped around the corner and confronted me, less than fifty feet away.

I could have ducked him I suppose, but I'd done enough of that for one night and Race Williams is often asked to explain his presence in such a neighborhood. The cops get used to spotting me, and now—well, he might have recognized me even at that distance and I didn't want to be raked in later and questioned on the murder of Sergeant Rafferty. Besides, as I looked behind me a motor-cycle cop with a boy friend in a side car was slowly slipping up the street. Also the boy in the side car was sporting a machine gun. I just caught the flash of it, but I knew those things and know that they are only trusted in the hands of men who know how to use them. I leaned against the pole and waited.

The motor cycle reached me first, stopped across the street and waited, the man in the side car leaning far out and staring at me with bull dog ferocity. He did it good too. I leaned against the pole beneath the light, pocketed my letter and lit a cigarette.

There's a false impression among the police that an innocent citizen won't notice such an attitude of belligerency, while a crook or a man with a guilty conscience will quake beneath such scrutiny. Of course it works backwards nine times out of ten. The innocent citizen gets nervous and blows

17

up, while the well-trained crook expects it and is prepared for it. And that's often the reason the innocent bystander gets hauled in so much.

In law every man is considered innocent until he is proven guilty, but in fact every man is looked on as guilty until he is proven innocent. And you take that as gospel from one who knows. I'm not quoting from books; I get all my knowledge from life, and when you get a lesson out of life it sticks.

The harness bull on the sidewalk didn't quicken his pace. I was being given time to think. Orders must have gone out quickly to question every one even ten blocks away—perhaps the whole lower city. I puffed my butt and waited. It was old stuff for me. Would this cop know me, and if he did would it hurt or help me? If I proved a stranger to him would he drag me in for the desk sergeant to have a look at? The commissioner was getting mighty particular lately with gun fights a nightly affair in most any section of the city, and the killing of a policeman no longer a national event.

I was deeply interested in my cigarette when the heavy hand fell upon my shoulder and a gruff voice snapped in my ear.

"I'll have a look at that letter you were reading—now!"

"Do you know any more jokes?" I shot the words at him without looking up, but before he could figure out an answer I swung and faced him beneath the light.

"Race Williams," he gasped. Then as the surprised upward curve of his mouth cut quickly down to hard straight lines, "But that'll do you no good. There's been mur—" He cut the word short, bit his lip a second, decided he'd better not say too much, and continued: "Shots and you go together like ham and eggs. I think you'd better have a talk with the sergeant."

"Had a lot of talks lately." I shook his hand from my shoulder. It was funny how he didn't ask to look at the letter again. He knew I knew my rights. "Of course it's up to you to do your duty. You know my business. I'm privately working with the law at present. You know I have good friends at

18

headquarters. Perhaps, after all, you might have to do the explaining." I sort of nodded over at the motor cycle cops. "Now, Delaney, I have business to-night. Young blood—a bad woman and worse whiskey. I won't add that he's a relative of any one in political circles; but his father's got the money to hire me for a job like that and his father must have good friends. Better think it over. Haven't you heard anything lately?"

And he had. So had I, for that matter. The whispered talk of the infatuation of a certain young man for an uncertain young lady. Besides, that man's father was rather well connected—too well connected for Delaney's peace of mind. That I hadn't been approached in the case and wouldn't be apt to touch it with a ten-foot pole if I had been approached didn't matter to me—and wasn't known to Delaney.

It was just a lie of course, but it might very easily have been the truth as far as Delaney was concerned. All the police read my character wrong. Not one of them would believe that I'd turn down a case there was money in, and that I didn't make a business of rescuing the perverted sons of wealth, whose scandalous and sometimes criminal escapades are looked upon as just the acts of big good natured boys having their fling at life.

Delaney was falling—slipping anyway. I saw the nod he gave to the motor cycle lad, who moved slowly away. So I pushed my advantage and added a touch of color to the story.

"It's a thing that won't stand for delay, or the newspapers will grab it. If that's the case I'll know where to lay the blame. Perhaps you can slip that blame along to the desk sergeant. He'll be willing to shoulder it, and no doubt thank you for it." I finished sarcastically.

"You have a tongue on you." Delaney shook his head and smiled. "I'm not one to have anything against your methods of business, Race Williams. I envy you your conscience at times and wish we of the force were allowed a little more loose shooting. There'd be more money in the pension fund then and less widows and fewer orphans." His lips were rather grim and I knew that he was thinking of Rafferty and the wife and children left behind. Delaney had no doubt picked up his information over a police box.

"They can't always hang it on you," he went on, "and they ain't never convicted you when they did get the evidence, but I dare say you've done for many a man who needed a killing. But—" wide blue eyes rested on me as a pudgy finger dug into my chest, "if you're lying to me and have had a hand in what went on to-night we'll know where to find you. I can't keep an eye on you to-night, even if I was so minded, but I'll get word of our meeting to Inspector Coglin, uptown."

With that final shot Delaney was gone. Inspector Coglin was down on me. Jealousy that I had so often succeeded where he had failed, or perhaps a real honest belief that I was more of a criminal than a detective—it didn't make any difference. He had sworn to get me—was laying for my scalp. But every time he had dragged me in for questioning I got my story over to the newspapers, which gave me considerable free advertising and gave Inspector Coglin a bit of the old raspberry. He'd let me alone lately. Vented his spleen on me by making faces and uttering threats. But I still followed my regular routine of business. When I wanted a man I stuck a gun in each pocket and went after him.

4

Within the Tenement Room

Delaney passed from view. The motor cycle cop, with his side kick, had long since disappeared; the street was deserted, but I backed into a near-by doorway and waited a few minutes. My letter writer was particular that I be not followed. He even saw his death if his whereabouts were known. The letter I ran over again in my mind. The wording was simple enough.

"If you will visit me to-night—one-thirty—at (and here was the address) you can render me a great service, which will pay you a great price. The knowledge of certain others of your visit or my whereabouts means my death. I have heard of you. I need you. I can't come to you. My God! Take a chance and come. Third floor, back hall, last door—right.

"D. D."

There's the music, write your own words. The last part told the whole story. Sincerity there? Maybe. Perhaps just a fear— even a hopeless sort of horror. Nearly every week some false case was offered to me. Mostly cheap tricks, where the enclosed check turned out to be no good when I tried to get it certified at the bank, before paying a visit to some lonely country spot. It was funny how these city killers went in for lonely spots in the country. And always the message was to come alone and secretly in the night. Still, most people who have business for me do not have the kind of business that can be shouted from the house tops. Blackmail, a great deal of it. Follies of youth demanding retribution in respectable and wealthy middle age. The skeletons in the closets of "the best people" rattle loudest. Now, I was searching for a client in the worst and cheapest section of the city. This smacked of one who feared the law.

I beat my hands across my chest a few times and started on my way. Another block up and a turn to the left, and I spotted my building. A searching glance up and down the street and I stepped inside, pushed open the door, breathed in a few of the smells, then shut out the winter night. But I didn't shut out the chill—a damp chill that was worse than the bitterness of the cold without.

A dull flickering gas light burned in the rear of the dirty hallway. I leaned against a rocky bannister and waited. Nothing special on my mind, but if the thing was a frame-up, a lad from across the street might drop over, plant himself in the hall and blow me out, coming down. No, I didn't suspect a trap but I was prepared for one just the same. It's not the expected in life that means death, but the unexpected.

Ten minutes were enough. I pulled out my flash, shot a splash of light down the hallway, then up the stairs. Lots of dirt but not enough for a man to hide under. The smells I couldn't see—but I didn't need to. I mounted the first flight of stairs. They creaked. I played the side of them. They creaked louder. I hugged the walls and the old boards still gave up their dead. Not so bad, you understand, but the slightest sound, if you fear a lurking enemy, is magnified to the pounding of a hammer.

The first flight—again my light. More dirt, but still emptiness. The second floor was safely reached and still without trouble, but I didn't get careless. Some guns like to play the ground, others feel safer at jumping roofs. The third floor took me longer to reach—real slow going there, and my gun was shoved into my hand. I'd listen most every step for sounds above or below. And the creaks were hard to place— you'd step on a board that would moan like a child—then another that would squeak like a mouse, and a third perhaps that would creak like a rusty hinge. Seven or eight such flights would get on a man's nerves. I was glad when I reached the top landing—I did my final stuff with the flash held well out to my side. Killers have a way of aiming at lights. I do it myself when dealing with the ordinary crook; and the novice always holds the flash straight before him. The wise man swings it far and wide and high or low. For my part, I always hold the light in my right hand and far to that side. The thinking gunman figures you'll play the gun in the right hand and the light in the left. Therefore he directs his fire to the wrong side of the light. That isn't just mathematical figuring or psychology. It's fact. I'm still alive, to prove it.

Just emptiness on that third floor but for the dirty smells, rounded in with the damp cold. If you wanted atmosphere, it was all there. Thick enough to cut. You could feel, smell and taste the odors that crept all over you like a live slimy thing. I shivered slightly, drew my heavy coat the tighter and pussy-footed it to the back of the hall and the door at the right. Light doused, head pressed close to the door, I listened. A dead silence, then a cough—low, hardly audible, but with a sort of rattle to it.

A minute's wait and I tried the knob; the door was locked. The catch clicked. A sudden squeak from the room within, as if some one had climbed from bed. Feet crossed the floor; bare feet that dragged along like the tread of a small animal. A lock snapped, the knob turned beneath my grasp, and relinquishing my hold on it I stepped back a pace. I was ready for most anything—expected most anything. There isn't much new that can happen to me.

The door swung open a trifle, and clutching my gun I waited for the man's head that would peer out of the darkness.

But no head came, and the door hung open a few inches only. There was just room enough for a man to stick his head out—or in, for that matter. If the party within expected me to oblige him by diving through that opening and getting crowned for my pains, he had a lot to learn yet.

So we waited. I wasn't in a hurry; the lad within was impressed, for his breath came in short, uneven gasps. Twice he cleared his throat—after the last, he spoke. There was a squeak to his voice like the boards of the stairs.

"Mr. Williams?" There was an unmistakable question in his voice. "I—" He started in again and stopped. If he wanted to make the conversation short and snappy I'd give him results.

"Yes," was all I answered.

"You have my letter—with you?" Then in a faint whisper, "D. D."

"Certainly." And before he got out his request for a slant at the paper I shoved it through the opening and dropped it to the floor. That was the first time I spotted the chain that held the door, for he pulled the door back to the full play of the chain and the flickering gas light pierced the darkness. An old rocker, a table that relied more upon the wall for support than it did on its three legs, torn wall paper that had been slapped back on the wall with a thick coating of homemade paste flashed into view.

He'd have to stoop to grasp that letter where I had dropped it. My flash was ready to shove on his face when he leaned over. But he didn't bother to pick up the letter. He let it lie there and pushed the door closed. I heard part of what he said.

"It is you, of course. Such a man would not have the letter taken from him." A slight bit of coughing, more words, and the door closed. Then the chain clanged as it was placed carefully down along the wall and the door opened again. Very slowly it swung back. Feet crossed the floor, the bed creaked again, and helping the door along with my foot so that it snapped back against the wall, I entered. It's a good many years since some one behind a door crashed me.

A bare-footed figure in a heavy bathrobe was climbing into bed—and the linen on the bed was clean. The blankets old, but clean also. Even the bed itself, which had long since lost its air of respectability, was free from dust or dirt; the black scars on the white enamel standing as grim reminders of hard years.

But the man was the thing. Those legs that disappeared under the clothes were thin, trembling lengths of bone. An arm that stretched out over the coverlet and a hand that waved me in were skeletonlike; the flesh drawn tightly, not soft and flabby. There were marks on the arms, too—tiny punctures too numerous to count, yet they seemed old ones. Then, as the emaciated little body turned and the hand waved toward me, I got a look at his face. White, drawn, sunken cheeks—colorless lips—and far distant, somber, searching, roving eyes.

Of course the thing wasn't new to me. There are thousands and thousands of them right in the city. One meets them every day—on the Bowery and along Fifth Avenue—from an East Side dive to a West Side apartment. I knew that I was looking at the ravages of dope. From the manner in which the back of his hand shot over his mouth before he spoke and the furtive glance over my shoulder as I closed the door behind me, I'd of spotted him without the telltale marks upon his arm.

"I'm glad you came," he squeaked. "I must talk—talk—now—some one must listen or I—"

"Just a minute." I raised my hand. I was in the thing now. I'd have to listen to him—a wild, fanciful story, no doubt. And perhaps it wouldn't do any harm. The warmth of the room felt good, the cleanliness of it was surprising, and the closeness of the two oil heaters that burned in opposite corners was not so stifling as at first. But I'm not the kind of story book detective who sits down, lights his pipe, folds his arms, and closing his eyes gets ready to digest a chestful. I wanted to have a slant about that room. There was ample

25

space under the bed for a man to hide; also there were cheap calico curtains that hung to the left of the bed and close to the musty window that was closed tight and plugged up around the edges with bits of paper and cardboard.

Haunted eyes followed me as I looked under the bed, and guessing my purpose his other hand came out empty and rested on the coverlet—but I kept my eye on him too as I looked behind the curtains. Just a glance—some clothes there and nothing more. I spotted books too, the titles of which made me kill a whistle of surprise. And there was no closet in the room—not another place to hide a cat in. This lad was there alone—unless he had some one tucked into bed with him, which, as I have two eyes, wasn't likely.

His smile was a weird, fantastic affair as I turned back to the bed and stood looking down at him. He sure was a mess, and yet his face had been a good one—a delicately formed hand twitched at the blankets. I'd let him begin, though already I was sorry I had come. "Got to have a million dollars by Thursday—Wednesday I don't need it and Friday will be too late," was already forming on those lips, I thought. Here was a sample of the very dregs of humanity. Still, out of the jumble I might get something that would serve me later. He had lived with the gang; deserted by them now, no doubt. Snowbirds have a way of hearing things—being treated by the big guns as so much stuffed furniture. But our snowbird was talking; gulping it, coughing it and squeaking it out.

"I thought you'd come. That was the first part of my trouble—to get the letter to you without any one knowing." A longer gulp. "A friend did that for me—a friend whom I can trust, for he'll forget so soon—though with me, I'll never forget. It's so like a dream." He stopped there and eyed me. What he read in my face couldn't help him any. But I was there to listen, not to talk. Once, by listening to the prattle of a child of four I caught a murderer. The thin man in the bed went on hurriedly.

"You have heard of Daniel Davidson. That is I." And I sat the straighter. "Is I" had slipped out so naturally, so unconsciously, it staggered me. I wasn't expecting that sort of English, even after spotting some of the books. But now my head half turned, and the gilt letters of Thackeray and Dickens and even the dry Macaulay glared dimly out at me. But the name Daniel Davidson didn't make me lie down and roll over. I'd never heard it before. Why he didn't pretend to be John D. or the President or the Prince of Wales I couldn't tell. In a hazy way his voice got over to me.

"My father was D. Perry Davidson. I am his only son. You see, in youth I lived with my mother in London. My father married again—but in his will he left me everything—everything. He had made that will before my sister was born." A pause—I lowered my eyes and looked at him. His listless gray eyes were glaring up at me. "You don't believe me. You don't—you couldn't—but you'll believe this when I tell you. Look at me—and here, look at this." His hand shot beneath the pillow—a bit of newspaper flashed into his fingers, then was crushed in mine. While the man breathed heavily I spread out the paper and looked down at the picture. There was a resemblance between it and the man upon the bed— nothing more. But the caption beneath it was interesting.

Thomas Henderson—escaped convict. Five feet, four inches—dark hair, dark eyes, weight a hundred and twenty-four pounds. Escaped prison, March 7th. $500 reward.

5

The Opening Door

I lifted my eyes from the paper. Everything but the weight might fit the lad upon the bed, but then it would fit a dozen other men. Here was the old story of the wronged convict claiming his own.

"This you?" I asked, tapping the paper.

"Yes," he nodded. "See how I trust you—one word and I'd go back to those walls for twenty-five years."

"And the crime?" I fingered the soiled paper.

"Murder."

"Of course you were not guilty." I thought that I said the expected thing. This lad might be snowed up enough to start parading the street in his night shirt, crying for justice.

"On the contrary, I was guilty." And his voice was very calm and very grim now. I saw his fingers close too and the slender, sharp, polished nails bite into thick flesh. There was a red flicker of blood on his lower lip—then his lips parted.

"I think," he went on, "that this will be your strangest story—your greatest hope of reward—and the righting of a great wrong. Not for me, perhaps, for my real identity means prison, and prison means my death. I am not big enough to die, even for a great cause—I am afraid of death. And yet the complexity of what I tell you is built on its very simplicity." With that he broke straight into the story, and I listened. Not that I believed it. But he told it well, and beyond doubt the man had an education.

"I was ten, my sister five, when my mother separated from my father. I would have chosen my father, but the choice was not mine. She took me to England with her. It was her hold on father's money that she thought of, for she left my sister. I recall my father's hand upon my shoulder—the look in his eyes when I left—the final words when he kissed me. 'Some day you will understand and come back to me.' And I did understand—but I never came back. My mother needed me. She was a weak, thoughtless woman—God forgive her—and the man that she left my father for was little short of a beast. He dominated her life and mine. She died—I would have sought my father—then came the war—the months in the hospital—and finally the word of my father's death."

A long pause there; the flicker of blood again on the lower lip, and again polished nails straining against tightly drawn palms. He would just clutch frantically at his hands, the nails tearing the skin—but no blood came. There was not much blood, I guess. I'm not one for sympathy, but I stretched out a hand and tightened it on his wrist. I understand such life, and after all this thing was real enough to him. So I let him ramble on; there were several hundred thousand involved. I laughed to myself and denied it as rot. But underneath it all was the semblance of truth. It was a story so fantastic and strange that even a snowbird couldn't have created it all. And the strangeness of it was what made it ring true. Get it as he gave it.

"My father's brother came to London for me, for I was sole heir—and, after many years, I was to see my sister who would be twenty-three then. I never fully understood that trip. For some reason or other it was necessary to put up at a cheap hotel along the water front when we reached New York. I registered under another name. The name on that paper—Frank Henderson. The explanation, I can't remember—there was champagne, a celebration; a girl and a fight—a gun in my hand, another gun in the hand of a stranger—and I killed him. I think he was to kill me."

"You imagine that. You didn't really kill him. It was a frame-up and they got—"

"No, no—I killed him. I remember that too well. The crime is mine. I was arrested. A lawyer was there—they said they would arrange it all. My father's memory, my sister's life—and I was convicted under another name and drew thirty years in prison. Even then I didn't suspect. Even when my life was twice attempted within the prison wall. They were working for me outside, I was told, and I would be free. Money would do it. Money would fix everything. Money—money—MONEY. Cursed MONEY!" And his head went into his hands and his hands went down on his knees.

"At last I could stand those grim walls no longer. I threatened to speak out—disclose who I really was—spend my own money in obtaining the best legal talent. They sent a little lawyer to see me who told me that a convicted murderer's money went to the state; that if I spoke out my sister could not inherit the money I would leave. It was a lie, of course—but I didn't know then. I was told that I would be free.

"They planned my escape by having me brought from prison to testify in a case, but they planned my death with it. A girl saved me. It's all too long to tell. For me to tell the truth now will mean prison again." He jerked his head suddenly erect—his eyes flaming, his cheeks flushed, his lips pale whitish lines. "To go to my uncle will mean my death. To lie idly by will mean the robbing of my sister. I don't want to die. I don't want to go back to prison. I can't. I can't stand it." He fairly shrieked the words. "Yet—I must face my God and my father, having protected my sister."

"Does she know all this—and your mother—your stepfather? What of them?"

"My mother is dead," he said again. "A broken, sickened,

maddened woman. Like Macbeth's wife, she died. My step-father—a drunken brute who disappeared in London when the money my father gave my mother was spent—a beast who beat me as a child until I lay a helpless heap upon the floor. I see him yet—his flaming eyes, great hairy hands and—" Again the head into his hands and again his cry. "Great God in Heaven, I am little better than the beast I feared. My nights are torture when I think of my sister. I can no longer hide the truth—yet—yet I fear to tell the truth. Here—" He turned sharply in the bed, and like a dog pawing for a hidden bone, dug into the mattress. A moment of hesitation, a sudden gulp of fear—then a hasty snatch, followed by a sigh of relief—and he faced me again.

"I got it—I thought for a moment—but no matter—name your price—name your fee and see the trust I put in you. Take it; keep it." He thrust a crumpled envelope into my hand. "Use it when I'm dead—for I have not the heart of a man now nor the blood of a son and brother. It is the truth— my will too—time it took—secret it was—one witness—a hopeless, dragging, dope-crazed creature—but he could write and he is a citizen—born here in the city, you understand." And he began to laugh as I shoved the envelope into my pocket. "Your word not to open it while I live. Her address— my sister's—on the envelope. I threatened them with that— first, a letter begging for help or I would seek you—then, threatening them—or him—my brother's father—my uncle— the lawyer—all. And if my sister is dead, that will avail them nothing; they can't touch my money when I'm dead." He cut off suddenly, coming bolt upright in bed and staring over my shoulder.

"I see him now—Raphael Dezzeia—my stepfather—the snarling lips—the great teeth—those hands—those hands— see—see—Raphael—my mother's husband." He clung suddenly to me like a frightened child, but his bony fingers still pointed and his weird, wild, searching eyes glared past me at the door.

Involuntarily I turned, and the hand that patted his back as I might have patted a dog swung to my pocket. For the face and eyes and great teeth and hands may have been an illusion. I didn't see them. But certainly the knob of the door had clicked, was turning there as I lifted my eyes from the jabbering, frightened, broken thing that was called a man and watched the door. Slowly—very slowly—yet very surely that door was opening. I jerked loose now and came to my feet; my hand clutched the gun in my pocket as I backed behind the other side of the bed, where I could watch that slowly opening door and also the man upon the bed. Nothing to fear from him, you think. Maybe not. Probably not. Almost certainly not. But I'm not of a trustful nature. All the great actors are not on the stage—besides, when I'm shot down I expect the coroner to find the bullet in my chest, not in my back.

Expectant, we both waited. He was looking for his stepfather, and I—well, one thing was certain—if this stepfather, this Raphael Dezzeia, did pay a visit after all the years he'd be less messy than usual. He wasn't related to me, you see, and I had little to fear. If the dear, long lost relative tried any of his beating-up tricks on me—why, the undertaker could pour him back in the bottle. So we watched the door—his eyes frightened, wandering, and pleading up to me. Mine, steady and ready for anything. But I didn't intend to cow our visitor with a look—I leave that to detectives to frighten women and children with. My finger caressed the cold, hair-tuned trigger of a forty-four, and I have yet to see the man that can frown a gun down.

Whoever was at the door was an expert at soft entry. There wasn't a sound as the door slipped open, far enough to admit a body—then it stopped, and I changed my position. I got the idea that some one might be playing Little Bo Peep through the crack. But I said nothing. It wasn't my game. Whoever opened that door intended to come in. If some one wanted my life or the lad's upon the bed, surely they didn't expect to get it by giving us pneumonia with the draft.

So we waited. No sound from without—no sound from within but the deep breathing of the man upon the bed. He was doing his stuff like an old lady with the asthma—and the worn door hung half open, and the cold wet damp and the musty smells of the hall and the winter night combined, drifted into the heated room.

6

The Girl of the Night

Generally I let the other fellow play the cards and just follow suit myself or trump when I can. But now I couldn't wait. I was afraid. Afraid for the lad upon the bed. His sunken cheeks had taken on a deathlike gray and his eyes, still blazing, had sunk far back into his head. His chest rose and fell and his heart beat like the town clock. He was the sort of a bird whose heart would just give a final jump up, forget to come down in time to catch the next beat and stop altogether. I had been standing alongside of one dead body already that night and I didn't want another. So I spoke out.

"You, behind the door," I snapped the word, "come in or I'll put a—"

And I didn't get any further. A voice came from behind that door—and believe me, it was no stepfather.

"You have company, Danny—I suspected as much—and I know, for Old Tim told me—Old Tim talks." And she came into the room. A slip of a thing, with a little hat that hid most of her hair, the strings of black just peeping out below the tips of her ears. Beautiful? No. Pretty? Certainly, in a sinister sort of way. I'd of spotted her any time. I knew the type. A girl of the night. She shot those snappy black eyes up at me— frankly hostile she was, and was willing for me to know it.

And when she closed the door behind her she locked it, hurried across the room to the bed, staring angrily at the man in it a moment, shook her hand at him, started in to rag him for something—then broke off with a pitiful little cry in her voice, and the next moment had crushed that emaciated body in her arms. She was crying too—sobs she tried to gulp down, but they came just the same. Here was real emotion, from one who was used to crushing the feeling of her inner being.

"You"—she cocked her head up at me like a bull pup—"why did you come and put him like this? Why, he could—he could—I know you, Race Williams—now go—go—he's mine and I'll take care of him—and protect him too. Why don't you go?" She jumped from the bed and stood before me, her little hands clenched.

"Easy does it." I looked steadily down at her, and then to the man. "Who is this girl? What is she to you?"

The girl jumped me again, but the man reached out a hand and gripped at her coat. His voice trembled.

"You mustn't mind, Mr. Williams. She don't understand. She fears—fears for me. Look at her, poor child. She's the girl I told you of—who helped me from—from them." He half glanced up at her. "It won't be long now." He turned to the girl. "Mr. Williams will help me—we'll go off somewhere for a long time—then when it is forgotten and things are cleared up—why, I'll take my own place in the world and you'll no longer have to work so hard, but live like a lady—a real lady. See, Mr. Williams, the haunted look in her eyes—poor child— poor child." And his weak, trembling arms sought to draw her down to him.

Poor haunted little child, eh? Some imagination that. A hunted look in her eyes maybe; a shrewd, appraising look, as one who is used to meet with and tackle the abuses of life— but nothing haunted in her eyes. A determined, hard, cold, calculating face—yet in it all the doubtful, frightened look of a mother chicken who watched her young. She patted the boy who clung to her as she steadily regarded me. Hardly more than out of her teens in actual years, but her soul had lived a century.

Davidson whispered to her. Motors, yachts and great houses drifted to me occasionally as I stood looking down at them. I was willing to leave. Here was the talk of a millionaire, or the ramblings of a snowbird all hopped up. You could take a look at this lad and you wouldn't need more than one guess to draw your conclusions.

"Of course, of course." The girl finally untwisted herself from his arms. "Mr. Williams believes and will help you—and now he will go, for you need your rest, Danny."

"Yes—yes." Danny stretched out a hand toward me. "You'll remember—you won't forget—won't think I'm a poor distracted soul who through the ravages of the drug contracted in prison—but now forever—See, she smiles at you—Milly likes you—that is good—for Milly doesn't like every one—hardly any one." And he patted her hand and held it to his lips. Did Milly smile? Perhaps. Her lips did, at least I think they did. Thin lips parted and showed even, white, well kept teeth—but her eyes didn't smile. Not by a jugful, they didn't. They watched me, hard and cold—and bitter too, I thought. Not with fear—here was the type who know little of fear—either physical or moral—just an uncertain, animal doubt and watchfulness of danger.

I took the bony hand of the man, dropped it and stepped to the door, turned the key and opened it. The air in the room was bad now. The oil mixed in with the other odors; the damp smell from without struck me full in the face. I shut the door behind me and stepped into the darkened hall.

Light feet crossed the room within, a hand gripped the door knob. I could feel it twist in my fingers. Just locking the door, I thought, as I moved down the hall. Then I stopped; the door had opened, the light illuminated the filth of that hallway. The girl stepped through, partly closing the door behind her. Once she stuck her head back in, and I heard her say:

"I'll tell him it's all the truth—but never worry—I'll have

36

you out of this hole in a—" The door closed, until just a dim thin sliver of yellow ran its length, and a hand gripped my sleeve.

"May I speak to you a minute, Mr. Williams—it's about him." Faintly I felt more than saw a little white hand shoot into the air and a thumb jerk through the sliver of light.

I nodded, then remembering the darkness, answered, "Yes."

"Down here then." She gripped my arm, and half dragging, half leading me, we stumbled along the darkened hall to the dirty window in the rear. Through the glass crusted with years of dust dimly came the outline of a distant sky and the bleak worn buildings of the block behind.

"I don't want him to hear," she explained. "What did he tell you?"

"Not much." If she wanted to talk to me, I was willing to listen—but if she wanted me to talk to her, that was a different story altogether. I remembered the hard, unfriendly eyes she had put on me. So she started in.

"He spoke of money—his inheritance—a sister—great wealth?"

"Considerable wealth—yes."

"You didn't believe it—believe him?"

"Isn't it true?" I evaded the question.

"What else did he tell you?"

"Not much."

"Anything?"

"About what?"

"Prison—for instance."

"Yes—prison, for instance," I repeated. "Isn't it true?"

"Of course it isn't. How could it be? Look at him—don't you understand? He's suffered—his mind wanders at times—but he'll come around all right. Forget to-night. Forget him."

"Do you think he should be sent away?" I tried that vaguely—just the hope of seeing how she'd take it, I guess.

"Sent away—him!" Little fingers bit into my arm. "No—

37

never—never—he'll be all right now."

"And you—you question me. What are you doing here? What are you to him?"

"Why—I am his life." I jarred back as she shot the words. There was a sincerity in them all right. But why did she follow me into the hall? Did she think for a moment that I believed such a wild yarn? Was she simply a poor distracted girl? No, she wasn't one to go into a panic—there was some truth in the story. But if there was, why didn't she want my help? Why wasn't she glad to get it? Did she think that I'd betray him or—? But she was talking.

"You understand his—his condition?"

"Snowbird." I nodded.

"Yes." And her voice was so low that I hardly caught the word.

"All hopped up to-night?" Somehow I wanted to stir her up. It hurt her to hear that word. "That's why he talks money—too bad." Then more slowly as I heard her quick intake of breath. "Snowed up! Bad!"

"No." It just broke from her. "Don't say that. I can't say that—because it's not true. He has been—but he's cured—it's that which ravages his body—plays queer tricks on his mind. But he don't touch the stuff—not now. He promised me—swore to me—and he wouldn't lie—not to me. He couldn't. I'd know—and—you don't think he touches it!" A change there. A pleading in her voice—a desperate sort of pleading, and the hands had slipped from my arms to my shoulders—her face palely dim in the dismal light from the distant sky on the blurred glass.

"I don't know. I only listened to you—you said it." I shrugged my shoulders. I'd be glad to get away from the whole drab business. The dregs of life are passed lightly over in a book or in a police court, for that matter—but here—when I faced it I didn't like the taste of it so well. I'm hard boiled all right—none more so, I guess, and I've seen so much that my heart is petrified to a granitelike hardness. The weakness must be in my stomach then, if you can call it a

38

weakness. But she was speaking again.

"You'll forget it all then—your visit here—and he didn't give you anything, did he?"

Here was a direct attack and I didn't like that. She suspected that envelope then—maybe wanted it back. Of course I could have lectured her on the ethics of my profession; gone into a long discourse on the confidence between my client and myself. But I didn't. I just lied to her. It came easier and saved time.

"He gave me nothing," I said.

"No—" There was enough of a catch in her voice to let me more than suspect that she knew that I lied, but she didn't seem to mind and I certainly didn't.

"I'll be going then." I lifted the little hands from my shoulder. Maybe she worked hard, for the hands were rough and coarse, with a smoothness at the heel of the palm—leaving the impression that hard work was new to her. "Of course," I added, "none of the story is true?"

"No." Then a sudden grab at me and a voice pitifully low. "About the money, I mean. The prison part—well, that's true. I've got to tell you so you'll not—" and a flood of words, so fast it was hard to follow them—pleadings and threats all mixed in together. "You won't betray him—what good can it do you? Poor, mishandled, ill-treated boy! They'd take him back—you won't—" A pause. "If you did—if you did—I'd kill you." And she didn't hiss the words; didn't shoot them out in uncontrolled anger or with the threat of an hysterical woman. Very slowly she let out the three words. Empty talk? Maybe. But I got the idea that she meant it. Yep—I believed her.

Then she grew frightened.

"There's a price on his head—I'll pay that—all of it—perhaps later in a big lump—at the worst in small weekly amounts—say, five dollars—maybe ten. Trust me—believe me—you'll get the money just as if you gave him up to the police—more even, for I'll—"

"Lay off, kid." I gave her the talk she'd understand. "If I

can't help a client I don't blackmail him. That's the difference between a Private Investigator and a Private Detective." I stooped—a voice was calling from within the room—plaintive, whining, cracked. Parts of it only drifted down the hall.

"Raphael—the beast—him—hairy hands." A moment of silence while we listened. "Milly—Milly—Milly!"

"There, you see." She spoke as if she blamed me for it. "I'll have to go to him. Be kind and generous and—" Then suddenly, "He didn't give you an envelope?"

I didn't lie to her this time. I didn't need to. The cracked voice within the room was calling loudly now—a disturbed roomer cursed and pounded on the wall. The girl left me—fled down the hall and into the room. The light for a moment—the frightened, childlike voice of the man and the answering, soothing notes of the girl—darkness and the click of the key—and silence. I stretched out a hand, found the bannister, ran my fingers along through the dust and followed the unseen trail to the head of the stairs. Dimly from below came the dull flickering glare of the single gas jet. The tenement house laws requiring a light on every other floor didn't disturb this landlord. A wealthy, drunken man at his club, perhaps, who couldn't tell offhand the number, or even the street the disreputable building he owned was on. And I didn't blame him overmuch. I'd try to forget that dump myself.

7

The Getaway Car

This time I didn't bother with the flash as I went down the stairs and I didn't bother so much with the creaking boards either. The next time a lad sent for me in that tenement I'd make him ship me a gas mask. The air was good as I busted right onto the street; a single blast and a deep swallow of it was like a course dinner with champagne.

And what had I received for my trouble, I thought, as I buttoned my coat tightly about me. Nothing but bad smells and the wandering talk of a drug addict who wanted to take his girl friend bye-bye on powerful steam yachts made from drifting dreams. Funny—I wasn't mad and I didn't laugh. There was something appealing about the boy on the bed—the education in his voice, the few books of a past that was no doubt filled with promise—and now; dope and prison and the dregs of life, with fruitless hopes and imaginary fears of the future.

The girl—yes, I sized up her anxiety. She loved the boy or thought she did, which for the time being would amount to the same thing. Something to mother and protect—the instinct of womanhood that is found among the rich and the poor, and even the woman of the night. The rich take it out on a dog, the poor on the children, and those of the underworld on some worthless man. Worthless; I didn't know about that—the boy appealed. If I were a philanthropist, perhaps I'd dig down in my pocket and send him away to a hospital which was supposed to cure the unfortunates. Then I'd puff with pride and strut about and get my clergyman to preach a sermon about me, and never stop to think that the money I gave the boy was being used to bribe the attendants to furnish him with dope. No—there's only one cure and that's manhood; a will power which is so seldom built into the racked brain of the weakling who becomes a sleigh rider.

And the girl? She was simply possessed with the fear that I'd send him back to jail. No—there was nothing in the thing for me. I'm not a charitable institution—so I stuck my hands deep into my coat pockets and turned down the street. What of the dead policeman? What of my alibi if I was questioned on that bit of shooting? I cursed the dreams of the boy and the hard-headed suspicion of the girl that put me in such a position. I remembered the cop who had questioned me a half hour before. Yes—I'd have to seek a telephone and fix that alibi. I belong to a high class club and I have a waiter who'd swear to anything for me. As to my chauffeur—well, before I got hold of him and straightened him out he'd done a term for perjury, so that wouldn't bother him any. Also there are a few good high class friends who I've helped out of trouble—they understand the mess an honest man can get into and haven't forgotten. Oh, I play the lone hand in everything but the alibi, and you've got to meet lies with lies. Not good ethics maybe, but common sense—and besides, I've said that my ethics are my own. No apologies, you understand—I don't try to tell any one how to run his business and I don't expect any one to try and tell— But back to the winter night and that alibi.

There'd be a dump open along the water front and I could slip into it and do my stuff on the phone. So I turned back; pulled up sharp and ducked down in an alleyway. A figure had slipped from the dirty tenement I had just left—a figure that stood irresolute; a tiny shadow only against the bleak

42

background of the door. But a white face turned sharply now and looked up and down the street. I didn't recognize her of course there in the darkness. But I didn't need to. I knew that slim build, the quick turn of that little head and the flash of the steady black eyes that tried to pierce the darkness. It was my girl of the night—Milly, of the smiling lips and the hard, cold, appraising eyes. Did she seek me? Should I show myself? And I decided to wait.

The girl had a coat pulled tightly around her and a little hat that was jerked down over her head like a basket. Even in the darkness I could tell that the coat was thin and cheap and that the winter night bit through.

The street was deserted; one more hasty glance up and down and a quick jerk of her head back over her shoulder and she was down the street toward me and the avenue beyond. She didn't exactly run—it was sort of a walking, jumping motion as she stuck close to the buildings. A suspicious gait that time of night, which of course had its disadvantage for one who did not wish to attract attention. But it was also a hard gait to follow; to pursue a speeding figure is easy enough, to shadow one is not so simple—almost impossible in the city streets. Was it that the girl didn't fear the law? Was it that she thought some one might shadow her, or was it that she was just in a hurry and didn't bother about either one of the reasons?

Well, I'd chance it—follow her at a distance. That bobbing head that jerked so often back over her shoulder would spot me all right. But she couldn't recognize me at that distance and there was the chance I might keep far enough behind her not to be seen at all. But what did I want with her? What was the use of following her? She was a dead issue as far as I was concerned, and there was my alibi and the—

My head shot back into the alley. Just in time, too—another was taking an interest in the girl. A man who leaned far out of a doorway down the street and on the opposite side from the girl. I needed good eyes to see him—just the whiteness of his face framed on the motionless outline of two shoulders.

Like a statue he was, so steady, so intent upon watching the girl. Yet, he too hesitated to follow her.

She reached the corner and disappeared, and I still crouched in the alley. The man stepped out upon the sidewalk; a hand dove into his pocket; a match flashed for a moment and a white face bobbed up between cupped hands. Then darkness again as the man sauntered up the street, paused opposite the tenement and crossed the street. He stood looking up at the building and puffing on his cigarette. Twice he moved toward the entrance and hesitated. Once he turned down the street in the direction the girl had taken and again he hesitated. Elbows akimbo, hands on hips, he waited.

There was the whir of a motor down the street. The man before the tenement and I turned our heads together. We both saw the approaching car. I looked back at the man in time to see his figure disappear into the hallway. A couple of seconds later a touring car with top down jerked up at the curb. There was no grinding of brakes, no squeak of old worn mechanism. Yet, the car was a relic. From the outside of the body alone you'd of thrown it away ten years ago. Still, the machinery was kept in good condition—brakes well taken care of, even if the engine did miss a beat as it panted by the curb.

It was the girl, of course. She hopped from the front seat, dashed into the tenement—and I ducked from the alley in time to hear her feet pounding on the stairs. Now, where did I fit into the picture? Certainly there was the smell of sick fish in the whole business. Should I protect the girl? Was she in danger from the man who lurked some place in that hallway? I thought not. He had seen her come from the house and hurry down the street. The street was deserted as far as he was concerned. If he burned with the laudable desire to knock her on the head he had his chance.

I'd wait. After all he might simply be a friend of the girl's. She feared the police would find Danny; here was the lookout maybe. A little too well dressed? Perhaps. But the boys on the Avenue were getting a bit flashy to-day. One couldn't tell.

44

Anyway, I'm no Sir Launcelot; this game wasn't for me. I'm not out to defeat the ends of justice—rather, the other way about. Still, I waited and listened for the girl to cry out, telling myself it wasn't my business, but knowing all the time that I'd duck into the tenement, crash the boy who was bothering her and see the kids safely away. Away? Certainly. The car was there at two o'clock in the morning for a single purpose. I know life well enough to know that the battered touring that stood so innocently against the curb was the get-away car.

It was a cinch that the girl felt their hiding place, or at least the boy's hiding place, had been discovered. Was it the man who had lurked across the street she feared—or did she fear me? And had the man across the street seen me duck into the alley? It was very dark there and I doubted that. Still, he may have watched for me, missed me, and was waiting in the hallway to warn the girl of my presence.

Silent? Yep, one always thinks the night so dreadfully silent until you try and listen through it. Noises pop up you never suspected. Somewhere far distant an elevated train rumbled by—almost overhead it seemed when I wanted to hear something else. A ship tooted on the river and the chug of a smaller boat came clearly to me through the nipping clearness of the winter night. But not a sound from the stillness of that house and I was close against the entrance now; braced on the iron railing ready to drop into the alley or vault the railing and dash within. I hate waiting—mainly I'm a man of action.

Five minutes passed, I guess—maybe it was only two minutes. I don't know—and the footsteps came—steady, light feet; then uncertain feet—feet that stumbled. I didn't need three guesses to know that my first thought was right. This was the getaway car and the girl, Milly, was bringing Danny down those stairs. A lesson there, though there was none to get it unless that figure lurked behind the stairs. Here was a young man, hardly more than a boy—and his feeble step and his jerking body told their story. Was it just weakness; the environment and association of the big gray walls, or—?

45

The door of the tenement jerked open, banged back, and I dropped to the alley, my knees bent to deaden the fall as I snaked along to the steps and in the protection of the stones a couple of feet below the sidewalk level, watched the pair come slowly down the steps and laboriously cross the sidewalk toward the waiting car. "Pair" was right! The lad who had slipped into the hallway was not with them—not a friend then. One who watched them—or—just another product of the night who lived there and who watched for other things.

The girl dragged the man toward the car and I saw that she wore no cloak now, but that her thin coat was wrapped around his shoulders.

"It's so cold—so very cold." Danny mumbled the words. "It would be better to stay here and—wait and hope—rather than—"

"No, no," the girl cut in. "They shan't get you. I'll have the money. Come!"

"What was that?" And though his teeth chattered, the man got the words off loud enough. Clear too—high pitched, with a ring of fear in them as his frail body straightened suddenly and he stood erect there on the sidewalk.

"Nothing—nothing." The girl dragged him forward. But I saw her glance over her shoulder. She was not far from the street lamp now and there was a look in her white face that would not easily be forgotten. Her eyes blazed and her cheeks showed chalky white as a little hand shot to the pocket of the sweater beneath her jacket.

"Bear up, Danny. Bear up." There was a hopelessness in her voice as the man seemed to slink there in her arms. "They shan't get you—shan't ever get you. Why—oh, Danny!"

And Danny was a pitiful mess; flopped like a drunk, he had—his knees on the sidewalk. His voice quivering, he pleaded up to her.

"If I just had a bit—the tiniest bit—never again—Milly—just this once—just this once. I've always kept my promise—but the cold and the street and the distant sky—just the tiniest bit."

46

He was crouched there a miserable little heap at the girl's feet. It was up to me to give her a lift. But I didn't—not yet. What of the man who had gone in at that doorway and hadn't come out? What of a trap? What if a blazing gun poked from the dirty doorway and Race Williams was stretched out to give Inspector Coglin an appetite for his morning meal that he hadn't enjoyed in years? So I waited.

The girl's head was jerking frantically up and down the block as her left hand dove into the little bag that hung by a strap at her wrist. There was a flash of paper in her hand, an eager whine from the man at her feet, and the paper was back in the bag again.

"No, no," the girl cried. "I can't! I can't! I can't! Come! Come!" And she bent her little body, clutched the man beneath the arms and dragged him to his feet—to feet that wouldn't hold him.

Even I couldn't stand it any longer. I'd keep an eye on the doorway and give the girl a hand. Not that I liked the girl or trusted her. I remembered too well the way those eyes rested on me. But I gave her credit for pluck. She loved that poor ravaged, broken body—hoped to pull him back and— My head popped suddenly down in the protecting shadows of the alley again. Dim lights were speeding down the street.

8

The Snarl of the Beast

It was a taxi, but a long, low, powerful cream-colored affair. It hadn't reached the curb, hadn't stopped, before the man was out of it. A huge, powerful body with long arms and massive hands that swung from side to side, reaching nearly to his knees. I didn't see his face—it was buried deep in his coat. But as he jumped from the closed car the slouch hat was knocked from his head and I saw the thick mop of hair, the high forehead and the wrinkles of coarse skin. It was the bullet-proof boy. Green eyes gleamed like a cat's in the darkness as he dashed toward the helpless boy and the girl who had dragged him to his unsteady feet.

I don't know if they heard him running over the pavement. His feet were shod with rubber this time and there was just a soft patter, like the tread of a heavy animal. But they heard him before he reached them, for the youth, Danny, let out a low moaning cry that would freeze your blood. The snarl that he had given back there when he was after me earlier in the evening was nothing compared to this. Like a beast? Yes, there was no doubt of it this time. Clearly, but low and whining through the night came the snarl of the beast.

And he was on them. Oh, the girl was quick. She saw him first, for she was facing that way, and her hand shot to her sweater pocket like lightning. I didn't need to be told that the girl was going for a gun—and where there was fear in her eyes there was a courage too and a steady, quick determination to match lead against those hairy hands that were stretching out for the boy.

She'd of had him, too. Bestial—madness—that snarl? Maybe. But there was method in it just the same. Whether the lumbering giant used it with a purpose, I don't know. But it wasn't just melodramatic. If it was used to strike fear, it served its purpose well. The girl was not to be cowed by mere noises—weird, uncanny or otherwise. She had lived in the underworld, knew death—expected it and was ready. Her gun was in her hand and sweeping upward; a good two seconds ahead of the hairy hand.

But the boy! When the girl let him go, he half slipped back to the sidewalk, his head twisted around on his shoulders, from whence the sound had come, paralyzed with horror. But when that snarl came again, it gave him strength—a strength built of fear, for himself or for the girl, I don't know—but a terrible, deadly fear just the same. He didn't see the girl's gun—didn't see anything but those stretching hands, those flaming eyes and twisted snarling lips. But it was of himself he thought.

"Not me—not me," he cried, staggering to his feet and throwing himself against the girl, winding his arms about her and pinning her arms to her side. It was too much for the girl—her fingers must have relaxed, for I heard the dull thud of her gun as it fell to the sidewalk. Then came the shriek of terror as the great hands closed upon the youth's throat. This was murder—right before my eyes. Or let us call it contemplated murder. One grip and one twist of those powerful fingers and Danny would be looking back over his shoulder—looking sightlessly over his shoulder.

Of course it all happened quicker than I can tell it. Mainly, as I said, I'm a man of action. I had a bone to pick with this hairy handed, snarling giant myself. Where I'm not a charitable institution, I do lend a hand occasionally—besides, Danny

49

had cried out in the room upstairs against the Snarl of the Beast. And here was the beast in person—so there was some truth in the story—some one certainly wanted Danny dead and—oh, we'll forget business and put this under the head of pleasure.

Those hands never closed. The big boy went in a bit too much for conversation. He hissed some words in the boy's ear before he finished him. And that was his downfall. One quick jump up, three leaps across the sidewalk—and I struck. Not with my fist, of course. I don't pack a sure enough wallop to prevent murder; not with the butt of my gun either, for I'm not anxious to have a bullet run up my sleeve—and besides, I hadn't forgotten that there had been a driver to that taxi, and also that man who might still be lurking in the dark hall of the tenement.

No—I just stretched up my hand and brought the barrel of the gun down on that thick mop of hair. Strong, powerful, proof against lead? Maybe. I don't know. But there was that single crash followed by a crack. The giant's hands fell to his sides and he hit the pavement like a stockyard steer. No surprise to me, that. I expected he would. Believe me when I tell you that wasn't any love tap.

He had the beef and strength all right. The blow was fit to split his skull open, yet he squirmed upon the sidewalk, wiggling and sprawling, his great hands clutching at the empty air and his fingers grotesquely opening and closing.

I swung quickly, my gun ready, for I had heard the fall of feet. The lad had come from the taxicab. I half raised my gun as I looked at his hands. They were empty. A stupid thug, this, or a frightened one, or just a real taxi driver after all. But I stepped forward, ordered him back to his cab in no uncertain tones and had a look in the back of the taxi. I didn't intend to have any one else bobbing up on me. You couldn't fool much with these chaps; murder was right in their line.

The cab was empty. I turned quickly, keeping the driver before me. The rumble of a noisy engine reached me. There was a chug and a gasp and the roar of a speeding motor as it ate the gas, missed once, nearly died, then raced quickly. You've guessed it; that girl had dragged Danny into the car, stepped on the gas, and now as I looked, a badly and quickly shifted gear clanked before it meshed—and the car was away.

The hulking brute still writhed upon the pavement but his clutching hands could reach nothing because nothing was there. The girl had even copped her gun before she dragged the boy into the car.

Would I follow them? A quick dash and I could easily swing on behind that old touring before it got fairly started. But what of the lad upon the sidewalk? Nothing to fear from him maybe. Then what of the taxi driver? Suppose he put a bullet in my back the moment I turned it to him. And also what of the stranger who had gone through the tenement doorway?

That last question was answered for me. The stranger came from the doorway; a fleeting shadow that dashed to the middle of the street and started in pursuit of the old touring. It was a close run, that—the man was quick and light upon his feet, but the old car was gathering speed and it looked doubtful if he'd make it. I could have stopped him, of course—a well directed bit of lead would have done the trick. It wasn't my conscience that stopped me from plugging him in the leg, ducking into an alley and letting the sprawling figure on the sidewalk explain the bit of gun play.

There were two other reasons that I held my fire. In the first place the man in the car wasn't a real client of mine. In the second place I didn't know how the lad stood who pursued the car. He might be a friend of the girl's who was protecting their retreat and now joining with them in flight. Also you can add to that the fact that he hadn't made the car yet.

With that final thought he made it. A last desperate plunge, a frantic leap forward, his feet dragging on the street—and I saw him clutch the spare tire on the back, hang so a moment, then pull himself up and into the circle of the rim. Two things flashed through my head at once. Would I turn over the tough giant who writhed upon the sidewalk and get a look at that face of his for future reference, or would I let him go and follow the girl in the car and find out just how the man on the "spare" fitted into the party? If he wanted to take a life as badly as the hairy handed beast had, he could easily brace himself on the tire, shove his shoulders over the back of the opening touring and plug the boy beside the girl. The hallway had been pretty dark for sure gun play.

And I decided. Things were ripe for pursuit. The taxi driver had climbed back into his car and was furtively watching me as he slipped the gears into first speed, preparatory for a getaway. That was fine. I opened the taxi door, climbed into the back, and shoving my gun against the driver's spine gave my orders.

"We'll follow the car ahead," I snapped. "Keep close to it, too."

"I ain't in this, Mister." There was a growl in his voice which changed to a tremor as I dug the nose of my forty-four a little deeper into the generous flesh of his back.

"You're in now," I told him. "If you lose ground, you go out and I drive on. Come—snap into it!"

9

A Pretty Bit of Shooting

The car sped up the street. I liked the hum of it as it raced through second into high. Here was one taxi tuned up to do its stuff. At the corner we turned and shot uptown. The figure on the back of the touring was hardly discernible in the darkness; crouched there so close into the tire it might have been an old rug or something. Just our curb lights were lit. I didn't want to advertise his presence to any passing cop any more than he did.

Of course he'd guess that we followed him after a bit; perhaps he might even recognize the car in a passing light. But he might also think that Hairy-Hands was in it or that the driver was alone. Provided, of course, that he was in with the enemy of the boy and the girl. That was something to think over. I'd decide that on his later actions. Most likely he'd climb over the back and join them. At present he might have the desire to join them and warn them, but lacked the physical strength; to be sure he'd had a tough run and would need to regain his breath. I'd await developments.

And the taxi started to slow down. My gun went to work again.

"Do you want to get tossed out?" I asked.

"You wouldn't throw me out of a moving car, Mister," the

53

driver whined. "There's something wrong with the motor. I noticed it earlier in the evening, before that lad picked me up." And as my gun tightened into his flesh, "You wouldn't throw a man from his own car—I might break a leg."

"Don't worry about your leg." And the tone of my voice brought his head the straighter and put more speed into the car. "The fall won't hurt you. If I drop you from this car, old boy, you'll carry a bullet in your back before you ever touch the pavement. You may be an innocent, law-abiding citizen but you're mixed up with some tough babies now, and I'm not the gentlest of the gang. Speed her up or I'll bump you off."

Did I mean it? But what of that? There was only one person who needed to be convinced, and he was. Lips smacked and teeth clenched, but the car gathered speed. We were running about thirty and holding our own. The car ahead was playing it safe. Neither one of us fancied being stopped by the police. I nodded my satisfaction. I always liked to play the game outside the law. I was probably the only one that night who could, under ordinary circumstances, stand a police investigation, and if the truth was told, I wasn't crazy about any such proceeding.

The car ahead was naturally suspicious or the girl or boy had looked over the back of the lowered top of the open car. The speed suddenly increased, the car turned down a side street, slipped across town, shot into Fourth Avenue and lit straight toward the Grand Central station at Forty-second Street.

The man with the gun talks! So my driver held his peace and kept the nose of his car pointed a half block behind the old touring. The picture remained the same. I leaning over the back, covering the driver and peering over his shoulder at the dimness of the tail light ahead and the shadowy form crouched close into the center of the spare tire. My driver was a good one. It was a cinch he was used to trailing other cars; maybe with a bunch of thugs hanging on the running board with drawn guns; maybe again just an innocent victim of

Hairy-Hands, as he now was of me. You can take your choice. I had my opinion, and at his first wrong move some undertaker would come in for an unexpected Christmas present.

No traffic cops were on duty at that hour of the night—or rather, morning. But at Thirty-fourth Street a blue-coated figure turned from trying a door, and coming to the curb peered after the fleeing touring. It was possible that he got a glimpse of the man crouched behind. At least he was suspicious, for he stepped quickly out and hailed us as we passed.

And that was all of that. My gun ran a tattoo up the driver's spine and we jumped forward, tightened up the hole between the car ahead and us by half the distance and left the cop standing in the middle of the road—undecided. He evidently wasn't sure of the lad on the "spare," for he let the thing slide. At least there was no bark of a gun or the sharp toot of a police whistle. We traveled on; a bit faster now, and a little slower as we skipped over the bridge by the Grand Central Terminal.

Slow? Maybe. But it's a sharp turn around the station and the touring gained on us. The girl took a chance and made it—you could see the car tilt slightly, hear the rubber on the hard pavement, and spot the jerk of the rear end as she straightened the old boat again and made the next jump out to the clearway of Park Avenue. The girl more than suspected now that she was followed.

I caught a better glimpse of the lad on the spare—he seemed to be climbing back into position. Another turn would have chucked him off, I guess. I'm almost sure he squealed. At least, a frightened yelp seemed to come from the car ahead; certainly the rest of the street was deserted. That baby didn't have much "guts" I suspected. Was he after all trying to tell those in the car that he was there, or did he for a moment get a glimpse of sudden and horrible death as the car and his body swung toward the stone balustrade that rose above the street level fifty feet below?

We didn't talk now, the driver and I. I watched his face and the car ahead. He watched nothing but the car ahead, his eyes straight before him—glued to the road. And we took another turn, over to Fifth Avenue; a quick slant at a light or two in the upper floors of the Plaza Hotel, and into Central Park.

That was bad. If the lad on the spare tire was bent on murder, here would be his opportunity. Deadly dark in the Park; few cars there at that time either. He could easily climb up over the back, plug the youth, Danny, and drop from the rear of the car and disappear in the bush and trees when the girl slammed on the brakes. That was only a thought, of course, but a mighty good one. If he wasn't a friend of theirs, which seemed sure now, certainly he didn't hop on the back of the car just to go day-day at two-thirty in the morning.

Nothing to see now but the dull splash of a tail light ahead, and the duller outline of the car near an occasional lamp. Central Park really should go in for murders. It's built for the job.

The touring didn't slacken its speed but its shadowy form seemed to be ducking and jumping from one side of the road to the other. Had a tire gone flat on it and was it hard for the girl to control the wheel? I tried to stare through the darkness. Was it imagination, or in the dull glare of a dim lamp post did I see that figure on the back gripping the lowered top of the car—struggling to climb over the back? I'd have to chance our headlights.

"Throw on the bright lights, fellow." I gave my driver a playful dig in the back with a bit of iron.

"They don't work—bulb's dead." The words sort of stuck in his throat, and I don't blame him. I'd take very little of his nonsense. Did he too see the figure climbing over the back of the car as it jumped from the left to the right, seemingly staying on the road with great difficulty?

My gun slipped up his back until the cold nose picked out a warm spot on the back of his neck. He spoke before I did. He said:

"If you don't believe me, lean over and try the switch on the dash." And when my gun bored deeper into the flesh, "You don't think I'd lie to you at a time like this,

Mr.—Mr.—" His voice faded out there.

"Williams"—I helped him out. I'm always strong for the etiquette of the occasion. "Race Williams—and I don't care if you're telling the truth or not. But—if you've been careless about the efficiency of your car to-night—why, it's your hard luck. I'll count three—and expect to see brights. If the lights are still out, then—so are you. One—"

"Great Heavens! you wouldn't shoot a man down in cold blood."

"If you're curious to find out, wait until Three. Two—"

"I—" And he lost his nerve. A hand shot downward and the brights snapped on. Just in time, too. Smack on the back of the car ahead they lit—that madly careening touring that was dashing back and forth across the road like a helpless ship in a storm.

But I didn't notice that. It was the figure on the back. I was right; he was climbing over the touring. At least that was his intention, for his feet were braced on the rim of the tire—a hand gripped the lowered top and the elbow of that hand rested on the top. But it wasn't that which brought my gun sharply up, directed through the smudgy glass of our windshield full on that wobbling car and the figure that clung to the back. It was the thing in his hand. Dully against the white of his fingers I caught the outline of a big black automatic. He was ready to use it too. For the arm of the hand that held the gun was already swinging upward, and his head had risen over the back.

It was our flash which made him hesitate and turn his white face back on us. But that would be only momentarily. A drawn, pasty, evil face glared blinkingly into our light. Wide, thick lips were partly bared in surprise. We could see him plainly but he couldn't see us. And then, when no toot came from our horn and no shot broke the stillness of the night, he figured we were friends and turned back again.

I fired of course—but too late. My bullet crashed harmlessly through the top of the taxi. Nerves? Hardly. A laugh in that thought. I haven't any. My driver had suddenly thrown up his right hand and knocked my gun arm into the air. And as he did, the boy on the back of the car poked his gun over the top. That would be the end of Danny, I thought, as my left hand shot out and crashed against the driver's ear. Fool! he was struggling for my gun. And now our car was doing its stuff crazily about the road. Our lights swung of course and were now illuminating the dead trees and deader grass.

"Pocket that gun or I'll wreck the boat!" The taxi driver screeched the words at me as his right hand tried to shake the rod from my grip as he held my wrist. With his left hand he clutched at the wheel, guiding the car back onto the road and the lights landed full upon the touring again.

Of course I lowered my gun. I didn't want a wreck then and what difference did it make? For as my right hand dropped the gun into my pocket, my left hand came quickly up with its mate. Simple, that. Simple, the driver, and—

We saw it together, I think—just as my left hand took the place that my right had held and the driver gained control of his car.

The man on the back was ready—well up on the lowered top, drawing a bead when it happened. A hand just shot over the back; there was the flash of nickel, a glimpse of wide black eyes and the white face of the girl of the night—Milly. After that the deluge, if you wish to be one of the literati. There was the darting stab of yellow, the dull roar of a shot above the motors, and a screech like that of a wounded bird. The man clinging to the top seemed to stand upright a moment. A hand clutched at his throat and as the car swung across the road he spun suddenly and crashed to the ground. The girl was able to take care of herself, you can kiss the book on that.

10

The Face by the Window

The thing was simple enough, I suppose. The events account-
ed for the swaying car. The girl had turned the wheel over to
the almost useless Danny, climbed into the back of the car,
knelt upon the rear seat and plugged her enemy. A horrible,
terrible deed, you think. I don't know. One hates to see a girl
mess up the public highways with a bit of well directed lead.
But really I couldn't hold it against her. It was a pretty bit of
work and no mistake. This youth, if he lived of course, would
never more believe that ancient stuff about the helplessness
of woman.

I had other things to think about. We weren't over twenty-
five or thirty feet behind the touring when the shooting took
place. It seemed certain that we'd run over the body in the
road. I braced myself for the jar—the jar that didn't come.
This driver of mine had some sense of decency after all. He
swung the wheel hard over—missed the inert form at the side
of the road—tried to swing back again when something happened. The steering knuckle, I guess—anyway, we shot off
the road, through some heavy bush, and taking another curve
careened madly for the thick trunk of a towering tree.

It wasn't until then that the driver reached for the emergency brake—and too late. We shot to the right, almost

missed the tree but not quite. The front fender was ripped from the car as if it was cardboard, the right front wheel tried to climb the tree, and I flung open the door and jumped for it just before the car turned over on its side and lay on the patch of grass beneath the winter sky.

There wasn't so much danger to it. The taxi hung before it went over. Then laid down on its side like a gigantic animal seeking rest, its two blazing eyes shining across the open park and onto the stone wall along the sidewalk. A dying grunt, a gasping throb—and silence. Then the lights went out and I saw the driver climbing from behind the steering wheel and pushing his way through the broken glass.

There was the distant throb of a motor, the grating chug of a motor cycle, and turning I ran across the open, ducked to the left, found the bare hulk of great trees and carefully made my way across the park. I didn't know if the man at the wheel stayed to explain the accident, but if that cruising motor cycle cop had come a couple of minutes earlier he'd of gotten a real story to plant down on the police blotter.

I chuckled a bit too as I made the distant road and later the stone wall that runs along Central Park and the Park itself. The girl had gotten clean away. A plucky, yet desperate little thing. Just the instinct that has been handed down through the ages. She was fighting for the life of her man and wouldn't hesitate to shoot down another to save him. Talk about her life and her mental condition and her environment and loss of God's greatest gift—womanhood! But give the Kid credit just the same. I couldn't see any harm in the girl. The man on the back of the touring sought the life of her man. He got what was coming to him. If ever a lad needed one good killing, he was the boy. I'm sorry if I appear hard boiled or cold blooded, but I couldn't get a sympathetic kick when that would-be murderer tumbled to the road. I must admit that I'm strong for a little loose shooting against loose thinkers. There may be laws of the state or of the government that aren't so good, but the laws of God and man can't be improved upon. Them that live by the gun should die by the gun, is good sound twentieth century gospel.

A few thoughts too as I slipped along the wall, found a gate and came out of the Park like a gentleman who couldn't sleep and had taken a bit of a walk. Cold? Man! Florida with all its hurricanes would look good when you got a shot of that Arctic wind along the broad thoroughfare known as Central Park West. Like most of the great city, they were still working on the street—and will be until the end of time, I guess. That sort of solves the problem of the unemployed in New York. The only lad out of a job at that time was myself. Did I have a client or didn't I?

I tried to figure that out a bit. Some place there was truth in Danny's story. Certainly he was a jail-bird; the girl agreed to that and he made no attempt to appeal to the police. What was his trouble then? For I greatly doubted that fairy tale of the inherited fortune—it fitted in too well with his drawn, sunken cheeks and punctured arm. But this is the civilized era, we must remember. Anything can happen, from the shooting down of a policeman on a black back stoop to the slaying of a district attorney of a big city with a Gatling gun parked in an automobile—or a bit of a hold-up of mail trucks in broad daylight. That's what I go by. If I have any rule pertaining to my profession, that rule is: ANYTHING CAN HAPPEN TO-DAY. NOTHING IS IMPOSSIBLE.

Still, it might all run into a simple bit of blackmail. This jail-bird, Danny, might have information on a gang; something that they thought would let them sleep easier if they gave Danny a first-class funeral. They couldn't slip information about him to the police that would send him to jail, because if they did he'd open up and talk. Again, who was head of the gang? Hairy-Hands—with the snarl of the beast?

The Snarl of the Beast. Food for thought there. Danny had hung that line on his stepfather. How true was it? Did Danny actually believe all he told me or was he framing up a story to get my interest and protect him against these birds who wanted his life? No—one thing I was certain of.

Danny may have been lying, but unconsciously. He believed every word he told me.

And the girl! Surely she wasn't working against his interest by telling me he lied if he didn't. I had thought that at first, but since she had dragged the helpless man from the tenement, escaped in the car and then shot down the lad clinging to the back, I couldn't believe it. No; she'd die for her man. She just thought I'd be sore when I found out that there was nothing in it for me and that I'd be out to collect the reward for his return to jail. Not flattering to my vanity, that thought, but natural just the same. She lived with crooks, understood their ways, and no doubt held their beliefs.

To them I was a man who'd railroad his own brother to jail or even shoot him down for a few dollars. And that's what I wanted them to believe. I never had railroaded a man yet. I may have been to blame for some birds taking a long stretch, or even roasting in the chair—but they deserved it. As far as shooting a man down—well, they could believe that because it was true. When a man goes gunning for me he takes his chances. I guess—

And I decided to quit guessing. I'd had a big night—a yawn now and the realization that I was ready to hit the hay—and there along the street was my house, less than a half block away.

It's in the lower Eighties that I live—and I'm up those brownstone steps, key ready to slip into the lock—when I stop dead. Two things catch me at once; my eyes and ears are working and both are rewarded. Through the thick curtained glass high up in the heavy wooden door I see the flash of a light. Just a dull waving flicker that climbs quickly down the wall in the hall, leaving blackness behind it. Almost with the flash of light a car speeds by the house, and as I turn and look out onto the deserted street a siren shrieks its warning to the emptiness.

Queer that. Three o'clock; a vacant thoroughfare and a warning horn. A party of youths toothing their defiance.

Maybe. Probably! But I shook my head. The light inside, my sudden arrival, and the blast of the horn. Too many coincidences. I don't believe in coincidences; they're not conducive to long life and liberty.

I'm not exactly a careful householder. But I had dismissed my chauffeur, Benny, earlier in the evening—also, I never leave lights burning. That flash in the hall might have been the blowing of the curtains from the library and a neglected light shining through. Might have been—but it wasn't. It was an electric torch held in some one's hand. It wouldn't be the first time I had visitors in the night.

My first impulse was to silently unlock the door, snake in, shove a gun through the curtain and sweat some information out of my early morning visitor. It's easy enough to make these lads talk. I have most persuasive ways. Not pretty or heroic, but after all it's results that count in life. You can't make ketchup without busting up a few tomatoes.

But I didn't obey that impulse. The shriek of the siren in the silent, respectable street made me slip the key into my pocket and let a gun take its place. I'm a man of action but I can think occasionally.

My first thought was that the car had waited down the street for me and that the driver had warned his friend within, that I was coming home. That would mean one of two things. The prowler in the library would either drop from the window into the alley, or facing the curtain put a bullet through me as I came in the door. But the light—I stretched and looked again. Plainly I could see it under the curtains—not much, but a dull steady glare just the same. This lad invited trouble—looked for it—hoped for it—and what's more he'd get it. I turned again, and sticking my head out the vestibule, cast a couple of searching glances up and down the street. It was as empty as a congressman's head.

Not a sound from within the house—not a breath stirring in the alley. Just the clear, windless, biting cold of a winter's night. But for the far distant, hardly audible rumble of the elevated train, the silence of a lonely forest lay over that section of the city. Slipping off my shoes I laid them with my overcoat in a corner of the vestibule; then crouching low I crept down the worn front steps. The hard stones were like blocks of ice and bit through my thin socks, but the fingers of my right hand sought my jacket pocket, and warm and comfortable wound themselves around the steel of a forty-four. No need to worry about my feet. I didn't intend to kick any one.

It was cold enough to freeze the tail off a brass monkey and dark enough for the monkey not to miss it as I hugged close to the heavy brownstone front and reached the turn and the narrow alley to the rear. My head shot around the corner and jerked back again—then more cautiously I looked out. The house next door was unoccupied and its slanting roof cast into deeper shadows the little alley. But a light—a single strip of it—came from my library window, and for the fraction of a second I had seen a face—just the whiteness of sharp features hidden by a dark cap. Something to think out, that. A figure worked within, and another crouched by the window without, looking into the room.

Again I slipped my head around the corner and this time followed it with my body. My gun was in my hand now—the business end of it drawing a steady bead on the thin strip of whiteness before the window; a silent, motionless figure that stretched a chin up to the sill and peered intently through the glass. Invisible from inside of course but a nice target from my position. He didn't know it, but his game was up when my gun slipped from my pocket.

He didn't hear me and he didn't see me. Lucky that? Perhaps—but for him, not me. I got enough of a slant at those coarse thick features, the whiteness of a hard-set chin lost in the depths of a high-necked sweater, to know that here was a species of the letter writers that kept cluttering up my mail with threats. I couldn't see his hands, so I couldn't threaten him if he heard me. Once that head turned—once those gimlet-like eyes that were staring steadily through the tiny slit in the curtains before the window turned toward me, he'd have to take his medicine. I couldn't tell what his hands held. He knew the game he was playing when he started out. I shrugged my shoulders as I slipped cautiously along. The funeral was his, not mine. Was it another of Hairy-Hands' friends? Surely they were bent on finishing the job.

11

A Masked Visitor

The man was standing on a small barrel, for I heard the galvanized iron creak softly as I drew nearer. Besides, he couldn't look in that window from the ground. As the barrel squeaked he moved his arms slightly, settled them more carefully along the stone window sill—and I sucked in a deep breath. This lad was there on business. I could put a bullet through him with an easy conscience. For the light within flashed slightly and a dull ray settled on the barrel of a sawed-off shot gun that was pressed tightly against the glass.

My lips set grimly as I pushed on. Just a few feet from him now; and then right beside him. I could stretch out a hand and touch him, but I didn't. It was a cagey game and took caution. Not that I had any personal fears. There was nothing new in this thing to me—my stealthy slipping upon an enemy in the night. A quick raise of my right hand and a quicker hammer-like motion down would tell the story.

It was the prowler within that bothered me. I didn't want to disturb him. I closed my lips silently. It was up to me to slap this lad away from the window without letting the friend within know that there was a change of plans. I looked back down the alley to the sidewalk without, the deserted street and the dull glare of the light on the pole across the way. Then I stepped closer to the silent shadow on the barrel, slightly to his right. He had a lean to starboard, so to speak. That's how he'd fall.

The light within flashed suddenly, leaving the man's head in blackness—then it came back again. Hit his face dully for a moment, and slipping by him shone past me and onto the high wooden fence along the alleyway.

I stepped suddenly back. Just involuntary, the motion was. No one could see me from the vacant house behind, and my house jetted out slightly near the front, hiding me from the sidewalk. There was no sound of my feet on the cold pavement. The light struck on me for a moment only and the man's back was to me. But something warned him of danger. Just instinct perhaps, or the slightest reflection of my shadow in the glass. I'll never know which—and I doubt if the lad on the barrel would either.

He started to turn his head, slowly, doubtfully, fearfully, too, maybe. I have had the feeling of being watched myself at times—nothing tangible, you understand, and no way to explain it. It simply comes from living close to death. And that man by the window was never nearer to death than he was at that moment.

If he had swung with the gun I'd of plugged him sure. But he didn't. Just his head was turning, in slow sharp jerks, like the mechanical store-window figures at Christmas time. Maybe he saw me—maybe he didn't. It doesn't matter. One look I got at thick lips, flat nose, and small, mean little eyes. Then I jumped forward and struck—not frantically or hurriedly, with fear of my life if I missed. I wouldn't miss; I knew that. It was all old stuff to me. Just one question only. How would he fall, and could I catch him before he and the can clattered into the stone alley, warning the lurking figure within who was making so free with my library?

The man on the barrel knew the danger, for the thick lips opened to cry out; the hands that held the gun swung quickly; dull little eyes snapped—and that was all of that. A lurch forward, a swish of air, and the barrel of my gun crashed

67

home just behind his ear. Nothing to do then but catch him as he fell. A right obliging lad he was, too—fell pretty, clutching tightly to his gun as his knees sagged and he toppled into my arms.

A bit heavy at first and some steadying to keep the barrel from going over with him. A minute later I had him on the ground, nicely rolled against the side of the house. No need to listen at his heart, no need to take his pulse. When I do a job I do it well. He would be bye-bye for some time; the little birds would be warbling in his ears.

I frisked him of course. A gat and a rather serviceable looking knife rewarded me. I pocketed them—the shot gun I slipped behind the ash cans in the back of the house. Everything was rosy, and using the unconscious man as a step I climbed upon the barrel to take a look—see in that window myself. Just a glance—nothing more. If that lad didn't mind being a target for some one on the outside, I'm a bit more particular.

One stretch on the up-ended ash can; a quick eye to the slit, and I knew I had plenty of time. The flashlight was on the floor in one corner of the room; no light struck the window now so my position was not a bad one. And such a room! Every book was out of its shelf—my safe hung open, with the papers scattered around the floor. Dimly, in one corner I spotted a pair of heels, but the owner of those heels was too close to the side wall by the window to be visible.

Now, what would some one look for in my house at three o'clock in the morning? And who would have nerve enough to take such a chance? I'm not conceited, you understand, and I'm only stating plain facts and not boasting when I say the thing was almost suicide. Besides, there would be nothing to find. Crooks have done it of course—gunmen have entered and searched my house in my absence. I never keep anything home—my safe is always open and no servants are ever present. Once a servant I had was tortured in an effort to get information and since then I've come down hard on any one I found in my house. The law was behind me there and I didn't hesitate to take full advantage of it. Now—I set my teeth grimly as I climbed from the window. I'd see that this prowler carried a message to the underworld of the city. Race Williams isn't one to play fast and loose with.

This time I came in by the back door; a well oiled lock made no noise as I slipped into the kitchen, and without bothering to switch on a light passed into the dining room which was directly behind the library. The hour was late. I needed sleep and no cheap crook was going to keep me up all night. I guess their plans had been well enough laid. It's my way to bust right in on a party. So—the lad by the window, who would shoot me down when his friend was discovered. Now that that little affair had blown up, I'd clear things up in jig time.

One glance through the curtains of the dining room was all I took. A little figure in knickers knelt close to the window near the flash, which was jacked up on a stack of books. And the figure bent low over other books—opening them—shaking them and tossing them into a corner—looking for something besides literary knowledge between those covers all right.

The gun too; I spotted that. A foot or so away, upon the floor—a classy, pearl-handled affair but a deadly serviceable weapon just the same. I stretched out my left hand and snapped on the light. A book hung in mid-air as a checkered cap straightened and narrow shoulders hunched suddenly. Then the right hand crept out along the floor toward the gun—a delicate, white little hand that was in tune with the slender ankles, the slim waist, and the delicate lines of the neck and shoulders. Here was a woman—a girl, and she was reaching for a gun. Was it my girl of the night? About her build. But, no; the thing was impossible—almost; impossible anyway.

"Leave it lay." My words shot out crisp and sharp. The fingers hesitated a moment, scratched upon the floor, then sought to move forward again. She was still kneeling on the floor with her back toward me.

"Madam," I said, very steadily but shooting the words fast enough to stop those itching fingers before they closed upon the pearly white grip of the revolver, "if you have any desire to leave my house alive, drag your hand back to your side."

Fingers hesitated; stopped entirely and went back to her side.

"You—you wouldn't shoot a woman." Her voice was very low, very steady, and without a tremor to it.

"I don't know for sure," I told her, truthfully enough. "But you make another grab for that gun of yours and we'll both find out. I'd look pretty running around and letting any gun-toting moll who wanted to make a hit with her sweetie take a shot at me. Now—come up! To your feet! Turn around and let me get a slant at you." It was a cinch this wasn't Milly. The voice was different; though there was an unnatural ring to it too.

She came slowly to her feet and I saw that she had a good three inches on Milly. She stood so, with her back to me a moment, then swung around. A checked cap covered most of her forehead; the rest of her face was hidden by a jet black mask. It didn't just cover her eyes and nose but hung down over her chin. There were two narrow slits for her eyes and a generous opening for her mouth. I could see the redness of her lips faintly, but the whiteness of her teeth clearly shone out. She faced me as stiff and as straight and as steady as a soldier on parade. Nothing of the novice in this girl. Young, she seemed; but old at the game—like Milly, I guess. Or was there a tenseness about her body—a stiffness that was unnatural? One thing was certain; she was not just a distracted woman, searching for some letters which she might have thought I had. And I passed my hand to my inner pocket where Danny's letter lay.

The graceful carriage of her body, the littleness of her hands, and the soft notes of her feminine voice made the plain black mask a ghastly thing indeed. Oh, I've seen lots of such girls in my day and expect to see lots more, but I never quite get accustomed to them. With men it's different. They shoot and you shoot—and the undertaker gets the laugh. It's just everyday business.

"Well—" she was the first to speak. "You've caught me, now I suppose it's the police." And with a toss of her head, "but I won't wait for the pinch. My visit was a fool one. I've taken nothing. Men don't shoot women, and I—" She half turned and edged toward the door. I thought that her lips curved into a smile. "You see, I count on the weakness and chivalry of the sex. It's rather unsportsmanlike, isn't it?" She was almost by the library door leading to the hall. I smiled grimly—what confidence she had. How often had she played such a trick and gotten away with it? This time it wasn't going to work. I just let the confidence ooze out all over her as I stood back in the shadow behind the lamp.

"You must play the game as you have learned it," I told her slowly, "and so must I. I don't know about turning you over to the police—there would be no thanks for me there. And don't count on your friend outside the window." And as she moved again, and this time stood directly in the doorway, I came forward leaning across the table, my gun slightly lowered and laying a straight line on one of those shapely legs.

"One step more and I'll ruin a perfectly good pair of stockings." Did I mean it? Don't make me laugh. A fine story that dame would have to carry to the underworld. Why, every lad who had a girl would send her gunning for me. When the coroner picked me up later he'd think I was doubling for a sieve.

It wasn't pleasant. I didn't like the idea but she had too much of a start on me to make a grab for her—and besides, the table was between us. But most of all it was the psychological effect. If I let this girl put her bluff over on me, the reputation for absolute ruthlessness that I had established along the Avenue would be gone. But I won't apologize for my thoughts. After all, it's my business. I'm no moving picture hero, with a big audience out front and the assurance that some one will double for me when the real danger comes. No—I've got to stand on my own legs.

12

Pounding Feet

The girl wavered there in the doorway. My gun was steady; so were my eyes—and there was a grim tightening to my lips. She smiled at first as she looked at me through the slits in her mask. I could see her teeth flashing—then the whiteness disappeared, leaving only a straight line of red through the black. She bent forward, peering intently at me. I heard the quick intake of her breath, saw the twitching of her fingers. Twice her mouth opened, disclosing the white teeth again before she spoke—and now her voice was lower, and for the first time her words shook.

"You—you—" She clutched at the woodwork for support. "You are—are Race Williams. Yes—I know—you would shoot, of course. What are you going to do with me?" There was a hopelessness to her voice now. The self-confidence was gone. See what a reputation is worth!

If she were acting a part she did it well. She wanted to leave me the impression that she hadn't known who I was before.

"You came to my house for what purpose?" I asked abruptly as she walked slowly back into the room.

"I didn't know it was your house." She recovered now and faced me—defiant if not confident.

"Then why the man outside?"

"Man—outside. I didn't know there was a man outside. I came alone."

"You laid a trap for me." I never took my eyes or my gun off her. "You came here, waited for my return, thought I wouldn't harm you because you were a woman. Then you'd trap me before that window, and your friend could shoot me. That's it, isn't it? Come! Tell me the truth!" I stepped around the table and stood close to her. "Let me have the truth and I'll let you go. The names of those who sent you. Who is back of it? Otherwise—" I shrugged my shoulders. "Even Race Williams can use the police at times."

"No one sent me." She jerked up her head. "I didn't know it was your house. You know the life—you know the game. It was just a job I intended to pull—an impromptu affair. The house was dark—the owner away."

"But the man outside," I cut in, stepping forward and laying a hand upon her shoulder.

She shook herself free and for the first time backed away, across the room and toward the window.

"Don't touch me." She half crouched against the wall. Not in fear but like an animal who, cornered, fights back. "I don't know about any man. Like you, I work alone." And with a shrug of those slender shoulders, "I'm on the other side of the line, that's all."

Her words rang true enough, but too many things had been happening for one night.

"Take your flash, raise the window and look below," I ordered.

Mechanically she obeyed me. Over her shoulder I stared down at the coarse, bloated face of the unconscious man. In a way it was familiar—the sensuous mouth, the plastered nose, and the rat-like eyes. A typical killer who for a few hundred dollars hunts down a stranger in the night. Too bad I hadn't shoved him over. If ever a lad needed one good killing that was the boy.

The girl gasped, jerked back, her little head bumping

against my chest. One hand clutched at her throat, the fingers of the other involuntarily folded about my wrist as she half turned. She knew him, I thought, but she was surprised too. Why? To see him stretched out like that? I chuckled softly.

"He's dead?" she murmured, her hand running up my arm and fastening on my shoulder.

"Stiff as a mackerel." I lied. "He can't harm you now. Let me have the story—and then the door. I won't lay the police on you." If she'd tell me the truth I'd make a bet that I had a case after all—and a good one. Why the desperate, repeated efforts to take my life—and at once?

"But I don't know anything—why he was there."

"You know him though." I tried to peer down through those slits—did I catch a distant sparkle of wide, staring eyes?

"Yes, I know him. It's Jake Minely. He'd of killed you too. He's dead—and that's right and good—but death always unnerves me. Funny!" And her laugh jumped up and down my spine. "I live so close to death, have seen, and even—Don't—please don't." She almost screamed the words, for my hand had stretched suddenly out and jerked off her cap. Blonde, bobbed hair clung close to a white forehead. My fingers were searching for the strings that held her mask when she cried out, tore herself from my grasp, and seeing that I was between her and the door, backed into a corner of the room, climbing over a jumbled mass of books. One thing was certain; this girl wasn't Milly. The same build perhaps; the same ethics maybe; but more class to her—more dog, if you get what I mean.

"Come, young lady." I was losing patience. "You don't think you can enter a house, search it thoroughly, plant a killer at the window to shoot me down, and then play the frightened heroine because I want to look at your face. I'm going to see who paid me this visit and I'm going to have you tell me why. I can't handle you as I would a man maybe, but I'll give you one minute to open up with the whole story. If I believe it you go free, if I don't"—I shrugged my shoulders—"there's the police." I glanced toward an old clock above the fireplace.

"You're a hard man, Race Williams—you're bitter and cold and cruel. It is useless for me to talk, for you won't believe me. Yes, I know the man below the window—why he was there I don't know. I came for something which I understood was in this house. I did not know it was your house." And with a sudden toss of her blonde head, "But I'd of come anyway. More, I can't tell you. I believe that you are being dragged into a case where for once your ready gun and brutal actions will not help you. If you let me go we may meet again—when it is possible that I can help you.

"Oh—I know your reputation. You need not threaten. I know you never bluff. I have heard stories about you that make me tremble even now. But I shan't talk no matter what you do—I've told you all I can—all I dare. I am helpless in your hands. If you wish to see my face I know that you will see it. But if you see my face now—a face that will do you little good—you will make an enemy of one whom you may need as a friend. For you are marked for death."

I don't know when I'd been so flattered. True—yes, and that's why I was alive to-day. But down in my heart I knew that only good had come to others through bad of mine. Marked for death, was right.

I bowed mockingly to her.

"I have no friends and many enemies; one more will not matter. Perhaps, as you say, I cannot make you talk—that we shall see later. But I can and will have a look at your face. Will you lift that mask or will I take it off? At least I will know my enemy when I face her again." I stepped forward; the books now held the space between us. It was not a pleasant task but a necessary one. Business is business. I'd be a pretty detective if I escorted every lady who felt like robbing my house to the door and assured her that the window would be open again any time she wished to return and convince herself that it held nothing of value to her.

This time she did not draw back, nor crouch low against the wall. She stood straight before me. Her eyes were blue and foggy—but steady, I thought. Certainly they rested full upon mine through the thin slits. And she folded her arms across her chest. A pretty picture—straight as a whip. "Outraged Womanhood" was the sub-title. It brought a smile. She didn't speak. Then I saw her lips tremble—her head sort of droop. She knew the game was up. I leaned forward, raised my hands toward the mask—and she did it.

She leaped suddenly over the books and into my arms. I had to put an arm about her to steady myself. At first I thought it was a desperate effort to make her escape. But it wasn't. She had lost in her attempted appeal to the fear of making her an enemy or the hope of making her a friend. Now she was playing the game that woman had played for centuries. A good game too, I guess. Most of my clients have some such stories to tell.

Her arms just went about my neck—her head rested on my shoulder, tightly pressed down so that the mask was against my chest. She didn't sob—there were no tears on her cheeks—but she clung tightly to me. There was a fragrance to her hair too—not just the freshness of youth. I felt sorry for her, I suppose. I have a heart as well as the next fellow; but I have a head too. She couldn't know the truth—couldn't guess that she was wasting her time. My life has been a mixture between the rich and the poor, the famous and the infamous; a social hash, so to speak. This girl didn't know that a Russian princess once clung to me like that, and that a now famous actress had pleaded with me, on her knees.

I half held the girl there. I wanted to let her do her stuff—there's the reading of character in that. How bad was she? What would she do to gain her liberty or protect her identity? But certainly she feared what I would see. Why? Would it connect up somehow with the past—an unfinished case, or—I smiled. For all the impression the proximity of her lithe young body made on me, she might as well have been a drunk hanging to a lamp post. Hands sought my cheeks, eyes searched mine. But if she intended to vamp me, she changed her mind—or the smile on my lips changed it for her.

She gave me a shock. Had I figured her all wrong? There was nothing of the woman in her actions now; the vampire of Kipling—or the flapper of to-day.

"Mr. Williams—Race Williams." She was shaking me by the shoulders as she talked, her words coming in quick, spasmodic jerks. "I wasn't always bad. I have been dragged into a terrible net. Won't you believe me—spare me—not lift my mask? I'll never do anything to harm you; perhaps lots to help you. You've seen people who wanted to be good, dragged into the bad."

"But I'm not going to harm you." I felt sorry for her and all that, but I wasn't going to let anything she said or did interfere with my plans. The more she wanted to keep her face hidden, the more reason I must have for seeing it. There was something big back of it all. I'm not just a brute. But see her face I would.

"I'm not going to broadcast your identity. You needn't feel alarmed." I tried to reassure her, half for the benefit of the girl, half for my own peace of mind. It isn't pleasant to maul a woman. Women mean nothing in my life. Some old mummy has said, "He travels farthest who travels alone." That's me. Venus de Milo or Cleopatra herself couldn't switch me from my purpose.

"Very well." She raised her head suddenly, her chin resting on my chest, the slits glaring up at me—the red lips slightly parted through the black and the white teeth gleaming bright.

"I'm a thief—a bad woman. I should be treated as such. To-morrow you will know and watch me and hunt me, and finally—but take it off and let me be gone. I will learn to hate you, I suppose. I had read much about you—thought you a hero and wondered if the day would ever come when I might meet you—that you might even help me; for I have lately thought of sending for you. You play at life and death with only gold between it."

I didn't answer her. There was a plea in her voice which made me wish that I could give the girl a chance and let her go her way with her identity a secret. But I couldn't. Years

77

ago maybe—now—my life might later hang in the balance. I raised my hand and gripped the cord of the mask, behind her head. It was tightly drawn and had no elasticity to it. I jerked once. The girl's head jarred back slightly but she did not speak. She kept her eyes full upon me—her chin tilted up. Generally speaking, I don't take so much interest in these things that come in the way of business, but now I was slightly curious to get a look at her.

My fingers slipped down to where the cord met the mask—one twist of it about my finger—again the jerk of her head, and the cord snapped. The mask started to slip. I caught the outline of the bridge of her nose—heavy eyebrows above—and her head went down tightly against my chest again. Damned if she wasn't crying; sobbing softly. I don't like the baby act and I'm not much affected by tears. But why hadn't she pulled them before? Why when it was too late? Why when I had only to step back and the mask would slip to the floor? But were the sobs real? I stepped back a pace, close to the wall—and the mask fell to the floor. But she followed me, clinging close, her head buried against my chest as I reached down and placed a hand beneath her chin.

She didn't struggle. Didn't try to pull away or place her hands over her face. She just held her head so, making me use force—not a great deal—there wasn't much to her. Slowly but surely I was forcing that head up. Her forehead was in the light now—and my hand stopped dead. There was the roar of a motor, the grinding of brakes, the pounding of feet along the alley. Heavy shoes were upon stone steps and a thumping against the front door, followed almost at once by the sharp ring of the bell. The girl's hand shot suddenly out, reached the wall, rested on the electric light button. There was a snap and darkness—but I still held her there.

13

Inspector Coglin—From Headquarters

Visitors in the night. Men who rapped and called to each other—hoarse voices that echoed unintelligibly along the alley and through the open window. Had I waited too long? Was this a rescue party? Too much noise, you say. But you can't always tell by that. Desperate men had stalked me in the city streets that night; more desperate than the usual run of criminals seeking vengeance. And they were strangers to me. Not a personal grudge! Then what? Had Danny's business more than punctured arms behind it?

The girl struggled slightly—broke from me. And I let her go. There wasn't anything else to do then. I heard her feet patter in the hall—stumble once—then run quickly up the stairs.

Was I angry at myself that I had waited so long; that I had missed seeing her face? I wanted to look at her all right—would too if this happened to be the police and their visit simply a check up on my movements following Delaney's story of seeing me on the water front that night. They hadn't been dragging me in much lately—not when they could get me to answer questions right here at my own home. I always saw that the newspapers got a hold of the story every time I was pulled over the coals and the advertisement didn't hurt my business any. I don't like the police—and they don't like me. Fair's fair! It's Even Stephen there. Still, there are some pretty shrewd men at Central Office and they know I'm not above breaking and entering a house if there's evidence I want. Now—I shrugged my shoulders as an electric flash sent a darting glare through the window.

I stepped back from the circle of light, swung my gun toward the window and jerked out my own flash light. The flash, the calling voices and the heavy feet smacked of a police raid and it wouldn't be good policy for me to knock over a flat foot.

My light blazed upon a bulky figure—the brass buttons and the shining shield. Big blue eyes grew larger and blinked wonderingly. A black automatic waved slightly—then emptiness. His light went out before mine did. The can crashed in the alley, a soft oath faintly reached me—then a loud shout as he warned his friends.

"They're in there yet."

That would be about all of that. Those at the door were determined men. A few more such crashes and the heavy wood would give, even if the huge lock held. The police were there on business, and I've had experience in waiting to collect damages from the city for a busted door.

Stepping close to the curtains I switched on the hall light by shoving a hand around the molding. A rookie might shoot in the excitement. Then I shouted—the pounding ceased and I called again. An answer this time and I recognized the voice of Inspector Coglin.

I didn't smile when I opened the door and let Coglin and two harnessed bulls rush by me. Guns flashed and red, excited faces came dully out of the darkness. Coglin opened his mouth to speak—got an eyeful as I stood in the doorway and gulped down his words. He tried again and did better.

"You, eh—Race Williams, eh?" He did more tricks with his pan than a burlesque comedian.

"Certainly." I glared over at him as I switched on the library light and led the way into the room. "You didn't think I had rented the house to some one, did you?" Then killing the laugh, for the thing certainly was nervy, "You've changed your tactics, Inspector—you have a warrant for this of course." And I knew by his face that he didn't. Coglin had come before—often enough—in the night too—but never like this. His visits had been orderly, if threatening.

Coglin didn't speak for a minute. In a way he was a clever man. His eyes roved about the room—took in the disorder of the books, the open safe, and the gun on the floor. He was pulling himself together before he spoke. There was surprise in his face, disappointment too, I thought. This visit was different than the others then; he expected to find something this time. Not just try to glare into me the fear of Inspector Coglin, the self-constituted terror of the lawbreakers.

"Well—" I finally spoke, putting on my dignity and high hatting him just a bit. "Why am I indebted to you for this visit—forcible entry, they call it?" Then running my hand along my chin and staring straight into that hard cold face, "Perhaps the newspapers will be interested." And I mentioned one paper in particular. That stirred him up. The newspaper I named had been riding the department generally lately—and Coglin in particular.

"You've got me wrong, Race." He shook his head. "I didn't intend to jump down on you to-night. I didn't intend ever to jump down on you again. We got word to-night that you had been given the works. We busted in here looking for murder."

"So," was all I said when he paused. I wanted to be sure he wasn't feeding me a line. Certainly he seemed in a hurry to find the corpse of Race Williams. Perhaps a natural desire, that. I hesitated a moment, then thanked him for his interest in my—death. But he cut in.

"It wasn't that, Race. One runs down murders in the mechanical department routine. The man with the motive mostly solves the problem. With you—well, I could name a hundred without much thought who'd be glad of the opportunity to do you in. The department would spend years chasing down possible suspects. You've got as many enemies as a dog has fleas. So we rushed things."

"Why to-night—why not bust in on me every night—make a habit of it?" I couldn't help being sarcastic.

He didn't answer me but walked to the window and looked out.

"Do you know the gent?" I heard him ask some one in the darkness, and saw his neck bob forward when he received the whispered answer. Then he turned to the men in the doorway. "Outside," Coglin ordered abruptly, and when the men had departed he produced a cigar and shoving it into his mouth walked up and down the room.

It was hot stuff to watch him. What a child he was! In his own stupid way he was putting the screws on me—giving me a chance to watch his hunched shoulders; his hard, cold, glaring eyes as from time to time he jerked his head toward me. An old timer was Coglin—heavy of jowl—hard of chin. He was getting ready to hurl a few questions at me. I threw myself in a chair and waited. Finally he swung quickly, jerked a hand from behind his back and shot a thick finger toward me.

"What do you know of Jake Minely?" he snapped.

"Jake—" I looked toward the ceiling. "I heard he had one of his little spells to-night and slipped off an ash can. Terrible how he came down in the world. A regular Peeping Tom now."

"What happened to him to-night—beneath your window?" Again the glare as sharp teeth bit through the cigar and Coglin deftly caught it in his cupped right hand before it reached the floor.

"I think he was overcome by the heat." I shook my head. "A sad case, Coglin—hot head and cold feet." I wasn't worried at all—bothered a bit perhaps. The police must have had a very good reason for busting in on me like this, and it was like Coglin to beat around before he came out with what was on his chest.

Again his eyes lit on the gun on the floor. He raised his head, and looking at the window moved indifferently toward that gun. It was just impulse on my part. The girl meant nothing to me. Yet, my business was my own and not Coglin's. I was out of the chair and across the few feet as Coglin bent quickly, and my foot landed on that gun before his hand did.

"I have a license to have guns about, you know," I said calmly as he glared up at me. "You have no right in this house, Coglin—now, state your business and be gone."

"You had a visitor to-night." He straightened suddenly. "What became of her?"

"She must have been frightened by the racket you made." The girl's gun was in my pocket and I was back in the chair.

"I think," the inspector said suddenly, "I think I'll search the house." He passed quickly to the stairs, and I followed him. His hand slipped into his coat pocket and I thought that I caught the outline of a gun.

"You'll have to have a warrant, you know, Coglin."

"I think not." He threw back his shoulders. "You and I, Race Williams, know each other well enough to dispense with such formalities." His foot landed on the first step—the other followed—hung in mid-air—then dropped back to the landing.

"Inspector Coglin," was all I said. But he knew before he turned; caught the ring in my voice and understood. When his head turned I was playfully juggling my own forty-four. I didn't threaten him; didn't point the gun toward him. I watched him suck in the deep breath and noticed the sudden color in his cheeks. His eyes wandered from the window to the door. He was thinking seriously of having a final showdown with me. But I knew my rights and he knew that I not only knew them but would protect them.

"Save your breath." I stayed the angry words on his lips. "There is no reason why your uniform should protect you or give you the right to trample on my privileges or the sanctity of my home." And seeing that he was planning on calling in the boys and going through with the search, "It won't make a pretty story in the papers if you find nothing—besides, I've got a few friends of my own high up."

Coglin thought that one out—then he shrugged his huge shoulders.

"Very well." He didn't try to bluff it out or threaten to get himself a warrant. Warrants to search my house were pretty well of a farce and rather frowned at down at headquarters. Coglin would have to have a mighty good reason before he'd chance flashing a warrant. Oh, he could get one all right. But would he?

"You call yourself a detective," Coglin sneered, "but you ain't much better than the crooks you hunt. I know what I know, and some day I'll lay the cuffs on you. Some day I'll send you for a long stretch. You're making a powerful enemy when you might make a friend." He was stealing the girl's stuff there. He walked toward the front door, placed a hand on the knob and hesitated—then turning, he stepped back into the library.

"I'll lay my cards on the table," he said abruptly. "Perhaps for once we can work together. Why do you think I came here to-night?" And being a man who asked and answered his own questions, "Because I had word that you were killed—murdered in your library here—by a woman."

"You should have sent flowers," I said—then more seriously, "Who sent you word?" It was odd. A woman was there—and certainly murder had been planned—not once, but at least twice that night.

"It came from the house next door." He jerked a thumb toward the window and the vacant house. "The De Voe maid."

I knocked that argument on the head.

"There is no one in the house next door. The De Voes are South for the winter, and the servants dismissed. If you opened your eyes instead of your mouth you might have seen that the place is boarded up."

"I know, I know." He nodded impatiently. "But they are returning next week. The maid came on ahead to open up the house. At least, that's what she"—and seeing the smile on my face he broke off and stepped toward the window. "Clancy," he bellowed, at the darkness without, "ring that doorbell next door, and if you don't get an answer, bust in—have a look around—try the window on this side for it. But I think you'll find a frightened maid there."

He did, but I didn't. Dully from across the alley came the distant buzz of the bell. Coglin waited by the window, scanning the darkened windows of the house next door. I saw him look up once where the sloping roof hung over the alley, the copper gutters of the De Voe residence and my brownstone house but a few feet apart.

"Not a light—not a sound—not a soul," I heard him mutter.

"Probably some one wanted to pull off a job and gave you the grand run-around." I tried to make him feel better.

"I thought of that when I got the message." He jerked his head. "And I put a double watch on all the joints in my district." For a long time he stood there stroking his chin, then he let the shades fall back at the window—stood so a moment, his eyes glued down on the floor. Popping they were—staring at something.

I followed those eyes but saw nothing. Then he bent quickly down again between a jumble of books and fished up a bit of black cloth. It was the girl's mask. He held it in his hand while he looked at me. His eyes bulged and he whistled softly. Coglin's face shone with elation now—emotion too. He couldn't hide his surprise and satisfaction.

"The scattered books—the man by the window—the gun—and now the black mask. You had a visitor then." He was examining the mask more carefully now, running his fingers over the material, sticking them through the narrow slits for the eyes and the more generous opening for the mouth.

"Don't be a fool." He turned suddenly on me. "There's a reward going out for the man; he killed a policeman to-night. Did you—did you do him in? I've been tipped off that he came this way. You're not holding him—trying to get information, are you? Forget our trouble; forget the department. The ten thousand dollars' reward is yours and—" His hands came far apart, his eyes blazed and his thick, dominant chin set tightly. He was looking for some one definite then.

"Easy does it, Coglin." I never saw a man more excited. "Some one was here—but has gone. I found the place like this. Who is the man you want?"

"The Beast." He fairly whispered the words. "You've heard of him perhaps—we've tried to keep it from the papers. A brute—who murders like the fiend he is. The most feared, the cunningest and cruelest creature that stalks the city streets at night. We call him simply, The Beast. You've heard of this man—know of him—have—have—?"

Yes, I had heard of him but just that night; met him face to face too. But I couldn't connect up the girl who had run up my stairs with the snarling, "bullet proof" beast that I had met and Coglin sought, though I wasn't any admirer of that little lady—she had too many lightning-like changes.

"Maybe you're mixed up in running him down, eh?" Coglin's cigar did a run across his face as his eyes snapped shrewdly. "But you'll get no information out of him. He won't talk, or can't, and even your methods won't get any—" The cigar took a sudden curve upward; the lighted end seemed to flick against his nose as the ashes fell to the floor. I too raised my head as Coglin reached for his gun and dashed by me and toward the hall.

14

A Hand on the Sill

From somewhere far above us in the darkness a chair had crashed to the floor. There was the patter of feet, a stifled scream, the jar of a closing window and the clatter of falling glass in the court without.

I jerked Coglin back. But it was too late to stop him now. There was nothing of the coward in Coglin—he feared no man; feared only censure back at headquarters and ridicule by the papers. Now he half turned and shouted to the men by the front door. Figures were in the room, heavy feet beat upon the stairs. From the alley without Clancy called shrilly, but none of us heard what he said.

A policeman on the stairs stopped; the officer behind him bumped against him and drew up sharply. Coglin spun like a top, his gun in his hand, his hat tipped to the side of his head, his cigar hanging from his lips. We all listened, heads raised, shoulders erect, skin tingling—the blood runs cold in brave men at times. None of us could be sure. A whining queer sort of animal sound had come through the open window—or was it just the whistling of the wind in the winter night; just the hum of the wind across the house tops? Yet—yet we knew that there was no wind. Coglin quivered like an angry dog. As for me—well, here was a good excuse to dig a hand into my pocket, and I sure took advantage of the opportunity. The queer, moaning note in the night was hard to place maybe—but I thought I knew that eerie cry, for I had heard it before.

Just a moment we stood so; then Clancy cried from outside. Coglin spoke in a hushed whisper to the men on the stairs and dashed toward the open window. He reached it too—pulled up sharp, and the bluecoated figure behind crashed into him. There was the roar of a gun; the glass above Coglin's head was punctured and a picture behind me smashed to the floor. This time none of us were in doubt about the sound. No one could mistake it for the wind—clearly through the night came the whining, hissing growl—the Snarl of the Beast.

"The Snarl of the Beast," I heard Coglin mutter—then as another shot broke the silence, he called—"Clancy, are you all right?"

"Yes, sir—I am that—it's the Beast, sir—himself—in person—there—he's jumped to the next house." Two shots almost at once, and Coglin throwing all caution to the wind ran toward the window, thrust his head and shoulders out and emptied his gun at the house across the way, shouting as he fired.

"He was there—in the window—surround that house—bust into it—all of you now." And he slid a leg over the sill, and followed by the uniformed men dropped to the alley below.

Good enough! That was his party, not mine. Something told me that the man would get away; be off through the next yard before the officers ever got there—and if they did get there—well, that was their funeral. The Beast—yes, a good name for him. A man who killed and got away. Brute strength, brute cunning, and the desperate resolve of one who does not know or does not understand fear.

Of course I wanted a shot at him. He was my meat. But I'd see him again. It was a cinch that he was here for one purpose. To get me. He had trailed me earlier in the night, and again now; right in the teeth of the police themselves. He must have tried to get in my house by jumping from the house next door. The girl had probably opened the window in the hope of escaping, and that was the crash we heard— when the window was hastily pulled down.

Maybe I should be out joining in the hunt. But why? I had other things to think of and it was in the cards that I'd meet this giant again. If we met now one of us would die, and I had a feeling that a well directed chunk of lead smack between those colorless eyes would be a surprise to the big boy who hunted his prey in the night. Then what? Then I'd be without a client, who wanted this man dead—maybe, who'd pay well for it—maybe, after all, did Danny know where there was a big piece of change that would be coming his way?

But the girl above! Was she in my house by accident? What was she searching for? A letter she thought I had? Then she was not mixed up with Danny, the girl of the night and the Beast, for there was no letter that— And I stroked my chin. There was a letter in my pocket. Yet, she could not know of that. Even if she had been told, there was not time—not time unless she suspected that I'd go for the letter that night. Hadn't Danny said something about using that letter as a threat over their heads? "Their"—who was "their"?

And the girl was still above and the cops were raising the very devil outside; shouting and pounding and calling advice to each other. Why, one good man with a steady eye and a quick finger and a handy ash can to wait behind, would do better than the whole force. Just watch and wait, and shoot the Beast down when he appeared. That would be my game—his huge form would make a mistake impossible. Nothing heroic about getting a man that way? Maybe not. But it's good business—and I'm all for good business.

For a while I stood in the center of the room, listening. The cries from without were dying away. Windows were flopping up and I daresay many a wire was buzzing frantic appeals at police headquarters. But no shout of triumph echoed through the open window; no more pistol shots either, for that matter.

89

The police were hunting down their man and not having much success at it. My ears were trained for sounds above, now. The girl! And there was no sound upstairs. Poor Kid; she was cowering in some closet most likely. Poor Kid, I thought again—and wondered if the "poor Kid" was sporting another gun in her hand and a bit of murder in her heart. She was a girl you might trust with your watch, providing of course that it was a dollar watch.

Somewhere off in the night, police and detectives would be getting in the way of each other—firing at their own friends and calling warnings to the prowler on the block. That was the law of the man hunt; fear of mistaken identity. I like to play the game alone; where every shadow is an enemy and each bullet I shoot goes in the right direction and reaches the right man.

Nothing but the cold came through the open window. I closed it—there wasn't enough fire in the furnace to heat the house properly, let alone trying to heat all outdoors. The tiny hole in the upper pane I stuffed a bit of paper into. Good clean shooting, that—just the single little hole and a crack the length of the glass. The bullet no doubt would be in the wall behind, where the picture had stood.

So much for that. A woman was hiding some place above. I wanted two things. One was a look at her face; the other a bit of a sleep between heavy blankets. And the first ran closely in line with the second. I couldn't get that sleep until I knew where the girl was. I didn't want to wake up suddenly in the morning and call a doctor to go digging the bullets out of my chest. So I stepped into the front hall and went whistling up the stairs, for all the world like an easy and undisturbed householder. You didn't expect I'd park myself in the kitchen with the ice chest shoved up against the swinging door to the pantry. Not me—I'd of gone to my bed if the Beast and all his friends were playing hide-and-go-seek under it.

The girl had been on the left side of my house, nearest to the vacant house next door; a room above and just back of the library. Witness the closing window and the crash of glass. The natural conclusion was that she wouldn't stay there but would skip across to the bedroom opposite or one further toward the back and away from the front stairs. She wouldn't run down the back stairs. The door from the hall to those stairs was locked. I always see to that. My house has been entered before and I make sure that prowlers don't run loosely around it.

You see, that's my advantage over the housebreaker. I know the ground and he don't. I know too when he runs up against a blind alley and is cornered.

Half way up those stairs my whistle stops. A door has closed softly; far back near the rear, on the side of the house I thought she'd be. I nod my satisfaction, and in the jet blackness trot on my way. I know where the girl will be now and I'm determined to see it through. She'd had the fear of the police put into her heart. If she won't talk, I'll let her expect a march to the police station. She could cry all over my shirt if she wanted to; I'd be changing it in the morning anyway.

There's a creak as I reach that closed door, grab for the knob, spin it, and feel the well oiled catch drop into its socket without a sound. No—she didn't lock it. I'm the only one who locks doors in my house—there's no keys in locks, to make it handy for crooks.

The slightest sound comes from within the room. The girl is there all right and at the window—slowly forcing it up. If she had worked a bit quicker she'd have come in for some good luck she had no right to expect. In way of escape, she couldn't have picked a better place. A pipe ran from the window to the back yard; a strong bit of copper pipe that would easily support her weight. But she couldn't have known that it would take her some time to find it. I'd often left and reëntered that way myself while servants were below. It was great alibi stuff for me when the police watched the house and I had a bit of business that needed secrecy. Some day I'll go in for secret passages and that sort of stuff, but I've never been able to find a deaf and dumb workman who knew his business and couldn't read and write and otherwise had no way of communicating with people. Oh, it's been done of course—books are full of it. But with me, I'm playing the game of life—yep, life and death—and there's only my gun, my fingers, and my eyes that make the grim reaper mark time on my little trip across the River Styx.

The door slips silently back—not a single sound—and hangs there as a draft of cold air hits me from the window. I can hear the girl—she's working just a bit faster now. She's got the window up and is out it. There in the dimness of the winter sky I get the faintest outline of her shadow as she does her stuff—uncertainly too. Was she an amateur or just nervous? That is, a physical amateur—not a mental one. The germ of the crook might be in her soul, but was it in her body yet? The mind directs the evil all right but the body can refuse to carry that evil out. Get the difference. You often have the will and the heart for a thing but not the stomach for it.

And she found the pipe. I could hear her foot ring out dully against it as I crossed the room, creeping silently toward the window. To call to her now might make her jump for it, and the least she could expect was a broken bone or two, or it might make her shout—which would be worse from my point of view. The court below slopes slightly from the street level and she'd have a good fall at best. If it was a man, I might jump, crash him, and pick him up later, when he was able to talk and no doubt willing. But this was reality and not what might have been. I hadn't fallen in love with that bit of fluff—not me. But it takes a peculiar mental twist to make a man crash a woman. Maybe it's a weakness; maybe it's a strength—I don't know.

The form slipped from the window now; the tousled head of the girl disappeared from view. Nothing left but a white hand that still clung to the sill for support. The fingers were trembling there; the other hand no doubt had found the pipe and clutched it—nothing left for the girl to do but grab the pipe with both hands and slide down. Nothing but that—yet it took courage. She had gone through something. The Beast with the hairy hands; the shots in the night; the police shouting to one another; and a pipe, the security of which was only problematical from her point of view.

Too late she made up her mind. I finished the distance in a quick leap that she couldn't have helped but hear, and clutched the wrist just as the fingers released their grasp on the sill.

"Surely you wouldn't go without saying good-by," I whispered sarcastically down to her. "Now just brace your feet on the ledge there—don't make the effort too hard for me while I pull you back into the room. Really—you'll catch your death of cold."

"Please—please—let me go," she sobbed—yet her teeth grated, in anger, I thought.

"I'm sorry." I gave her the conventional answer. "But you've made your bed—if it pricks you've got to grin and bear it." I started to haul her up as gently as I could.

"Oh—oh! that hurts," she cried. "Don't—please don't." There was a whimper in her voice; a low, grating tone that could not be hidden even in the sobbing of her words as her other hand shot up and clutched at my wrist—and her full weight hung upon my arm.

I'm a strong man—the suddenness of it jarred me forward a bit but not enough to pull me through the window. Still, to have a dame hanging to your arm and swinging about like the pendulum in a clock is not so easy. I reached out with my other hand, caught at the wrist that clutched at mine, straightened her out a bit and proceeded to lift her in the window.

She didn't resist any more now. She was frightened. I couldn't make out her features over well, but a white face with tightly set lips was staring up at me. But this time one thing was certain—I was going to have a look at that face. Things came easier as her feet found the ledge again and rested on it. I gave her a chance to get her breath back—tightened my grip on her wrists—and got ready for the final tug that would bring her over the sill and back into the room.

15

The Man in the Blackness

And I didn't pull her in. Some one was in the room behind me. Did I hear the step? I don't think so. Did I hear the man's deep breath? Maybe. But I'm not sure of that—not positive that I heard anything. I don't always have to hear things to know that another presence is close to mine. There's a tingling comes with it. Maybe I do unconsciously hear, feel or sense that presence—and then I was sure. A heel scraped the door jamb—very slightly of course, but enough for me to know. Visitors in the night don't have to write me letters.

Would I drop the girl and let her take a chance on the fall? That was my first thought, I'll admit. It wouldn't kill her, and what did I owe to her? Suppose this was Hairy-Hands—The Beast coming back again! He'd have the nerve for it. I didn't doubt that after his action that night; from lying flat on the sidewalk down town, to the roof of the house next to mine, and a swing down it to the second-story window in about one hour or less is some traveling for a boy who's felt lead on his arm and steel on his head, you'll admit. No—there wasn't anything I wouldn't put a-past that gent who the police slated as coming from the animal kingdom.

But another thought came with it. Hardly The Beast. I have ears that are tuned as fine as the Navy wireless station. He couldn't have made the house without my hearing him—and without the police seeing him either. But I'd have to drop the girl—then the thought—the solution no doubt to my silent visitor in that room. Coglin had played the game well; one of his men had stayed behind—hidden across the hall down stairs in the dining room. That was it. That must be it. Least-wise I told myself that was it and gave the girl a chance. Strange for me. Yep, there's no way to explain why I didn't let her go, and reach for a gun.

"Grab the pipe and finish the job you started," I told her as I bent forward, putting my lips close to her ear or where I thought her ear was. "Silently too—or the people next door will— Come! snap into it, Kid—here's the chance for freedom you've been sobbing about."

I released one hand, steadied her with the other—and reached for my gun. Was I fooling myself by thinking it was a cop who had remained behind? And what was the girl to me? Was I playing the idiot because of a bit of lace; the same that had knocked the ambitions of great men on the head throughout the past centuries. I don't know—but somehow I just couldn't drop her. A soft, delicate, cold hand in mine! Good to feel? Not so you could notice it! I wished with all of what I am pleased to call my heart that the hand was big and rough and hairy.

Certainly I could be seen there in the window as I half turned, lowering my gun so that it and my hand were in the jet blackness beneath the sill. It was ridiculous for me to tell myself that I was invisible. The morning was still dark, and all that—not much to see—and yet I had seen the girl in that same window. And her hand found the pipe—the other sort of squeezed mine—her voice came up to me.

"Thank you—I'll never forget." And she started down the pipe. I could hear her all right—and the man in the room, could he? I ducked to one side, into the darkness, when he spoke.

"Don't get funny, Race Williams," he snapped. "I'm a Headquarters' man—where's the light?"

I breathed easier as I slid into the darkness. I never did envy the life of the force. Take this poor unfortunate lad for instance. Here he was trailing me, and the moment he thought that I spotted him he had to give his presence away. Probably had orders not to fire unless I went to shoot him. Think of that—as if I'd write him a letter, telling him to start in searching for his gun. No wonder so many of the cops get knocked off. He wasn't permitted to just plug me and explain afterwards, and he didn't know if I'd shoot or not.

Knowing my reputation, he must have spent a bad ten seconds or more when he saw my face framed in the window. Had I discovered his presence, and if I had, would I shoot? Fine thoughts for a guardian of the law. Now, as I slipped deeper into the darkness, the grating sound on the pipe came clearly to me.

"I'm going to that window and I'm going with a flash." The man in the dark tried to make his voice ring with assurance and his feet heavy as he started to walk forward.

"You'll pull no flash here and you'll stand your ground." I shot the words out of the darkness as I moved again to avoid the possibility of a shot striking from where my voice came. "As soon as you show a flash, I'll fire—that's gospel." I finished as the feet drew up quick and clicked on the floor.

"You're defying the police—Coglin just wants an excuse to take you in—better keep still and—remember, I speak in the name of the law."

"Do you now?" I was out to gain time. "And how do I know that? Of course, if you're really from the department— why—wait and I'll switch on the light. But don't move."

"Some one went out that window." He fairly hissed the words, yet his feet jerked back again. "I'll—if you shoot me, Race Williams," and he played the old stock company voice, "you'll swing for it."

"Don't be silly." I edged further around to his side. "I don't believe you're a policeman at all. If you were, you'd know they don't go in for hanging in New York. Why, Man, any school child knows—"

"I know, I know—if you dare to fire, you'll get the chair."

"Better!" I stepped a little further around him. "But you're only guessing. I've got to be sure of you. I'm the last man in the world to defy the law of the state. I have great respect for its august—" I broke off as his feet scraped. "Another move and I'll plug you."

He stopped dead—there was a dull thud outside the window. This cop had courage all right. He threw all caution aside, pulled out a flash and dashed toward the window. A brave man, that; somewhat of a foolish one also. I don't go in for murder. Still, if I had doubted— Well, even policemen can't run around my house without a warrant. I felt almost sure that at the worst I'd get a disagreement by the jury in case of a little killing. But the girl was in the court—safe from him at least, and my fingers already rested on the electric light button.

As he reached the window I pressed the switch and flooded the room with light. No need to argue with him further. No plain-clothes man, this—but a harnessed bull.

"Some one dropped from that window." The officer turned angrily toward me. "What do you know of this?"

"I thought as much." I looked down at his gun as I dropped my own into my pocket. "And I'd of had him too if you hadn't come stamping into the room." He had the grace to blush at that crack. "He was trying to climb up from outside—a detective, I think."

"You'll pay for this," he said; opened his mouth for a flow of words—closed it again—tried once more and repeated with a gulp, "You'll pay for this." Certainly he wasn't any orator.

What kind of a discussion we'd have gotten into I don't know. But our little party was broken up by the ringing of the door bell and the pounding on the front door below. The harnessed bull hesitated, his gun half raised toward me. It was in his mind to stick it in my back and shove me ahead of him down those stairs. Not a pretty picture that, so I saved him the trouble.

"I'll lead the way down," I said. "This will be Inspector Coglin, returning—and no doubt he carries a bit of paper with him; they call it a search warrant." I threw the final words back over my shoulder as I started toward the stairs.

"He told you that?" The cop behind gasped and I had found out what I wanted. If anything suspicious turned up at my house Coglin was ready to grab himself off a warrant. Now, who was the judge who had so little respect for his own slumber that he would stay awake waiting to sign such a warrant?

I shrugged my shoulders as I preceded my friend down the stairs. I gave Coglin full credit for finding at least one high official who looked with an unfriendly eye on my activities. Still, the thing had a few advantages. My house wasn't such a small affair. I'd had at least one visitor; I couldn't go to bed without searching it for others. Inspector Coglin and his friends would save me that trouble. Yep, I've got to admit that even with me there are times when the police serve their purpose. That he wouldn't take me to the jug was fairly certain.

Of course it was Coglin at the door. And his smile of pride and derision as he presented his warrant was wiped clean off his map like you'd pulled a mop across it when I killed his enthusiasm.

"Yes, yes, dear man," I yawned. "I know about it. This good soul here told me all about it." I glanced at the officer behind me, who was yelling his head off about hearing some one drop into the alley.

"I did not—I never did." And the harnessed bull burst into an explanation that sounded pretty lame under the hard eyes of the inspector. I tried to caution them about having a row in my house—even advising an investigation about it, and then dropped the matter entirely. But Coglin had lost his enthusiasm to search the house. If I hadn't of seen that paper I don't doubt for a minute that he'd of buried it deep beneath his coat.

"Just one favor, Inspector," I said as the boys started in to do their duty. "Take my bedroom, upstairs, first. I'm tired and I want sleep—the front door will lock itself when you go out, and I won't need to be disturbed."

He was about to refuse, then changed his mind with a scowl. It was a cinch what was passing through his head. He never did anything I asked him to, therefore I was trying to get him to search my room last. Why? Of course he couldn't figure that out—but he decided there was some reason for the request. Anyhow he searched my room first—made no objections while I slipped into my pyjamas, saw him out, locked my steel lined bedroom door, pushed over the great steel shutters with the narrow slits for air, and climbed into bed.

Some one stood outside the door, I think, but I can't be sure. But an easy conscience is a great thing—my room was safe. A man must be sure when he seeks his rest. Five minutes at the most and I was sleeping like a child. But I always sleep tight—come fully awake in a second too. So it was I heard Coglin at the door shortly after dawn.

"We're leaving," he growled, and nothing more.

And nothing more was needed. I turned once in the bed, called a cheery "Good night" and asked him to shut the door quietly when he went out. Did he go then? I don't know—before he could have reached the front door I was fast asleep again. No—poor old Coglin didn't have the guts to drag me in—not him. He feared neither man nor devil, did Coglin, but like the elephant who fears the mouse, so Inspector Coglin went in terror of the newspaper reporters. After all, jobs down at Headquarters—even the jobs of inspectors—were none too secure. Crime ran unchecked through the city streets and the police traveled in fear of their jobs as well as their lives. To give them credit, I guess the thought of the job came first. A New York City policeman hasn't much time to think about his life to-day. No, sir. I'm not down on the police as an individual—not me. It's the system. But no thoughts ran through my head then—I did nothing else but sleep—and I did it well.

16

By the Alley Door

Benny, my chauffeur, was on the job at twelve next day and he's an all-around man; good at the car, good at bacon and eggs and coffee, and can handle a gun when the occasion warrants it. He didn't bother me until I had finished a couple of eggs and was on my second cup of coffee—then he laid down the mail, the morning paper and chirped:

"Two men watch the house—dicks, both of them."

"Central Office men?"

"Yeh—they make no bones about it."

"And the paper this morning, Benny?"

"A harness bull croaked—sergeant; a murder in Harlem and a girl in Brooklyn cut with a knife. Your name don't appear."

"Anything else—automobile accidents? Central Park?"

"Inside page—twelve."

I waved Benny away, took the paper and turned to the item. There wasn't much to it. The police were laying low or my taxi driver had put over a bedtime story on that innocent motor cycle cop. Yet it was a plausible story at that. I read it over again. The substance of it was that there had been a slight accident when the steering knuckle of a taxicab snapped in Central Park. The "fare," seeing the danger of striking a tree, had thrown open the door of the cab and attempted to jump—but unfortunately just as the car swerved from the road, he was thrown violently to the roadway. The story went on.

"He was not unconscious however, and the taxi driver, having driven for him many times before, knew his address and the man was taken to his home in another cab, called by the officer."

Not bad—not half bad even. He'd have his own doctor who'd pull out the bullet, and the police record would carry a fractured leg or a broken collar bone. Well—it didn't make much difference to me. These were pawns in the game—the game of Hairy-Hands. A big game too, for even a pawn was bent on murder. But was Hairy-Hands the leader? I doubted that. Brains, not hands, were searching for my death. Why?

What of my client? In broad daylight, over a second cup of coffee, his story didn't seem so impossible after all. If it wasn't for the tiny punctures on his arm and the girl's denial, I'd be tempted to believe it. Hairy-Hands, The Beast, had never taken an interest in me before. Was it just coincidence that he should be after me and the boy at the same time? No—I don't go in for coincidences. But the girl—

I stopped and laughed. If it were true, what good would it do me at that moment? I didn't know where the boy went to. It was a cinch that he wouldn't come back to that dirty tenement, and it was a cinch too that his lady friend didn't want me mixed up in it. Would he write? But how? She'd let him think that I was all right that night. No doubt she'd have the mailing of the letters and would probably slip them into a convenient refuse can, in a mistake that it was a post box.

So much for all that. I'd look at my mail anyway. A quick glance convinced me that there wasn't any from the boy—perhaps it would be sent to the office. But one letter interested me greatly. The left hand corner of the envelope made me open it eagerly. No disappointment either. A check for a thousand lay in my hand; right on a New York bank too, and there was no necessity for having that check certified. I knew Barton Briskey and had had business with him before. The letter was short and to the point.

MY DEAR WILLIAMS:

Will you call at my down town office at 12:00 (twelve) midnight to-night. I will discuss something which should prove to your advantage. A copy of this letter goes to your office.

Respectfully yours,
BARTON BRISKEY.

Not a word concerning the check. It was just there and that was all. We understood each other. Barton Briskey was a lawyer—a criminal lawyer—and I don't mean that last crack as a pun. There wasn't any question that he had been about a block and a half ahead of the district attorney for the past ten years and was likely to hold his distance too. He knew the difference between right and wrong and knew just how far he could travel on the wrong road without tripping over the top step of a jail entrance. Barton Briskey was the mouthpiece of more high-class crooks than any ten other lawyers in New York City. And he wasn't any shyster either. I daresay there weren't any lawyers in the great city that had anything on him for knowledge of criminal law and the best method of beating a case. Twice he had been up for disbarment, yet each time the great legal minds found the evidence insufficient. Not that he wasn't guilty. They all felt he was—but "insufficient evidence" landed him back practicing again. An uptown office and a downtown office—and believe me, few people knew where that down town office was—when too many found it out, he moved.

Yes, sir—I can't say that I'd fully trust him—but I had to admire him. He could have been head counsel for the biggest corporations in the east and done credit to it too—but he wasn't. He liked to play the game he knew so well—some day he'd get knocked off—that was certain. But we had one thing in common. So far the police couldn't get anything on either of us.

I read his letter over again. I liked the way it ran. No mention of that check for one grand. That was his way of doing business. And the time? Clients who have something to hide like the hour of midnight—but why him? Still, I didn't care. My work is always better in the dark—eyes are always watching—guns always ready. It's a great life—this business of always watching for death. Like eels getting skinned. You get used to it.

There was no hint of secrecy in the note. But of course that was understood, if for no other reason than that his down town office might be discovered and raided. Though they'd find nothing. Barton Briskey's knowledge was all in the back of his head; his files were some place above his ears. Every crook knew that he kept no questionable memorandum, and never once had he tried to blackmail a former client. He was a hard man against you—but if you were his client, then you were a lucky man indeed. I tucked that letter alongside the one in my pocket—the one that bore the address of Danny Davidson's sister, or suddenly adopted or even imaginary sister. For no such name appeared in the telephone book, though Oscar Merrill Davidson hung his hat at that address.

At my office I got the duplicate of Barton Briskey's morning letter. He was a thorough man and so was I. I'd be in the neighborhood of the lawyer's office a good hour ahead of time. One can't be sure—he might be interviewing his client and I might get a slant at that client. I've worked for Barton Briskey before—blindly, and I didn't like it. It might be a case of losing the job or keeping his client's identity secret from me. This way, I might spot the one who sought my help through Barton Briskey—in a way, then, I'd know about what to charge and how big the thing was.

I made it easy for the dicks who followed me that day. I just didn't notice them, went home at dinnertime, took a nap, read my paper, and at ten-thirty did my stuff. It was time to shake the shadows. It's not a matter of being clever or slippery. It's a matter of timing things just right. The city sleuths would have a car down the street all right. They had, for Benny spotted it. I worked it like this:

I waited in my vestibule for Benny to come with the car; and I spotted his lights as he turned the corner down the street. Not my own car of course—that would be known and followed even before I got in it—this is a hired one. And it never slowed down as it approached my house at exactly twenty-three miles an hour. That's my margin of absolute safety.

Practice told me exactly at what moment to dash from my doorway; just as the nose of the car passed the second street light down the block. Then I made my run for it—out onto the street, a quick spurt and I grabbed the door, swung up on the running board, and Benny stepped on the gas. It was almost a straight run to the Park from there and Benny hit the entrance at nearly fifty miles an hour. What's a ticket or two? But the chances were he wouldn't get that.

It was the jump I made as Benny slowed down as he turned north in the Park that carried danger. I had to skip across the grass and drop behind the wall before the high-powered police car gave chase. But practice makes perfect—I made that wall as the police auto flashed through the Park entrance. The police were sure on the job and they'd overhaul Benny before he got a hundred yards. As for me—I skipped along in the shadow of the wall, waited until I spotted a taxi, slipped back into Central Park West, climbed aboard and shot over to Broadway and so up town. At the Ninety-sixth Street subway station I left the taxi and entering the underground—roared my way to the lower city.

I doubt that the police were overanxious to follow me; more likely they wanted to watch for any visitor I had—preferably Hairy-Hands. That was nice—it isn't often that Race Williams sleeps under a police guard. Really, I'd have to write the commissioner a letter of thanks for it.

It wasn't so cold but there was a rawness in the air and the feel of snow. This time I played the lower West Side, not far from Wall Street. Few tenements there; mostly worn old structures that housed through the centuries the great lawyers and brokers of former days. And even yet prominent and famous names stood out on the windows of buildings whose only claim to distinction was the glories of the past. Pitifully shabby, these three-story structures looked—sunk into the midst of New York's great skyscrapers. Yet, there was a staid respectability about them that was not to be denied.

An occasional light peeped down through the musty window of some young American who was destined to make his name in the Street as he worked in a cheerless, cold office. Dim lights too in the back of shops; musty old holes where bespectacled and long-haired book worms spent their days with their noses bent into ancient books that had little to recommend them beside the date they went to print.

The building that housed Barton Briskey's office stood on a corner. A saloon had once graced the entrance and it still did business under the title of OYSTER BAR. But not at night—no shadowy forms drifted in and out of that dreary doorway. The main office entrance was on a fairly wide street; the side entrance, which I guess was Briskey's way in and out, was on an alley so narrow that if two cars wanted to pass, one would have to climb up a pole and wait until the other went by. But I'd come in by the front entrance when the clock struck the hour. I wasn't supposed to know much about that back entrance—and I didn't. But I thought it more than likely that that little door in the alley led directly to the rooms of Barton Briskey. At all events I'd watch and see if he came in that way—that is, if he wasn't already in. Not any special reason in my mind. I'm just a careful man, that's all.

Across from that little door was a busted wooden gate and the back of a covered truck in the driveway. That was inviting. I slid around that truck and listened. No movement from within, so I climbed aboard—noted the stacks of tightly bound volumes that were catalogues or magazines, and I saw too the heavy matting that was tossed into the back and partly flung over the books. It wasn't so clean but it was warm.

Besides, from there I could watch that little door without being seen myself. The radium dial on my watch told me that it was just five minutes after eleven. There was some time to wait yet before I put in an appearance at the lawyer's office.

There was time to think too. The check had been a generous one. Flopped in sudden after my talk with the youth and the attempt on my life by Hairy-Hands. I wondered if the youth, Danny, had sought out Barton Briskey and if Briskey was financing the deal. If he was there was real truth in the matter. Of course my visit there might not have anything at all to do with last night's experiences, but—

My thoughts quit and I eased forward on my stomach, peering out and trying to look down the little alley. Footsteps were creaking along—not pounding on the pavement as a man who walks about his business—but a gent whose attempt to slip noiselessly along was somewhat killed by the musical shoes he sported. A sheik whose vanity was betraying him to my straining ears.

He was a long lanky bird and I had a hunch that I had seen him before; last night—the dirty panhandler who had tried to get me in conversation while The Beast jumped me. Not much of a lad either, if it came to a show down; a cowardly sort of a boy. Surely he wasn't on my trail; yet, what was he doing in that neighborhood and why was he so stealthily approaching that doorway?

17

A Rescue

Just a coincidence that he was there? Not a chance. In some way Barton Briskey was connected with Danny Davidson. On which side was the question? It was possible that the panhandler had gotten wind of my coming—that some one had even trailed me. Not that I believed that, but as I said—ANYTHING IS POSSIBLE TO-DAY. Of course there was the idea of a trap. Barton Briskey wouldn't be above such a thing for his own benefit. But it wouldn't be for his own benefit. I don't suppose there is any one who knows me better than Barton Briskey, and he knew that if he trapped me and I lived, I'd come back for him. He knew also that when I go for a man I get that man.

Then what? But I'd wait and see; perhaps this lad was there for an entirely different purpose. He was a leaf from the old days—a costume player—for to-night he was dressed in the livery of a chauffeur. Maybe to-morrow he'd play the rôle of a baby in a perambulator. He might just as well try that. His stooping shoulders and slouching gait couldn't be disguised and I doubt if the crack in his voice could, when he got excited. No—if any lad wanted a try at my life there could be no one I'd prefer to this duck. He didn't have the stomach of a louse. The gang should use him to frighten women and children—and very young and nervous children at that.

He took up his stand by the little door across the street; close to it too, so that he could not be seen from either end of the alley; yet, he could stretch out his head and look up and down it. The place was as silent as a morgue. Strange too—a few more hours and it would be alive with push carts, hustling men and lagging boys. I daresay in the daytime you could buy anything in that alley from a ham sandwich to an automobile, to say nothing of a handful of oil stocks that were guaranteed to rob widows and orphans of their last nickel. No—all the crooks didn't hang out in this neighborhood in the night—the boys that worked there in the daytime had them skinned a mile.

This fellow didn't have long to wait. Things were about to happen. I crept to the front of the truck as he crouched back against the wall—and the little door opened. A figure framed there a moment; a figure that looked up and down the street, then closing the door behind, it stepped toward the single step which led to the sidewalk. It was a girl—of course I couldn't be sure, but if I were a betting man I'd lay pretty good odds that it was my girl of the night—Milly of the smiling eyes and hard mouth.

As the door closed, the man came into view again—an arm shot out and wound quickly about the girl's neck; and I was close enough to hear the voice that hissed in her ear, though I couldn't get the words. But he sure was an obliging cuss, for he half carried and half shoved the girl across the alley and straight through the gateway, and right smack up against the truck where I lay. I could have laughed but I didn't.

The girl fought a little—after her first involuntary gasp she didn't cry out, though she could have. The man's arm was about her neck but the hand had missed her mouth. He released his grasp when they reached the protecting sides of the gate and were hidden from view in the alley.

"Not a peep, lady." And I could see the gun shove into her side; not a gentle shove either. It hurt, for though no protest came from the girl, her lips clicked with a snap.

"We ain't a-goin' to hurt ya, lady," the man whined on. "It ain't a kidnaping nor yet an elopement. Just want to borrow a bit of change—let me see what you have in that bag there." He snatched the bag from her, tore it open—dropped it with a curse and ordered the girl to throw up her hands.

"You got more than that, ya little rat. Come—give it up—quick—do ya want me to smack you one?" He snatched her hat suddenly from her head. I drew in a deep breath—if he had of been a vaudeville magician he couldn't have pulled a better act. It rained money there on the walk—big bills too—right out of the hat.

"Ah!" His gun lowered for a moment as he snatched at the bills. Then he thought of the girl. Just in time too, for her right hand had dropped and was creeping toward her pocket.

"Ya would, would ya?" He jumped up, with his arm raised and his fist closed. "Your sweetheart'll wait a bit for ya to-night. I didn't intend to crash ya, but now I—"

"Won't." It was I who finished the sentence for him as I jumped out of the truck, grabbed his hand and twisted it behind his back. I was slightly ashamed of the girl too. One quick look she took at me, then dropping to her knees gathered up the money. Money! The god of her kind. It came before her life even, I guess. She was still on her knees when I knocked the gun from the dirty lad's hand, spun him around and stared into his face. He knew me too, for his face turned white.

"Race Williams!" he gulped.

"You're going over," I told him as I shoved the gun against his chest. "You tried for my life last night—you know my law—if you've got a prayer say it before I pull the trigger."

What a rat he was! He didn't stop to think that I couldn't just kill him there in front of the girl. He didn't know that it wouldn't be good policy for me to startle the neighborhood with a pistol shot; that my business there was far more important than knocking off a cheap gun. But nothing like that went through his head. He just saw death—sure and sudden, and he slunk to his knees and began to beg for his life.

And the girl! She fell for my talk. She was on her feet now, clutching at my arm.

"Don't kill him—please. After all, it's me that he harmed—not you."

But I shook my head.

"He tried for my life and he's got to take his medicine." I couldn't very well just let him go, and I couldn't very well knock him on the head either. I'd of liked to have questioned him but that wasn't practical there. Not with the girl about and—if I let him go he'd think it was a weakness on my part. It wasn't my way to let up on an enemy. He'd know that—the word would get around and—

I jarred up straight. You could have knocked me down with a rotten tomato. The girl had shoved a gun into my back—hard too.

"Let him go," she said. "And you"—she turned to the man who was staggering to his feet—"keep your face shut on to-night."

"Also"—I added, for my gun was still trained on him—"if you're in the city to-morrow I'll find you. Your life isn't worth mine—make tracks—and remember, I'll be looking for you if it—"

And that was all of that. The man was out in the alley dashing wildly down it. Before I could finish my sentence he'd of been in Harlem. The girl had given me an excuse for letting the bird go. He didn't know that. She didn't know that. So it was good. But the girl! Just think of it—I'd saved her money; perhaps even her life—and now— She laughed there beside me; and I turned sharply as the gun bounced into her pocket.

"You wouldn't have killed him—besides, I couldn't let you go that far for me. I'm not worth it." She stared down at my feet. A slight bit of wind swept around the open gate and a crumpled bit of paper hung about my ankle. I got to it ahead

110

of the girl. It was a century note. I whistled softly as I held the bill toward her. This girl had come down the little stairs that must have led to Barton Briskey's office, and she had come down dough heavy. There's food for thought for a thinking man. I never jump at conclusions—not me. But I wouldn't need a brick wall to fall on my head to let me know that Danny Davidson, the girl called Milly, and Barton Briskey were all mixed up in the same business. Also, that where Barton Briskey was—there was money.

"Keep the hundred." The girl looked up at me; steady eyes that shone through the darkness. "If you want more, name your price—you helped me, I suppose."

"You suppose!" I gasped as I shoved the century note into her hand. "At least you have to admit that I saved you the money."

"More, my life, I guess." And there was an earnestness to her voice. "That money was for Danny—Danny's life maybe. It wouldn't have been taken without blood on it." And then very slowly, "Yes, blood on it."

Danny, the girl—and now Briskey. Had she sold out to Briskey? What she sold out I didn't know—but had she sold out? Blood on the money—her blood, or Danny's blood?

"Are you sure," I stared straight down at her, "that there isn't blood on the money now—that it isn't just blood money?"

The corners of her lips slipped into a queer sort of smile.

"You won't take money from me—perhaps because you think it's blood money. After all though, I might have died—and then Danny—" she spread her hands far apart. "Here's the advice I can give you. Make what you can out of Barton Briskey—I did. Danny is entitled to nothing—there is no money coming to him—nothing in the future but the prison gates or what I can bring him. There—my hand and my word on that."

And despite the cold of the winter night it was a warm little hand that slapped itself into mine. So different from the cold fingers of the girl hanging from the window the night before. And her voice, too—nothing of the cultured training there perhaps, yet a musical ring that was sweet and natural—as if for the first time Milly's real self was speaking and not the hard, cynical girl of the night, who was ever on the watch for danger.

"Where is Danny?" I asked. "Surely you'll let me see him. Where is he?"

"I could lie to you of course." Her head cocked up. "And I would, too—should have now maybe—for you might follow me. Yet, I won't lie to you to-night."

"If some one hasn't anything to fear from Danny—then why the attempt upon his life?" There was a stickler for her and I wished for a light to watch her face—nothing but whiteness—shining eyes and glistening teeth, and the faintest semblance of red lips.

"Because on his life hangs the life of another. There—I've said too much now. To-night I fought tooth and nail for this money." She still squeezed some of it in her hand. "Forget me—forget Danny—at the first opportunity we will leave the country. Take what you can get. You can't fight alone against such odds—think of one man, determined to kill you if he must sacrifice his own life for it—then think of a city of men—for, Race Williams, there will be such a price on your head that even the most chicken-hearted sneak thief will forget your reputation, his own fear of death, and shoot you in the back any hour of the day or night. Such orders will go out. I know it."

"Will go out!"

"Will go out to-night—after your visit with Barton Briskey—unless you are reasonable—and sensible."

"Then there was some truth in Danny's story of half a million; there is real money involved."

"Real money—yes—more than that—twice that—and perhaps double again that sum. But none of it is for Danny. Do you think I would see him robbed—"

"But there was some truth in his story."

"He thought so—you heard it—do you think that a father

112

would forget his daughter—leave all to a son he had not seen in so many years. Be—" She broke off suddenly, her head shooting up in the air. Steady feet came distinctly down the alley. I didn't have to look to know that this was a flatty—a patrolman making his rounds.

"I must be off—good-by—thank you—and—"

"I'll see you to the subway," I said. Perhaps I was gallant—perhaps I had an admiration for the nerve of the girl—perhaps I just wanted to think before I left her. Maybe I thought I'd keep an eye on her. But, take it any way you want—I followed her out into the alley.

We didn't walk together and we only cast one quick glance over our shoulders at the policeman who pounded along, trying the doors. He saw us, of course, but he didn't hail us. I daresay he knew of that truck with its warm blankets, and had stirred up more than one couple there. But what he thought didn't matter. He didn't bother us. We turned out to the wider street—the girl crossed it slowly and I followed her. Danny might as well get his money.

She didn't hurry and try to give me the slip, and I didn't try to overtake her—just kept my distance, to the subway. I had lots of time yet. When she reached the subway entrance she turned, hesitated a moment, and stepping toward me took me by the hand. Did her eyes just glisten with the brightness of youth or the thrill of battle? Perhaps—but I thought not. It was hard to believe that that hard little face would give way to emotion. Yet, when she spoke I knew that there was at least moisture on her cheeks—two drops that came from shining eyes. Tears? Yep. It sort of gave me a jar inside—and her voice shook when she spoke—and her face seemed to grow softer; but perhaps it was the dull light of the subway entrance.

"Thanks." She gulped the words. "I shouldn't say what I'm going to say. It'll fetch a laugh, coming from me to you; or perhaps it will just sound like—blasphemy. But I got a get it out or it'll tear the very insides from me. I don't believe bad of you—nothing but good; and, blasphemy or not—God bless you, Race Williams." Fingers tightened for a moment in mine, the erect little head lost is cockey tilt and dropped to her chest. And she was gone—turning suddenly; dabbing at her eyes and running down the steps.

Theatrical? Maybe. Playing for the gallery, like the woman of the stage? Perhaps. But I didn't believe it. My own stomach gave a bit of a jump as I turned and plodded back down the street. Then with a shrug of my shoulders I dismissed the girl from my mind. Big things were in the air. Instinct had kept me interested. Now—we'd hear what Barton Briskey had to say.

18

The Car with the Drawn Curtains

It was five minutes to twelve when I turned the corner toward Briskey's. Things had changed just a bit on the quiet street. A huge closed car was drawn up across the way—curtains drawn tightly, too. Briskey might have just arrived, for the man at the wheel sat silently, looking straight ahead into the darkness. His head didn't turn as I passed. Unnatural that. An honest man should take an interest in a passerby at that time of night. But perhaps Barton Briskey's chauffeur was not permitted an interest in things.

Over my shoulder I watched that car—the driver, the drawn curtains and the closed doors. But the curtains in the windows of the car didn't waver. That was good—there was glass between the curtains and me. Why good? Well, one can't tell when bullets will come sizzling from a closed car—a rapid-fire gun might even spit lead through the glass, but the aim is never so good. So I hung close to the building, walking a bit rapidly from one doorway to another and with both hands sunk in my pockets. If things started, two guns would be necessary—maybe not half enough—but we'd have a try at it anyway.

115

And I made the doorway that led to the stairs and Barton Briskey's office. A tiny light shone from the top of the long flight; that was encouraging. I'd much rather walk toward light than away from it. At least I could be sure no one lurked in the darkness there at the foot of the stairs—and I was sure before I plodded up them. Musty this place, but clean just the same. Simply the dampness of years gathered in the old wood despite the well-swept floor and polished woodwork.

I stopped and listened once when I reached the upper landing. Then I stepped boldly toward the wooden door where gold letters bore the notice—JAMES SMITH—COLLECTOR. I nodded. Perhaps James did a legitimate business there in the daytime; perhaps he was just an old law clerk who worked for Barton Briskey. However, I raised my fist and brought it sharply down upon the heavy wood. And as the echo of my blow died away a distant clock struck the hour of midnight. You can't beat that for timing things—not by a jugful you can't.

Quick steps came softly across a rug, pounded for a moment on wood. Came the snap of a bolt, a twist of the knob, and the door opened. Was Barton Briskey careless about throwing open his door without investigating who stood without? If he was, the thing was new to me. I didn't like his assurance that I was the visitor. Oh, he expected me and all that, but he was a mighty careful man. Had some one let him know that I was on the stairs—could he have seen me from the window above? But no light had come from that window. Shades, or shutters, or what have you, were carefully drawn, shutting out any light. I surely had given that window a good look-see from the street below.

"Ah, Race—my boy." A bony hand shot out and gripped mine. It was a damp, cold hand—something like you'd picked up a handful of already shelled clams. "This is good—very good—one is glad to see friends. Do you know, I hesitated to send for you. You're such a vicious sort of a devil, and I was afraid you might misunderstand." Barton Briskey stood aside to let me enter, carefully shot the bolt to behind me, and

116

rubbing his bloodless hands together stepped over toward the open fire. Little he was; bent, too—the long-tailed, black coat wrinkling up on his back as he jerked up and down before the fire.

He didn't seem to watch me; just stared straight into the fire, his neck going in and out of his collar like that of a curious old tortoise. Yet he wasn't old—less than fifty, I guess. It was the yellowness of his corrugated skin and the deepness of his eyes, and the straggling ends of gray hair that just crawled down through the wrinkles in his forehead. He didn't speak for a minute, and I understood. He was giving me a chance to look the room over. He knew my ways.

Of course it wouldn't offend him if I searched the place; and I wouldn't care if it did. I trusted Barton Briskey as much as I did any man—which was very little. But it was unnecessary to search that room; a quick hurried glance was sufficient. He had set the stage to make me welcome. "Make him feel at home" sort of business.

The two closets in the room had their doors thrown wide open. The one was shallow, with books upon the shelves—mostly old copies—heavy stuff, too, which added an air of reality and respectability to James Smith, I suppose. The other closet was a deep affair, and inspection had been made easier for me. The door was thrown open and knickknacks of one kind and another were piled upon the floor. I did take a walk to it and shoot my flashlight within. Nothing there of course.

The shelves along the wall which sported curtains had those same curtains thrown far back. It was as if a magician assured me that he had nothing up his sleeve; and, as usual, with that assurance comes the suspicion that trickery is planned—else, why the preparation to show me how secure I was? One curtain, however, remained drawn. I suppose I should have been too much of a gentleman to disturb that, after the generous display of all other possible hiding-places. But I wasn't. I jerked that curtain back and disclosed a door. A bolt was drawn tightly across it—I pulled on the knob. The

117

bolt was real and not a dummy. Satisfied, I turned to the man by the fire.

"It's cold out." Barton Briskey swung and faced me. "Not so cold as yesterday but mighty raw. That door now," he jerked a thumb toward the still waving curtain, "we will talk of that later. It leads to an alley without—privacy for me, you see—few know of it."

I just looked at him. Few, maybe—but at least three, of which I was one. He went on:

"Sit there by the fire so you can see both doors. I know your peculiarities and your objections to having your back to a door. I hate drafts, too." And his laugh cackled like the logs on the fire. "I wish to save time. I don't want you sitting nervously about. Thus my preparation. You and I are alone, Race." He turned to his desk drawer, jerked it open as I took the offered seat by the fire.

One hand in that drawer, he watched me before he spoke again.

"The weather is cold and you do not look your best. A trip south now might do you good. Have you got the time for such a trip—with adequate pay? In other words, Race—can you go south"—he snapped his shrewd little sunken eyes at an old clock upon the mantel—"this morning?"

"I might—but I think not."

"You have a case then—another case?"

"Maybe—but I am here to hear your business, not discuss mine."

"Quite correct." Colorless lips snapped; the hand shot out of the drawer and a tightly bound stack of bills flopped upon the desk.

"Suppose I sent you away on a case, and later you discovered that there was no case—what then?"

I smiled easily.

"Probably I wouldn't go—but you wouldn't fool me more than once. You know that, Barton Briskey." Was there a warning in my voice? I don't know. I didn't mean to put one there, but he jerked his head out toward me, fastened those gimlet-

118

like, steel-colored eyes on me. He was trying to read what I was thinking. He may have been good at it. I don't know. But I wasn't thinking anything just then. It was up to him to make a break.

"Suppose—" he said very slowly. "Suppose I should trap you here—put you in danger of your life—and that life was saved; what then?" And though he smiled there was an earnestness in his voice which I didn't like.

I answered smile with smile—but my smile was a grim one.

"Then I'd come back and stick a bullet straight between your eyes." Did I mean it? Don't make me laugh. Barton Briskey was known to tote a gun, and was known to be mighty quick with that same gun. I'd give him a chance to try out his hand against mine.

"Good—very good!" He broke the band on the bills and ran his fingers over them—century notes they were—with a freshness that told they were not long from the bank. Little brothers to the roll Milly had carried. Certainly Barton Briskey, whose god was money, was in a generous mood that night.

"You simply think of yourself, Race—not selfish exactly; I don't mean that. But you must at times think of the other man. Of course I am a firm believer in law and order. That the pen is mightier than the sword, was written for me. But"— the eyes again were fastened on me—"I do not also believe that the pen is mightier than the gun. You have heard of course that I can reach, draw and shoot in just one second. Now—what do you say to that?" He chuckled as if he joked, but I knew that he studied me keenly, and that there was something behind all this chatter. But he had asked a fair question and I gave him a fair answer.

"What do I say to that?" My hands never moved from the sides of the chair. "I say that you'd be exactly one-half a second too late."

The wrinkles in his forehead curled up to one big single ridge, and his eyebrows raised with them—but his eyes pecu-

119

liarly remained the same small shrewd little points of steel.

"Yes—perhaps I would." It was as if he thought aloud. "So then, if I ever trap you it must be certain—sure. But the talk is stupid and ridiculous. Our paths have only crossed in friendship—mutual understanding and mutual profits. Forget my whims—it is my insatiable appetite for psychology—the study of— But no matter—back to the subject of your health."

"My health is good."

"You think so—but no. If the trip south does not appeal to you, there is Alaska—deep snows, pure health-giving air and the big game hunts upon the stretches of mountain ice. Expensive, you think? But no—you have been most fortunate. A fairy godmother has waved her wand, and all things are possible. Two thousand—three, perhaps—come, I'll not be stingy. I'll make it four. You should travel like the gentleman you are."

19

The Trap

I hesitated a moment before I spoke. The game was deep. Barton Briskey was offering me money to leave the city—drop an investigation—a client that I had. He couldn't know that I didn't have any client—but there could be only one case that he meant. Danny of the weak brain and the punctured arm. I'd make him place his cards on the table.

"Briskey—" I stroked my chin, "circumstances are such that I can not leave the city at this time."

"For how much will you go?" He waved a finger reprovingly at me. "You're keen, Race—bright; you think you smell money and this talk with me convinces you that there is money just around the corner from your reach. Just let me assure you that the case you have—the wanderings you listened to, are nothing short of a disordered mind. I give you my word that you can make nothing—on the other side."

"Then why do you fear the other side—fear me—my investigation?"

"I, my dear boy," and he pulled the indignant, "have no interest in this. Money had been put in my hands. To put it brutally, it is to buy you off. The man you have seen—the man who claims to be the rightful possessor of great wealth, is the rattling skeleton in a family closet. Look, you—and I tell you only what I am told—though most of it I have investigated for your benefit. Police headquarters will convince you that the man is a wanted criminal."

"Is the man's right name—his real name—Daniel Davidson?"

Barton Briskey weighed that question in his mind as well as in the upturned palm which he held before him, moving it slowly up and down. Then he spoke.

"I believe that that is the man's right name," he said very slowly.

"And he had a father called D. Perry Davidson?"

"I believe that he did."

"And that father left considerable money—half a million, say."

"I am not sure of the sum—but my investigation disclosed that the amount was a substantial one."

"And now you offer me money so that I shall prevent justice being done and allow this poor boy to die of want—deprived of his rightful inheritance. Without going into the case thoroughly, Mr. Barton Briskey, don't you believe that if I get him his money—straighten out his trouble—he'll pay me more than ever you could afford to?"

"Not me—not me." His hand fell upon the desk as his brow scowled. "I am paid to offer you this money—that is all. It might as well be by me as another. But you are wrong. D. Perry Davidson left nothing to this son—not one penny."

I straightened suddenly—then smiled.

"You don't expect me to believe that yarn—after that." I pointed to the bills.

"You work with the fingers and with the eye." Briskey smirked over at me. "But there are times when the brain serves a purpose. I expect you to believe nothing. If you had visited the Surrogate's office you would learn that no money was left this son. Common sense would tell you that. He went away with his mother—never came back to his father.

122

When D. Perry Davidson died he left every penny to his daughter. This Daniel Davidson came from England to start trouble. He was a thief and a dope fiend, I am told—and then came a gun fight—over a girl. A lawyer, wishing to keep the Davidson name clean, got him to plead guilty under another name. He went to prison, and—"

"And they helped him to escape—I know the story," I cut in.

"A girl helped him to escape." Briskey corrected me. "Now, you see my point—or my client's point. Daniel Davidson had disgraced the family. That he is alive has been kept from his sister—until recently. He wrote to her, I believe. Her uncle has been paying out money to keep the scandal a secret. He is willing to pay more, but others have learned—and there is blackmail. Now you are in it. If you go on with your investigation the whole thing may become public. My dear boy, this will be the easiest money you ever earned. Come—we'll make it five thousand dollars—higher, I can't go."

"Who seeks his life?" I flung that at him as a starter.

But it didn't stick Barton Briskey. He had an answer for everything.

"Fortunately I have access to the gossip of the underworld. Yes, I fear that his life is in danger—so we would get him out of the country if possible. In prison he learned a secret— through a girl he has blackmailed certain people—desperate criminals."

"I see," I nodded. "The girl who was here to-night."

"What of her?" He came straight up this time—and the whiteness of his face had turned to a pasty yellow. "You— you have been spying on—" And suddenly taking a grip on himself, "But there was a girl here—how you knew it—" and he was smirking and smiling and watching me.

I sniffed the air.

"Your nose knows." I laughed. "Surely *you* don't go in for dainty perfumes. So—" I spread my hands far apart. "But back to business. These people who seek his life also seek mine. Can you explain that?"

"I can." He was very emphatic. "Simply through intuition and not what I know as a discovered fact or even gossip. But if I held a secret you would be the last man I'd want to find it out. Yes, Race Williams—under such circumstances I believe that I—one who abhors physical encounters and whose stomach sickens at the sight of blood—would seek your death. Do I make myself clear?" There was a new note in his voice. And his eyes bored into me as if—well, as if he suspected my knowing some secret of his. Certainly he would take a life if in taking that life he protected or profited himself. As for his stomach—fields would have to run red with blood before you could sicken him. That was my belief anyway.

"Well," he said after a bit, "what do you say?"

"Why—I say nothing—except that it will be impossible for me to leave the city at this time."

"Aren't my answers to your questions satisfactory? Now be reasonable, Race. I am not paid to answer your questions—simply to offer you the money. But you have done work for me and I like you; want to see you make some money. Also—I am paid according to my success—come, I won't hold out on you." The hand went into the drawer again. "Here's the rest of it," more bills upon the desk, "ten thousand—just my ten percent. Don't be a fool—play the game. Ten grand for not working—think of it—ten thousand dollars to stay idle and leave the city for the winter."

"For the winter." I thought aloud. "Then—Danny Davidson will be dead, I suppose."

"It is not for us to speculate upon the workings of divine providence—or the other kind." He rubbed his hands together. "Suppose nothing—except the money."

"And what proof must you have of my integrity?"

"Nothing—nothing more than the envelope with the enclosure, that if I know anything about you is still in your pocket."

"You know a lot," I told him. "Perhaps you know what that envelope I am supposed to carry contains."

"I know what I am told." His voice rasped a little. "It contains a will."

"And what good is a will if the maker of it has nothing to will?"

"It would make a dirty scandal—make the life of a young girl miserable—ruin her health worse than it is now. If I can't appeal to your head, let me try for your heart—or are both hard and—"

"I'll think the thing over," I told him as I stood up and half turned toward the door.

Barton Briskey came from behind the desk and clutched me by the sleeve.

"You must decide now."

"Must!" I turned suddenly on him. There was a threat in his voice—my hand crept close to my coat pocket.

"Exactly." He bit his lip. "I said 'MUST.'"

"Must—or lose the opportunity, eh?"

"Must—or—or lose your life." He leaned forward and there was no levity in his voice, nor in his eyes. He was in deadly earnest—his face white—not a plain, ordinary white but the whiteness of milk—a thin, watery sort of milk.

"You threaten me?" I watched his hands as I tapped my pocket. Then I shook his grip from my sleeve, stepped to the door and shot a hand upon the bolt. "Remember that half second, Barton Briskey." I smiled with my lips but my eyes were steady and hard. "Indeed your love for money must be great when you threaten me. You have neither the strength nor the courage to attack me—and you know it."

"It's not me, Race," he whispered. "God knows I wouldn't threaten you—but don't go out that door until I have talked a little more. I shouldn't talk—I may pay well for it. But Hell itself lurks in the city for you to-night—lurks beyond that door."

"So—" I swung so suddenly on him that he backed up against the desk—and some of the money fell to the floor. "You mean—mean that you have trapped me here. Why, Man"—and there was no mirth in my laugh—"I have a good mind to—and by God I will." Feet had run from the door—feet that made no effort to hide their pounding upon the steps. This little runt—this Barton Briskey, who knew me so well—had trapped me there. Sure—I was to get the money and be murdered for it afterward. No wonder the offer to go bye-bye was so generous!

My gun was out, pounding against his chest. He was leaning against the desk—his breath coming in quick uneven gasps.

"Don't shoot—don't, Race. I didn't know—didn't suspect. Didn't, until it was too late. I saved your life—it's the truth—listen to what I have to say."

"Well—speak up—if those without, want a dead body to satisfy them I'll feed them one. So that's what the car meant below!" I stretched out a hand, gripped Briskey by the neck and drew him to me. He didn't resist—just wilted up like a rag as I frisked him; pulled a long-barreled, foreign make of gat from the tail pocket of that frock coat and chucked it far back in the closet.

He squealed on.

"They came to my place to-night—one man—a desperate, wanted criminal with a price on his head. 'Race Williams is coming here,' he told me. 'Keep your face shut—he's learning too much—to-night he goes out.'

"I tried to protect you, Race—argued with the man and found it was the Danny Davidson affair—that Danny held a secret which, if it came into your possession, would send three men to the chair. One, the worst the city knows—not a man at all, sometimes I think." And he shivered slightly.

20

I Decide to Face the Enemy

But shivers wouldn't get Briskey any place. He was a great faker; what could have possessed him to double cross me like this—could his story be true, or some of it true—or were the Davidsons, The Beast, and half the underworld of the city mixed up together in this thing and working for one common end—the death of Danny, and incidentally the death of Race Williams? But Briskey was still talking—the words barely coming from his parched lips. Being a man who is always ready to listen, I loosened my grip on the crooked little mouthpiece's windpipe. The words shot out then like escaping steam.

"I saved you—feeling sure that you would give up the case. I don't want to see you killed; you've been valuable to me. I told this man that you would be fixed right to-night— that you would see Danny Davidson no more, and that you would leave the city—until—until all was over." I suppose by that last crack he meant the murder of Danny.

"They stayed just the same. Why? They didn't believe you?" I tried a couple of questions.

"They believed me—but were doubtful of you being bought off. That little light there—" He pointed to a queer looking red lantern on a shelf. "If you agreed to my price—

agreed to drop the thing—then I was to put the light in the window. Agree, Race. It's the easiest money you ever earned. Give me that will and go your way in peace—I'll put the light in the window and they'll fade away. Hesitate, and your chance of life is slim indeed. Every criminal hand in the city will be stretched out for you—there is a big price upon your head. If you did escape to-night it would do you no good. Death is sure; not as if one or two men hunted you down— but some one all powerful has called for your death— unless—" He looked up at me eagerly. "Will I light the lamp—now?" A boney, trembling hand felt out for the little lantern—a fragile bit of glass that looked as if it'd bust in your hand as soon as you touched it.

"Sure—" I said. "Light the red lantern and flag the train."

"And you'll take the money?" He crossed to the fireplace.

"No—I won't take the money," I told him.

"But you'll go—drop the case?" He looked suddenly up at me from the fire.

"No—I won't."

"But the light—I can't light it if—"

"That's your party." I nodded grimly. "You may explain afterwards that I changed my mind or you were a bit muddled—anything at all."

"They'll probably kill me," he gasped.

"Probably." I yawned. "But you won't be buried, forgotten. I'll send flowers."

"You joke."

"Don't put the light in the window then, and you'll see how much I joke. I'll save those birds the trouble of knocking you off. It's your own fault, Briskey—now do your stuff."

He went to the front window, threw it open, and smacked back the shutters. Then he returned to the fireplace and picked up the lamp.

"You do it." He extended it to me with trembling hands.

"I don't know the trick." I shook my head. "Maybe you have to wave it—maybe you have to put it in a certain position—maybe the boys in the closed car might even take a shot at it—or me. No—you're the boy that knows the trick. Go to it." My finger closed slightly upon the trigger and the hammer rose and fell with a dull click. A pretty trick, that!

He hesitated a moment—then struck a match on the stones above the fire. I watched him; watched the match too as it hovered near the wick, the flame wavering from the draft of the open window. But the match didn't go out—for Briskey suddenly cupped it in his hand and described a half circle with it. To save the flame—or a signal? For he was directly in a line with the window. Not that they could see him from the car in the street; he was too far back in the room for that—but—there was a house across the way; a house with windows. As for me—I stayed to one side of our open window. If any bullets came through it I'd let Barton Briskey do the ducking.

I suppose you call it conceit—I like to call it pride. But I had put fear into Barton Briskey. Or had I? I watched him carefully, to make sure he wasn't acting. I didn't know, never even thought that he'd go to pieces like that. That cold, bloodless, heartless little lawyer. Back of all the threats and gun play there must have been money—big money.

He was having difficulty in finding the wick—his fingers and hands shook like the old time bar-flies used to. Once he looked over at me, for he heard the click of steel upon steel as the hammer of my rod slipped up and down. He couldn't be sure that I wouldn't plug him. He'd of plugged me in the same situation. So the match darted forward, touched the wick, and a tiny flame sprung up. As that little flame licked at the wick, caught and grew steady—from the street below came a cry. The cry I heard the night before, and would remember for a good many nights to come.

A whining sound at first, which broke gradually as it reached a high note and finished with a snarl. Low this time—but clear enough. It was The Snarl of the Beast. I half turned toward the window. They couldn't intimidate me with any stage tricks, nor with the bestial cries of a half mad brute that roamed the streets; real or stage properties made no difference to me—beast or man.

And I swung back to Barton Briskey. The cry had hardly died away in the night when his head came erect.

"Not that—not that!" I heard him mutter—but it was the slight ring of glass on stone that made me turn—made me swear softly too. The little red lamp had slipped from his fingers before those snarling notes had died away. Had it busted? Man! you couldn't have found the pieces with a microscope. The glass had just evaporated—mixed with the red of the stones before the open fire.

I shouldn't have hesitated maybe. Put it down as a weakness that I didn't shoot the little crook and be done with it. But I didn't—I just stood there juggling the gun and watching the terror-stricken form by the fire. Before I could make up my mind what to do with him and decide if he was faking the trembling or not, he came erect—jumped to the window and slammed it down.

"I did my best," he cried, turning to me. "Take the money, Race. I'll call out to them—anything—let the leader come up—I can't let you go out there. The Beast—you heard him— he'll tear you limb from limb—I can see it—see it all." He fairly shrieked the words as he tore at the few streaks of hair that hung over his forehead. It was heavy stuff for Barton Briskey, and although he did it well somehow it lacked reality.

Maybe you could see me torn limb from limb, but I couldn't. I wouldn't let him lean out that window. Not that I feared for his life. I could watch them plug him without getting a kick to it. But he might signal them in some way. So I waved him back from the window.

"Don't think I'd double cross you." His voice was stronger now, his carriage more erect, his face still white, but the hand that sought my arm steadier. Was he after all playing a part? Had he actually planned to trap me there—or was he trying to affect my nerves so that I'd take the money and make a deal with him?

"Will you—will you take the money?"

"You can't buy me," I told him. "And I don't—"

"I have it," he cut in. "The little door there—none know of it; at least, very few. They will never suspect—go—you must."

"I have a final word for you." I planted myself firmly before the curtain. "I'm going to try to believe some of what you told me." I laid my hand on the bolt of the little door. "But if you've lied to me—trapped me here; and I'll learn the truth—then I'm coming back."

"Yes—go—for that Beast and the wolves of the underworld are on the stairs—there in front. They are ready for you—waiting for you. See, I saved you. What will happen to me I don't know—but I sent for you, and I will sacrifice myself rather than you."

Maybe it was true. Maybe it wasn't. Hand on the bolt, I hesitated. I was smiling in derision at his terror but the smile was going now. My lips were tightening—my eyes narrowing. That others knew of that little back entrance I didn't care. I didn't think of that—didn't think of anything. Anger was swelling up inside of me—something that seldom comes to me. Something that I nearly always control—and fear too. When I spoke it was as if the voice came from another—I did not think out the words or frame the sentence. It just came, that was all.

"You say they're on the front stairs, Briskey? How many of them?"

"Five—maybe more—and perhaps The Beast himself—certainly he will be there. A man whom lead—"

Good! My left hand left the bolt of the little door, slowly sought my pocket and snapped out with another gun. If Barton Briskey had trapped me there to-night, he'd get an eyeful now that he wouldn't forget in a hurry. Guns are my business—action my meat. The Beast was wanted—the price on his head was large. He and his gang had taken pot shots at me as often as they liked. He had tried to kill me and also the youth that I was pleased to look on as my client since talking with the lawyer. Well—the police wanted to drag me in, did they? I'd give them something to work on. The dregs of the

131

underworld were after my hide, were they? Now—I'd give them a chance to get that hide, and may the devil take the carcasses that were left upon those stairs. So I stepped across the room and clutched another bolt. The one of the main door—the door which led to the stairs and the waiting gunmen.

"What—what are you going to do?" Briskey's upper teeth began to wobble in his face. Now I knew why they were so straight and even.

"Why," I flung him a defiant look over my shoulder, "I'm going to meet the boys. You never knew me to dodge them yet. What's five or six, more or less—one shoots oftener and doesn't waste so much lead." It may have sounded foolhardy, but after all there was a lot of common sense. Meet lead with lead and it takes the heart out of the potential murderer. Sometimes even the soul.

I don't think my voice shook, but maybe it did. With anger, not fear. Passion is a bad thing. But I was mad now—mad clean through. I've often said I'd fight it out with any gun in the city, any place, any time—and that isn't just wind. It wouldn't be the first bit of lead I'd exchanged—not by a long shot it wouldn't.

"You can't—can't. It's suicide."

"Not unless it's in the cards." I shrugged my shoulders. "Watch, Briskey, and take a lesson from tonight's work. If I win through—and you're to blame—start traveling, and no matter how fast you go remember I'm only a few hours behind you. If you know any undertaker, get a flat rate for the crowd." It all sounds like braggadocio, I suppose. But I can't help that. It's just the way I felt. Truth is truth, you know.

Briskey made a run for me—changed his mind as he smacked up against the mouth of a forty-four, and backed slowly across the room.

"That's a good kid," I told him. "Another break like that and I'll start in with you—for one more or less won't matter to-night. Better get going at that back door." With that I snapped the bolt of the office door and pressed the electric light button, pitching the room into blackness.

21

Action!

There was a thrill to it as I jerked open the door and stepped to one side. The game wasn't a half bad one at that. The boys that crouched out in that hallway were probably all killers— every one with a long police record. Others wouldn't dare lay for me. You wouldn't be able to get a jury to convict me even if the grand jury did indict, for lawlessness ran riot in the city. Maybe I'd come in for a vote of thanks. About getting killed myself—that was possible of course. Better die now than forty years from now, with pains in the stomach. Besides—I'd be shooting from darkness into light. The boys would have to shoot blindly, while I could account for a man with each shot. I don't go in to miss, you know.

Silence out there beneath the light; silence on the stairs too, and as I shot my head around the door no lurking figure greeted me. Had they lost their nerve? It would be like them of course. I didn't think they'd have the stuff to meet me face to face. I know those rats too well.

Perhaps they lurked on the dark stairs. Not so good that. I'd counted on copping off at least one as soon as I threw open the door. A dead body tumbling down the stairs among the others would have a good mental effect. Psychology and corpses go well together. And not a sound!

133

I stepped into the hall—well away from the stairs, reached the bannister and looked over. Dimly the light from above shone down to the landing below, and dully I made out the emptiness of the little hallway that led to the entrance. Funny that—had the boys quit altogether? Was Briskey after all just a plain bluff? Did he expect to get away with that stuff on me? Did he take me for a child? But the cry in the night—the Snarl of the Beast. That was real enough.

A bolt jarred—not below, but in the room behind. The room I had just left. And I knew the truth—not just a guess. I knew as well as if I'd heard Barton Briskey arrange the whole thing. And I knew too that the thing was big—very big—to make Barton Briskey take the chance he did. But the main part was that I understood why he had wished to send me down the little back stairs to the alley. The gunmen weren't in the front at all. They were waiting there on the little alley stairs. No doubt the door leading to Briskey's room was lined on the outside with a thin shell of steel. The boys would just shoot up those narrow stairs as soon as the door closed behind me—or perhaps there were even hidden side passages where they could do their shooting in absolute safety. Heavy padded walls probably, that would keep the crack of the bullets from being heard in the alley without. Nice game that. Nice little playmates Barton Briskey had.

How did I know all this? Well—some of it was just guess work; some of it putting two and eight together; some of it plain intuition—but most of it a certainty from the sound of that bolt in Briskey's room, and the whispered voices of men and the patter of many feet. When I left the room, Briskey shot that bolt and let the boys in. Now he was explaining the situation to them. Some would be following me to the stairs—others would be ducking around the front way, from the alley. I could make the street before them, I guess—dash out, seek a convenient doorway and hold my own until dawn or the coming of the cops. But I did neither of these things. They would be expecting action—and I wondered if other men lurked in that curtained car, waiting to open up with guns when I made my appearance. Barton Briskey was most sure of his ground before he chanced making me his enemy. I set my lips tightly. If it came to a fight to the death I'd see if I couldn't save one bullet for Barton Briskey. Surely he was entitled to it. And I'd bet a pretty piece of change that he'd have a dozen or more reputable citizens who'd swear he wasn't within five miles of Wall Street that night. Such is an alibi—when you hold secrets of those who perjure themselves to hang onto what they call "respectability."

So I decided to stick around; decided just as the sneaking feet reached the door of Barton Briskey's office and paused there. Who would be the first man to step into the light? That was my question. And their question also. Feet scraped by the door—came to a stop as other feet stopped behind them, and a voice whispered.

"Better wait till he reaches the bottom—Ed Jackson will get him and beat it—besides," and so low that I wasn't sure of the words, "The Beast is there too." That's what it sounded like—at least there was awe in the speaker's voice and a real hushed murmur of others.

Then those behind began to push, I guess. Such is the start of a gun fight. The lad in front is shoved forward, protecting the *brave* fellows behind. Like a subway rush or a riot—the fellow behind, who feels safe, pushes his friends into action. That was my cue, and I took it as a figure appeared in the doorway. I just slipped back in the hall, found the stairs that led to the floor above and went slowly up them—sort of sideways, watching for an attack from above as well as from below. But it was dark there and I could not be seen.

It took them time to reach the head of the stairs and look down them. I could lean over the bannister and see them—a hard looking lot they were. Each one toted a gun in his paw—five, I saw—huddled there by the head of the stairs, beneath the light—looking into the hall below. Then an intake of breath, and the leader spoke.

"There by the door—ain't that Ed—or—give him a call; did he let the dirty skunk, Race Williams, slip?" And in a hoarse

135

voice, "Hey, Ed—did he—did the meat come that way?"

There was an answer from below that I didn't get. What sort of birds were these fellows? Did they think they could stand there and plan my death? But at that moment they could, without interference from me, for I had climbed to the top of the flight of stairs and could no longer see the little huddled mass below. Of course I couldn't be sure how the thing would come out—with death certainly. But I'd give a good account of myself, and planted there at the top of those stairs the chances were not unfavorable. It's too bad some enterprising promoter didn't get an option on the show and post bulletins outside the building, with the list of dead and wounded, and the shooting averages.

Just one thing bothered me. In this fight Barton Briskey would probably win out. That is, in tying my hands for the next few weeks. Danny Davidson's case needed immediate attention. At the best I'd wind up in a police station. Lead wouldn't fly long before the police would be on the job. The dead line too—that imaginary line drawn across the lower city, that the police had so many years ago laid out. It was for the protection of the lower city with its great diamond brokers—but really the thing was instituted for Maiden Lane.

This time the cops would surround the building. I half envied the crook and the murderer, who can shoot down a police officer and run for it. But I couldn't do that. That the end justifies the means was made for me all right—but no end would justify the taking of an innocent life. Now—to crash one on the head is a different matter. Sounds brutal and all that, I know; but I'm not above it just the same. We can't be too particular and—

They were coming. It took them long enough at that to figure the thing out, and I'll bet that Barton Briskey did it for them, and then beat it. I could hear the boys moving toward the stairs which led to the third floor, and to me. Then the lights went out. Briskey knew that I was onto him now. It would be a fight to the death. I nodded and shrugged my shoulders—then lying full length upon the floor and burying my cheek close to the worn old carpet, I extended my arms full length to the edge of the first step. It was a good position. I could fire without being hit. If a light went up below I had only to raise my head for one quick shot—but mostly I'd just shoot down the stairs—blindly of course—but the stairs were narrow and the chances of a hit were better than those of a miss.

Of course I'd fire low and close to the steps—the boys would be snaking up; sticking close to the floor—crawling on their stomachs. It was possible that one might make the grade without getting plugged, so I prepared for that even—slipped out my flash and laid it ready, the button beneath my chin. There might come a time when I wanted to take in the situation. So I waited.

Nothing new in the whole business? No, perhaps not—but I can't honestly say I was bored or that the thing was drab and uninteresting. My blood runs warmer at such times; a pleasant thrill tingles through my body. A hard, cold business? Maybe. But there's a kick goes with it. The animals in the jungle must get it at times, when the hunters are on the trail—that's why they so often jump out and make an attack themselves.

The stairs creaked—no other sound. They knew where I was now, and they weren't going to talk about it. Doors were opening below too. I wondered if that was to deaden the feet upon the stairs or just to make sure I wasn't hiding some place on the second floor. Came a pretty loud creak of the boards as the approaching gunman slid nearer to an early grave. That disturbed the others, and a voice came out of the darkness; trying to kid me into believing that they thought I had escaped.

"No use, boys—he's skipped from the roof upstairs to the next one. We'll have to look around the block and then give the thing up for to-night. Come on!" The speaker had hardly finished when the stairs creaked again—much nearer this time. And then stamping feet in the hall below—as if a lad was doing the Charleston. After that, feet again on the stairs

of the first flight—and a mumbled voice of one who descend-
ed to the ground floor. One—yes. But one who tried to give
the impression that a dozen or more were leaving the building. What children they were after all! What right had they to
play at the game of life and death? Shooting defenseless men
in the back was their favorite pastime; not trying to corner a
man who knew his business. But that crawling body was
coming on.

There was no way to avoid the thing, I guess. I'd have to
open up. And then I decided to give them a chance—at least
this one lad on the stairs—that is, if there was only one.

"You on the stairs," I called. "Stand up, drop your gun,
turn your back and walk down."

As if I were the captain giving the order to fire, things
started—half a dozen guns rang out at once, almost before I
had finished speaking. Pounding lead whizzed into the wall
behind me; dull splashes of orange blue flame darted up for a
full two seconds. That was the plan of battle. The one—or
those on the stairs were to dash forward under the protecting
shots of the men behind. They wanted to finish things up
quickly and make a get-away before the police came.

But the lad on the stairs didn't do his stuff on time. The
roar of the bullets had passed away and I heard his feet as he
ran for it—not back down the stairs, but up them toward
me—showering lead before him as he came.

And the fight was on. If they were going to rush the stairs
like that I'd need a light. I didn't think they'd take such a
chance; but they were all coming—shouting now too—firing
wildly. There was nothing to fear from the shots behind the
leader. That was like the old time holdup men of the Western
Plains, who fired into the air as they rode around the outside
of the train. Of course these boys couldn't shoot up the stairs
at me without hitting the lad who led the attack. They just
fired high.

I changed my plans at once to meet the new danger. I just
leaned forward and set my chin on the button of the flash.
The light darted straight out and landed full on the coarse,

unshaven map of a wild eyed baby who held his left hand on the bannister and in his right clutched a gun. He fired, I think—wildly too—but not me. I don't shoot to be spectacular. I let two shots go at once. One skipped by him and down the stairs—the other didn't. It wasn't meant to.

That unshaven baby just picked himself up and turned a back hand-spring. Remember, he was less than ten feet away from the mouth of a forty-four, and believe me—that same little forty-four is no Christmas toy for a young child. I've picked two hundred pounders right off the ground with a bullet in the shoulder. But he did his stuff into the gang below, and from the grunts and groans I could tell that there was one sweet mess at the bottom of those stairs. And then I snapped out the light.

22

The Shriek of a Siren

There were curses and cries of pain and threats of skinning me alive—and a final burst of flying lead. But I just lay there and waited. Like the handful of Americans at the top of Bunker Hill, I was sitting nice and pretty. These boys only knew the one game—to shoot and run. As they had planned things it was sure death for me. When things went differently they couldn't figure out a new plan. If they had taken their time; just watched those stairs, while they sent a couple of guns to come down on me by way of the roof—why, they could have had me between two fires. But, no—they were playing the game as they saw it. Ten to one looked like a sure thing. Now—they were not so certain.

I grew impassioned as I waited there. I was pretty easy on them, I thought. Here they were chattering below, trying to find out who was hurt and if any were dead, and in the meantime I waited; waited their pleasure. And that's the reason that these boys shoot many in the underworld—especially the police. The poor cop knows where they are half the time; walks right up to them on the street, to make a pinch—and gets shot for his pains. Then what? The commissioner and two or three big officials duck into high hats and help carry the casket. Great stuff that?

No, I can't see it. I'm all for justice and fair play. I'm not out for vengeance. There wasn't a rat in that crowd who wouldn't be the better off for a permanent home in the ground. I'd been enough of a hero for one night. Besides—there were the police. I didn't want to be dragged in and held, even long enough for Danny Davidson to get the works. And why hadn't some one heard those shots already and notified the police? A deserted, empty building—certainly. The gang had seen to that all right—but in some of those little shops along the street a store keeper must have slept. They weren't all brokers with fancy apartments in the upper city.

Of course I'd know as soon as the police were coming. The boys had a lookout ready. If I didn't hear the clang of the wagon or the shrill blast of the whistle there'd be a shriek of a siren from the car in the street. But back to my first thoughts. I'd played the ten, twenty and thirty hero long enough; had let them fire first and obeyed all the proper requirements except for the bullet in the shoulder, which generally comes before the hero does his stuff. But this was life—and there they were planning below to take my life.

Truth is truth. Call it murder if you like—a disregard for human life. I don't care. I'll run my business—you run yours. I snaked along that narrow hall, found the bannister, shoved both my guns through the uprights and let four quick shots slip down those stairs. Results? I should say so. I was talking the kind of language they understood. Did I kill any one? I didn't know, but I sure made a hit and started things moving at the foot of those stairs. Mad! They were raging lunatics, and they coined words that the best dictionaries never heard of.

Shouts of pain—curses of rage—flaring guns and roaring bullets. One nearly got me too—just luck that, for a bullet seared along the side of my hand, like some one had drawn a hot poker across it. But they didn't get mad enough to dash up those stairs and finish me. And what's more they took their conversation back into the hall and out of my line of fire. Surprised? Why, they didn't expect the other fellow to fire

141

except when they attacked. No—they figured that I was too respectable for that—or too much afraid of the law. Now—well, they'd have different views on life; some of them, perhaps, on death.

They didn't beat it though. The thing was desperate—they had to have my life. After a bit they quieted down, dragged their wounded or dead back off the stairs, and got into a regular football huddle, I guess. Anyway their voices buzzed up to me. When would they think of coming around from above? And when would the neighborhood be alive with the police? What had happened to them? They watch the city pretty carefully these nights. A period of silence—then a voice from below.

"A truce, Race Williams," the fellow who had done the talking in the beginning called up to me—and he flattered me by not sticking his head around the stairs. I could tell from the distant sound of his voice. "The money is still yours—if—if you concede to the original plan that was suggested to you." And he didn't go into detail. A hint there. The rest of the boys weren't in on the whole show—it wasn't necessary to tell them the facts to get them to hunt down Race Williams. They all hated me—all feared me too. My standing wouldn't be hurt any in the underworld, for these *little things* get around.

I dropped back in the hall a bit before I answered them. I hadn't heard any noise but I couldn't be sure that one of them hadn't made the stairs and wanted to find where my voice came from.

"You give me terms!" I laughed. "Really, it's too kind of you—and if I don't agree, what then?"

"Then," he said very slowly, and in a deep voice which was meant to be blood curdling, "you die!" He got my laugh, and realizing that his logic was pretty weak, enlarged upon it. "We will get you to-night, if we all die for it."

"That suits me," I told him. And when he didn't answer right away I tried to egg him on. "If you don't get busy pretty soon, I'll come down after you. How are the rest of the boys?"

And that last crack started the cursing all over again. Each one took a turn at it. Like children they were—and I sat on the floor and waited. The cursing died away—a gasp came— a little ripple of surprise—followed by footsteps, queer kind of footsteps, that scraped on the stairs of the first flight. A sort of a smothered squeal of triumph came up from the gun- men—which was answered by a whining note that was fol- lowed by a low snarl. Here was The Beast in person. They respected, feared, and stood in awe of him.

Well, I'd show him a little respect myself. So I slipped back to the head of the stairs—got the flash ready—spread myself at full length again—saw that my chin rested close to the but- ton of the flash, and waited. They treated this lad like the con- quering hero on a college football team. I'll admit I got a bit of a thrill out of his coming myself. Not that I feared him, and not that I simply wanted vengeance—but there was a price on his head—dead or alive. Inspector Coglin had told me that. Now—when the police came I'd have a good story. The Beast was wanted. I'd be sitting on his chest, ready to claim the reward—and what's more I'd tell the papers that Coglin put the idea into my head. After all, I'd get paid a bit for this night's work.

And The Beast came. That steady, shuffling, foot-gliding noise reached the landing below—slipped along it and with- out a word to the men at the bottom of the second flight, turned onto the stairs.

Superstition runs high in the underworld. These lads prob- ably half believed that The Beast couldn't be killed with lead. Perhaps they'd missed him often enough. And it was no doubt that superstition that saved his life. Fear, when they fired—fear of that belief that they couldn't hurt him. Fear of his face and swinging arms and snarling lips too. But I shrugged my shoulders and waited. His mouth didn't bother me. I didn't expect him to bite me. As for those long arms with the hairy hands—they'd never reach me. Another few seconds now and I'd flash the light and put a bit of lead between those colorless eyes. Only one thing bothered me. I'd have to follow that shot up with a dash down those stairs. I couldn't afford to have the boys cart that body away. Gruesome to think of that at such a time? Maybe. But shooting is my business. It was bad enough to hunt The Beast alive, but if I had to run around the city trying to get the remains—why—

And he was half way up the stairs. No snarl now—a low whining note, as if he sniffed at the air. And his feet beat faster—like four feet instead of two; he must have had his huge hairy hands on the stairs also. Good! His time had come. I leaned forward, ready to set my chin on the button when it happened. From the street below came the shrill blast of a siren—three times it cut through the night. I couldn't hear the steps of the man on the stairs then—the warning blast of that siren was followed by confusion below. A gasp—a shout—many shouts—running feet—cursing men—and the thud of a heavy body as a couple of them dropped a wounded companion in their flight.

My chin missed the light and I fired—blindly—wildly. For a moment I had visions of those hairy hands upon my throat. But there was no danger. The warning notes of the automobile horn had reached The Beast upon the stairs as well as the others, for I heard his feet again—heavy they were as he pounded down the stairs. I had missed him, I guess—and for a moment I thought of that superstition. But I hadn't seen him, and in the darkness I couldn't tell which side of the stairs he was on or if he stood erect or crouched on all fours.

The police that these rats defied brought terror with their coming now—some of the gunmen dashed to the lower stairs, to run madly back again and seek Barton Briskey's room—that would be their escape of course. Did the police watch that little alley door? And my escape—well, I'd try the roof. So I too hurried for freedom toward the stairs behind me, and dashed up them.

I used my flash generously now as I neared the trap door which led to the roof. One foot on the ladder, and I paused, to drop quickly back on the landing again. Men were on the roof—men who tore at the trap and beat upon it with heavy clubs—night sticks, I guess.

The police had worked it well—that is, if they guarded that little alley door. As for me—I was in for it. No use to try and fight my way through. I'd tell a story of how I was trapped there by a fake letter—and then the gun play. They'd never convict me. So I sought the hall—found a door and spun the knob. It was locked. I hurled my weight against it. It gave slightly, and at the second attempt busted open—and I pitched into an empty office or studio of some kind.

Closing the door I searched the room with my light—then I spotted the generous window and looked out. A fine sight in the street below for an honest citizen. It looked like a police parade. The emergency squad? Maybe. Yet it seemed quite a crowd to be handy at the first alarm. I could see the truck in the gateway of the little alley entrance, and there were half a dozen blue coated figures there. Hard to explain that. It almost looked as if this raid was planned in advance.

Feet were pounding in the halls now—running up and down the stairs. The room contained two or three chairs and an old table. I pulled a chair up to the table, put out my flash, pocketed my guns, and sat down—my elbows on the table, my hands against my face. At the first flash of a glim, the cops could see that both my hands were empty and that I was not looking for trouble. I frowned slightly too. I'd have to hunt myself up a new mouthpiece now. Something told me that Barton Briskey would not help my case any.

My thoughts suddenly went flat—the door burst open—a figure was framed there a moment and a flash shone full upon my face. I blinked into the light, smiling grimly. Here was the pinch. I didn't know who the officer was. I couldn't see him but I heard his little gasp. Surprise? Maybe. But I thought it was more of satisfaction. He didn't speak and I didn't speak. Then he backed from the room, closing the door behind him. What do you make of that!

There were whispered words in the hall and the thud of heavy shoulders against the door. That was more like it. Some one had been put on guard. Why? And my heart jumped a bit. I had a few good friends on the force. Had one of them seen me, taken in the situation, and was ready to protect me? But that would be almost too much to expect of any man. Yet—it was the only thing possible. Still, there was a guard at the door.

23

In the Hands of the Law

The tramping in the hall went on—hoarse shouts that turned into whispers before they penetrated to the little room, came from the alley below. But there was no roar of guns—nothing to denote that there was a capture. Yet—many cops stood guard by the little alley door.

Five—ten minutes passed. Things quieted down in the house—then feet along the hall without—a muffled voice said something to the guard on the door and the knob rattled. Again I had a visitor—but this time he did not show a flash. Simply pulled the door closed behind him; then snapped a switch, and the room was lighted from a swinging electric globe that hung from the ceiling above my head. I blinked up at the green shade that threw the light down on me—then saw the man who pulled forward a chair and sat opposite me. It was Inspector Coglin.

"Here we are again, Race—my boy." And there was a beam to his eye and a light, airy, fluttering movement of the cigar as it traveled back and forth across his face. He was pleased with himself.

"Made a haul?" I asked. "Got—The Beast?"

"No—" he frowned. "Got away. Barton Briskey has put it over on the force again. That little alley entrance was a blind—there's a door on those back stairs—half way down them—and that door conceals a passage to the house across the alley." He jerked his head toward the window. "No"—his eyes narrowed now and stared unblinkingly at me—"we didn't get The Beast, but we got—you—Mr. Race Williams—this time."

"Me! For what?" I elevated my eyebrows. "I came here in answer to a letter."

"Sure—" he nodded, with a smile; "and so did I, Barton Briskey's letter."

"He wrote you?" I didn't try to hide the surprise in my voice.

"Not exactly—not exactly. I couldn't say that and tell the whole truth. No—the letter wasn't addressed to me. To you—he wrote you two letters. I read the one at your office. An expert opened and resealed it for me."

"So—" I let it go at that. Inspector Coglin was improving. "But what have you got on me?"

"Murder—double murder."

"Some one dead?" I questioned.

"Exactly—two of the nicest stiffs you ever set your eyes on. One behind the ear; the other—not so good. I know both of them well. You've saved the state a big electric bill."

"One must protect one's life." I shrugged my shoulders. Years ago I got over trying my case before the officer who made the pinch. But Coglin hadn't made the pinch—he had kept my presence there a secret from the others. Why?

"I daresay you'll be a free man in the next eight or ten months," he said calmly. "But they'll hold you without bail—I can fix that—at least for a long stretch. Now—that would be too bad, wouldn't it? I'd hate to arrest you."

"Why do it then?"

"Yes—why do it?" He leaned far forward. "And I haven't done it yet. I hope I won't do it. Come, Race—I'll be honest with you. I can't cry over the pair of guns that you stretched in the hall below. It was Briskey who trapped you, wasn't it? I had the place covered all night. But I was after one person—

one thing. The Beast—I've sworn to get him." His hand crashed down upon the table. "I waited—even let you have your little fling with the gun, until I thought a war had broken out. And then he came—I saw him come in." His upper lip shot down on his lower lip. "And all the time he was within my grasp—hidden in a car with the shades drawn. He skipped out of it and into the house here before we could even get a shot at him. I'd know him any place—he put me in the hospital once—I—"

"But what about me?" I yawned.

"I'm willing to let you go free—and help you. Your path and The Beast's are sure to cross—I know that—your life is forfeit in the underworld. The story is around—a stool pigeon brought it to me. You're playing the game against all the forces for evil—playing it alone. How would you like to play it differently for once—play it with the whole force of the law behind you—with me behind you?"

"What's the price?" I asked.

"Simply that you work for me."

"Join the force?" I smiled.

"Hardly." He smiled back. "But we'll join forces for this one instance—then—enemies again if you will—for your ways and my ways would never fit together. I'm too old fashioned, I guess—but this once. I want the credit for the capture of The Beast—I don't care if he's dead. Here's your chance to go gunning legal-like."

"You get the credit and I get the lead, eh?"

"Maybe." And his face grew stern and grim—a hard, determined, honest face he had at that—stubborn too. "No, Race—I don't fear his lead nor his hands nor his bullet-proof body. But his path and mine don't cross. I'll face him any time I can—I just want your help. Where you are, he'll be. It's the common gossip of the underworld. If you don't—"

"If I don't—what?"

"I'll put the screws on you—good." His fingers clenched, the nails biting into rough hands. "I believe you're in a case now that means something to you. I believe too that this man they call The Beast is closely involved in it. I'm willing to help you—if you're willing to help me. If not"—again the clenched fist—"I'll tie your activities up for a time at least—hang this killing to-night on you—and make you explain before the grand jury what you were doing in the neighborhood of Sergeant Rafferty's killing last night. You may have fooled Delaney but you can't fool me. Take your choice. Come—all I want is the credit—and—"

"And the money too." I grinned.

"No—" he shook his head. "You can keep all of that. You'll get credit for his capture or death if you make it. Three policemen have fallen prey to this creature—you haven't got the conscience nor the orders they have. It's the end of this murderer that I want. But you'll be working for me—all the money is yours."

"H-m-m." I thought that one over. "And about my other business—do you want to know about that—have some one with me wherever I go?"

"No—you're a free agent. We won't follow you—ever. But we'll be ready if you call for us—if you find this Beast. And I'll face him with you. The thing's too big for you alone, Race—or maybe it isn't—in a great many ways you're a remarkable man." And that was some compliment when coming from Inspector Coglin. "Come—will you go in with me; work with me when possible until we get this man?" He snapped out his watch. "It's late—what do you say?"

There was Danny's envelope still in my pocket. What a stir-up the opening of that might create! Of course I'd be searched at Headquarters. I could draw a gun on Inspector Coglin and make a bid for freedom. But what good would that do? I'd be a wanted man. No—the thing sounded good. There'd be lead and blood and death before this game was over. It wouldn't be so bad to have the law to fall back on. Coglin no doubt had been given the special handling of the capture of The Beast; maybe they were ragging him at headquarters. It wasn't a half bad deal. To shoot and feel certain that later twelve men wouldn't be listening to a police version of how it happened. Just one thing I resented—and I let him have my objection.

"I'm not a murderer." I laid a finger out toward his chest. "I shoot to protect my life or the life of another. But I don't go out to kill. Am I to understand that you're giving me my freedom now to kill this—this Beast?"

"Hardly." He shook his head. "But I think you will—and I think too that he may kill you first—that's why I offer you my help—not to protect your life but to be sure of his—or his capture."

"And you'll take the blame for any shooting that comes in the way of my duty—duty to the force, eh?" I couldn't help but smile. The thing seemed good—just my fear of being in with the police; my distrust of them and their distrust of me—and my years of running alone.

"I'll shoulder all the blame and protect you to the extent of my position. Also I'll stand side by side with you whenever you call for me. Just a ring of the phone, and the greatest police force in the world is behind you." His voice rang with pride.

There was a long period of silence. I liked to run the thing over in my mind and enlarge on its possibilities; Coglin misunderstood my silence. He leaned across the table.

"There's one thing else—stick to me and I'll let the Kid go—the one we picked up to-night at the foot of the subway steps, after you left her." He straightened with a smile; for once he had caught me off my guard and he noted the surprise in my face. "She's not been booked yet," he went on. "Have her outside now—don't know how you feel about her—but I'll keep your name out of to-night's work—that is just between me and the commissioner. And the girl. What do you say?"

"O. K. by me," I told him.

"You agree?"

"Yes—on one condition—we'll split the reward on The Beast."

"No—I want you to—"

"That's the only condition that I'll go in with you." I cut in on him. "We split the reward."

"Very well—and we'll split the danger." Our hands met and clasped. It wasn't until later I found out that Rafferty, the dead sergeant, had been married to Coglin's sister, and that there were two little girls—who now had no father.

"I could have squeezed you, Race." Coglin came to his feet. "But I didn't. I know you'll play fair with me. My job depends on my success in the running down of The Beast. Not that they'd fire me. But I'll quit if I don't grab him." He turned toward the door. "Shall I bring the girl in?"

"Yes—" I said. "Fetch her in—and leave us."

"Right." He grinned broadly. "You'll be able to walk out, a free man, when you wish. You're working for me now—give me a ring in the morning. Night!" The cigar jumped up against his nose; he jerked his collar tighter and turned toward the door. I still sat there as he passed out. The door closed behind him—remained so a moment as two pair of feet tramped along the hall and started down the stairs. Then the door opened again. Milly, the girl of the night, stood in the doorway.

"What have you done for me, Race Williams—what have you done?" She ran toward me—stretched out her little hands over the table and clasped mine. "Coglin told me that—that my freedom depended upon you. Oh—it's too much to ask."

24

Inside the Taxi

For the first time the girl faltered; she half leaned against the table and her face was white. What dark eyes she had too—with the sparkle of life still there—and that was all that was left of her youth. Not that there were lines in her face—no—she had a finely chiseled face, now that I got a good look at it under the light. For the first time too I saw that haunted look that Danny had spoken about. It was there—and I had laughed at that idea before. Perhaps things had changed, that was all. She trusted me now—but did I trust her?

I came to my feet and stepped around the table to steady her a bit—she was wobbling there like a drunken sailor—and then she did it. Flung herself forward, her little black head just reaching to my chin as she clung to me—shaking like a leaf and sobbing like a child.

A hard, calculating woman, I thought. And now she had blown up. Certainly this wasn't acting. And certainly again it was hard to believe that this was the same girl who had leaned from the back of that swaying car and shot a man into the roadway. Hard to understand women—I gave it up years ago. I just take them as they come—watch them and—

But there I stood, one arm about that slender body, the

153

other hand patting her back—and trying to comfort her with silly talk.

"Brace up, Kid." I finally took her by the shoulders and held her off at arm's length. Her face was red; tears still rolled down her cheeks; and it was somber, painful, black eyes that looked into mine.

"What of Danny?" I asked her. "He'll be needing you." And with a sudden thought, "The money—the cops didn't frisk you for it?"

"No—I've got it—it'll go to Danny. And you—you—" she reeled forward again but my hands stretched out and held her off.

"Please—" two little hands sought the lapels of my coat. "Just let me lean there again—a minute only—I shan't hurt you. I'm bad, I know—but it's not like a disease—don't just despise me. For a moment I felt safe, and forgot." With a quick, convulsive shudder she ducked under my arms, flung her hands up about my neck, and clung to me—her head buried in my coat.

What sort of game was this? I can't say that I got a kick out of the little velvet hat that brushed my cheek. I put a hand down and felt her forehead. It was burning hot. I jerked off her hat—hair brushed my chin and she clung the tighter, boring her face hard against my chest. But she never spoke and she never looked up at me, and somehow I got to brushing her black, bobbed hair back and sort of holding her.

But her hair wasn't intoxicating to me. It tickled my chin a bit and the fragrance of it was honest and hadn't come from the five and ten cent store. It was a funny situation—there we stood—she, hanging to me without a word, for the sobs had stopped now—and outside the police protected us, and off somewheres in the cheerless city was Danny.

"There's Danny," I told her. "I'd better see you home." And when she did not move I shook her up a bit. "There's Danny—the man you love. You owe something to him."

"Love!" She jerked suddenly erect. "What right have I to

think of love? Owe something to him! Yes—my life, I suppose. I owe all of that to him. For the wreck that you saw the other night is of my making—God will punish me for that, I suppose." She laughed sort of hoarsely. "If God can—but the fires of a dead man's hell can't be any worse than the fires that torture a living soul. Come!"

So we turned toward the door. I could think that one out. The hall was quiet. At the bottom of the first flight we met a policeman. He looked suspiciously at us but did not move. At the front door another—a vaguely familiar face turned away as we passed. What a change just a few hours make—or a few minutes for that matter. Inspector Coglin's influence was already being felt.

No one bothered us. A dozen or more policemen were guarding the block—and Inspector Coglin, from across the street where the car that had contained The Beast still stood, nodded to me. Down the block there were a half dozen taxis to choose from—the echoes of bullets travel quickly; the curious were already in the neighborhood. But The Beast and his friends had made good their escape.

We didn't speak as I put the girl into a taxi and climbed in beside her.

"Where to?" I said. "Surely I'll get another chance to talk to Danny now?"

"The Grand Central Terminal," she told me. I passed the information on to the driver and the car shot away. But my question about Danny was ignored.

We were up to Thirty-fourth Street when I spoke again.

"You won't tell me where Danny is?" I asked.

"I think I will—if you still want to know, to-morrow." Her voice was very low. "I'll give you a ring—in the morning—or maybe the next day. I want you to get a chance to learn things—and maybe you won't want to see Danny again—or even me—even me!"

Yes, I'd learn something in the morning—something about the will of Danny's father, D. Perry Davidson. We finished the trip in silence. She, crouched there in one corner of the car—

while I lay far back in the other, trying to reason things out. If Danny wasn't entitled to any money, why the rumpus? But of course his father's will would leave him money. Did they think I was a fool altogether? Probably Barton Briskey thought that such a story would ease my conscience into throwing up the case and not bothering to look the will up at the Surrogate's. But why had the girl told me there was no money for Danny—and what did she mean that she owed everything to Danny and that her soul burned, and that sort of chatter?

I jerked erect in the car. Barton Briskey had said that Danny's gun fight was over a girl. Was this the girl? I turned suddenly to her as we pulled into the station.

"Are you the girl—that Danny had the fight—the shooting over, when he went to prison?"

I could see her white face jerk up in the darkness as the driver leaned back and opened the door. But she didn't answer. She climbed from the cab; then leaned back in again and beckoned me toward her. I bent down, sliding along the seat, until her face was very close to mine. I could even feel the warmth of her breath on my cheek.

"I am the girl—the girl that drove him to prison—and to murder. God forgive me—and you forgive me too, Race Williams." Her face snapped up; I caught the flash of great black eyes, then two red lips—lips that I saw for a moment and then felt. Yep, get a laugh out of it if you can. I couldn't. The girl had leaned forward and kissed me suddenly full upon the lips. Was it the warm kiss of a woman who loves, or the cold kiss of a woman who plays? Neither—more like the soft lips of a young child—memory must serve me there—for such a feeling knocks off the years and brings a picture of dirty, unkempt children—a hard, cruel face—and the bleak walls of the orphanage where I learned to coldly calculate the frailties of man.

That's that. And quite enough for one night, you'll admit. Did I suddenly discover that I was in love—madly and blindly in love with the most beautiful woman in the world? No—

not me. And I didn't laugh either. Somehow the Kid got that kiss over the way she meant it. Or—and I turned sharply to the driver and gave him a look that wiped the silly smirk off his face. The girl was gone—it wasn't the first woman who'd kissed me and I daresay it wouldn't be the last. I may be no winner of a beauty contest, but my face wouldn't turn your stomach either.

The girl disappeared in the station and we drove on. This time when I reached my home, Benny was waiting for me. There was no news. The police had stopped his car, looked in and gone on. Benny wanted to enlarge on the story but I cut him short. As Samuel Peppys would chirp—"So, to bed!"

Before I was up in the morning Inspector Coglin called me on the phone. I was awake in an instant and my mind was clear; I have learned to snap into things quickly.

"I thought I'd let you know that the gang got away last night. Had any threatening messages—or—oh, anything?" he asked, and there was an anxiety in his voice.

"Not a thing," I told him. "But here's a hunch for you. What did you do with the bird you got under my window the night before last?"

"You mean Jake Minely?" he said—and then, "I'm still holding him."

"Will he talk?"

"No—we tried to sweat him—Barton Briskey showed up as his lawyer and he shut up tighter than a drum."

"Briskey, eh?" I gulped. "Did you lock him up?"

"No—better wait. I got a hunch that Barton Briskey not only protects criminals with his legal knowledge, but profits from their crimes."

"You've had that hunch for years." There didn't seem much to that, but he was wise not to drag the lawyer in yet. And then I got a sudden thought. "Look up Jake Minely's record; I think he's an old offender—if he's got three convictions against him, threaten him with the Baumes law and the life sentence. If he won't talk to you, see if he'll talk to me— give him his freedom if he will."

"I'll do that," Coglin snapped, and I could picture the cigar racing by the telephone mouthpiece.

Not so bad, this working for Coglin. I might get some needed information—but first off I'd make a trip down town and have a slant at D. Perry Davidson's will.

And I did—just that little thing. I won't say I walked out of the building reeling like Charlie Chaplin in the days of the custard pie comedies. Not a physical reel anyway—but I sure had a mental one. D. Perry Davidson had left everything to his daughter, Muriel P. Davidson. And what's more he particularly mentioned that his son got nothing; "who has neglected and forgotten me in my advancing years and failing health," was the way it read. You couldn't get around that. Danny Davidson was left as flat as a poet's pocketbook. So I took the air—and what's more I needed it.

25

A Certain Lady Again

Could Barton Briskey's story after all be true? That this sister, Muriel, simply wished to protect her brother and the name of Davidson. And did Davidson hold some information that made the underworld thirst for his blood? Was a will after all contained in the letter that I still carried, and now placed in my safe deposit box, or was it information that I might have if he died? I had taken it in trust for Danny. He believed me. Foolish that I didn't open it? But I have my own code of ethics. Danny's envelope, whether it contained a will or anything else, was safe.

Now—what? Now you have a case, now you haven't. I didn't know where I stood. By ignoring Briskey's offer, had I slipped up on a real piece of change? But I shrugged my shoulders. I'd have to await developments. A pretty mess it would be if I'd just walked in on a nest of crooks and would spend the rest of my life killing off the gang, without getting a nickel for it. But thinking wouldn't do me any good. I set my lips grimly. I had a little business to attend to with Barton Briskey. I'd told him I'd come for him, and now I'd keep my word.

Oh, I didn't intend to simply walk in and shoot him down. But I wanted him to think that I would—wanted him to know that I hadn't forgotten—wanted him to be forced to strike back. Sick this Beast and the gang on me again—open up and let a little daylight through the blackness of the case I thought I had. That he'd be "out of town" was certain. And "certain" was right. A holiday had been declared in his "public" office. It was empty.

With that little duty off my mind I skipped up to my own office. No mail to amount to anything. What of the girl Milly? Where would she call me up—at the office or at the house? But Benny was waiting at the house—and the phone rang in the office.

As the soft feminine voice drifted to me over the wire I thought of Milly, and then I didn't. But the voice had seemed familiar at first.

"Mr. Williams—Mr. Race Williams?" and when I verified the anxious note in her voice, "this is Miss Davidson speaking—Miss Muriel P. Davidson—did you wish to see me?"

Stumped? Sure I was. What do you think? Did I want to see her? I didn't know. And why? But I ducked her question the best I could with a pretty weak come-back, I'll admit.

"I—did you wish to see me?"

"Yes—I think that I would like very much to see you. I have not been over well, though not so bad as people think—but I can't come to your office. Not my health, exactly—there are other reasons—I never go out on the street." She didn't dodge my questions so I tried another.

"You—you wish to consult me on business?"

"Well—" she sort of gasped, "I did think the business was yours—but I have heard from some one who refers me to you—some one who—who claims to be a relative—and I am in great doubt. Can you come to see me?"

"Yes," I said, "I can—where?"

"Why, at my home here—my uncle's home—Oscar Merrill Davidson."

"To-night—late?" I sort of wondered if this was to be a back door affair, while the household slept.

"Late? No!" There was a surprised note in her voice.

"When you can—this afternoon—I'm always home—and I'll be waiting—but the sooner the better. If—if—"

"Yes—" I encouraged when she did not continue.

"I see little of the world, Mr. Williams." She tried again. "If I must pay you for this visit—so, advise me and I'll be glad to—"

"That is hardly necessary," I cut in. "I'll see you then, this afternoon."

"Yes," she said. "And thank you—ever so much."

With that she hung up the receiver. At first I put the call down as a fake, but then this girl seemed so pitifully befuddled and rattled—that was natural under the circumstances. She had given me no address either. Honesty of purpose that—I had simply to look up the Davidson home in the telephone directory. And it was there all right—right on Riverside Drive. Had this girl tried, through Barton Briskey, to buy me off and failed—now would she make the attempt in person? After all was it true that Danny had gotten in touch with her?

At all events it seemed I was going to learn something, and about time too. I'd of liked to have gotten in touch with Milly—heard a word from Danny, but that seemed impossible now. Strange thoughts were pounding through my head. Could the will of D. Perry Davidson have been forged, and now the determination of Danny to have his own stirred up a panic in the camp of the enemy? Again if there was nothing coming to Danny, why fear him? And why had Danny been told once that the Davidson fortune was his—or had he been told it? I shrugged my shoulders. I'd listen to what this sister had to say and keep my face closed.

Thoughts of another trap came to me, certainly. Anything was possible—the game was big. I thought of Inspector Coglin and looked toward the telephone. The Davidson house was on Riverside Drive. It might be nice to have a detail of police waiting outside. Yet, I'm used to working alone and taking care of myself. Besides, this was not in line with "my" police duty. This was private business, and the

161

police had no part in it. Danny and the police wouldn't fit. But I sat down and wrote a little note before I returned home.

"Benny," I said when I was back home, "we're going visiting this afternoon. You will wait outside in the car for me. I won't be in the house over an hour. If I don't show up in two hours, take this letter straight to Inspector Coglin." And I slipped the envelope into his hand.

Did a feeling of security and an easy indifference to danger come with this new found police protection? I should have felt easier, but I didn't. Suppose something turned up and this girl wished me to go with her to meet her brother! Maybe she had heard from him; maybe the house would be watched and she'd want me to slip off somewhere with her. What of my note then? What of Benny sitting out there in the car? What if Inspector Coglin burst in, looking for me, and the whole mess became public? No—these people wanted secrecy. Yet—what a great protection the police would be! At least, I tried to tell myself that as Benny and I rode uptown.

I tried to think of other things as we swung onto Riverside Drive and along the Hudson. The newspaper account of the gun fight last night. Just a description of a feud between two rival gangs, it read to the busy man who glanced over the headlines and remarked to his wife about the epidemic of crime in the city. He'd smack his lips with satisfaction when he read of the death of two of them. Barton Briskey's name and my name were missing from the account. Inspector Coglin came in for the credit of busting up the party. There was the usual announcement that the police had a good description of the men and that they would all be apprehended within the next twenty-four hours. Of course that would be the last the "busy man" would hear of the affair. But he wouldn't mind. A jeweler killed or a bank messenger shot down on the public street would drive that "gang feud" into oblivion.

The Davidson house was only distinguished from the line of others by the number on it. The regular solid stone front, the curve to the steps and the stone bannister and the double doors. I drove half a block by it and had Benny pull up just around the corner. No use to make my entrance too conspicuous. If the enemy followed me there, good enough; they might think that things were coming to a head and act accordingly. "Accordingly," meant to me another crack at my life. Fine stuff that—Coglin could explain the dead for me afterwards.

Before I stepped from the car, I said to Benny:

"Give me that envelope." And his eyebrows shot up as he extended it to me, but he didn't speak. He watched me with interest and a sort of approval as I tore the note into tiny bits, and lighting a match burnt the message to Inspector Coglin to a fine white ash in the little receiver beneath the window of the car.

Benny sighed with relief, I thought. So did I. I wanted my mind free to act as I have always acted. I couldn't get used to the police being behind me—the further behind the better, I guess. It didn't seem right and natural. There's no other way to explain it. Oh, I'd work in with Inspector Coglin as I had promised—let him horn in when The Beast and I had it out. But this was private business, and Coglin didn't belong—not yet anyway.

Did eyes watch me from the heavily curtained windows as I mounted the front steps and stabbed the door bell? I don't know. I saw nothing suspicious. How could people like this be mixed up with the scum of the underworld, Barton Briskey, the wreck Danny, and The Beast? And who was The Beast—just a killer who worked for others in the night, or was he in reality the fears of Danny's youth—the man who had married his mother?

I'd know when I spotted the girl how deep she was into the thing. You can't trust any one these days. The "best people" have been known to rob their own mothers and the "socially elect" are not above going in for a bit of murder at times.

The butler opened the door for me and my suspicions should have been lulled to slumber. He was dressed in black trousers and white coat, and bent and bowed and scraped as I stepped into the hall. He was done up like a Belasco stage setting, and the map on him was old and lined and as beaming as the setting sun. But if you get too close to the sun it'll burn you, you know. One of his hands clutched at my hat—the other started to drag my coat off my back.

I swung and faced him. In a situation like this I wouldn't turn my back to the angel Gabriel.

"I'll keep my things," I said as I jerked back into my coat. "I won't be long. Miss Davidson is expecting me. I am Mr. Williams."

"To be sure—to be sure." His hands rubbed together, his shoulders bent a bit more, and he turned and led me back through the large hall and to a door at the right.

His tap was low and methodical, and if he got the word to open the door it came too low for me. But he swung open the door, motioned me to step within—and chirped:

"Mr. Williams is here, Miss Muriel."

That was that. My left hand sunk into my pocket. My right held my hat as I slipped sideways through that door. But there was no need to watch the butler. The door closed behind me and footsteps beat along the hall without. The room was fairly bright and I held my back to the door as I took in the situation.

"Mr. Williams." A voice came out of the corner, and again I got a start. There was something familiar about that voice. I knew before I stepped forward and faced the speaker that it was my blonde visitor of two nights before. Her voice was lower and meant to be disguised. Still, I knew her—and she knew that I knew her, for she tore the shawl away from her head and I spotted the blonde mop of hair. She sat erect on a couch and extended her hand toward me.

26

The Gun Behind the Curtain

I stepped across the room and took the outstretched hand. Nothing could happen to me there with Benny outside in the car. At least, I told myself that—as my left hand wound itself a bit tighter about the grip of my forty-four. I'd rather count on the cold surface of a rod than the propriety of a young lady inviting a gentleman to her house to have the roof of his head blown off. Remember, ANYTHING IS POSSIBLE TO-DAY.

She was talking, telling me to sit down beside her—and I was shooting my eyes about that room. Just one thing disturbed me. The curtains behind her. Oh, they seemed to be drawn across a window. The temptation to walk directly up to them and jerk them back was strong. But I didn't. Somehow I wanted to leave the impression with the girl that I trusted her—which I certainly did anything else but, once I spotted that yellow roof of hers.

I ignored her invitation to sit beside her, and pulling up a chair placed it before her, so that her head and shoulders were between the curtain and me.

"You know me of course," she said, and her lips shot back, the redness of them setting off the pink and whiteness of her skin and emphasizing too much perhaps the dimness of blue eyes—a hazy sort of blue; nothing definite about them. Yet

165

she was good looking in that baby-doll sort of way, if you fancy them soft and pasty and marshmallow like. She was speaking again.

"I was going to try and keep my identity a secret—that is, that I—Muriel Davidson—and the girl who visited you the other night were one. But there has been enough sub-terfuge—lying and cheating. I am through with it. I am sending for you before I send for the police. I do not question your purpose in this case—your determination to see through to the end the claims of a young man that have nothing to recommend them but the shame of a sister. Of that I shall say nothing." But she talked on and I watched that curtain. It seemed like something pointed and round and hard was smack up against it and that it moved and tried to get a line on me as I kept the girl between it and me. Of course that round, pointed thing may have been a putty blower—but probably wasn't.

I couldn't just slip a bit of lead through the curtain. Under certain circumstances, maybe. But if the girl were honest, what would be more natural than she have herself protected? She already knew enough about me to feel the need of a gat-tling gun handy. She droned on—about her early life, her brother's neglect of her father. At length she hit the interesting part, and I listened intently.

"You no doubt have looked up my father's will. You have learned that my brother is entitled to nothing. Now—to the point, and why I sent for you. You represent this man who claims me as a sister. Perhaps it is true—perhaps not—but he has written to me of you. I owe him nothing—but I owe something to the name of Davidson. Bring this man to me—let him bring his proof from England—but blood is thicker than water. Once I see him face to face I shall know. If he is my brother I shall give him money—make a settlement to have him leave the country—your fee shall be paid too. If he is not my brother, or if he is and does not stop blackmailing me and my uncle—then I shall go straight to the police—scandal or no scandal."

166

She bent forward when she finished and I bent with her. Not swayed by the power of her words but swayed by the power of that pointed object that still dug itself against the curtain. But she had spoken out—straight from the shoulder. She expected me to answer, and I did. If it was the first time I had seen the girl, I'd of admitted that her words rang true enough. Just a high spirited woman. Now—I could not forget her visit to my house that night before—her attempt to steal something there—no doubt, Danny's envelope and the will, or whatever it contained.

"May I ask you a few questions?" And when she nodded, "In the first place, how do I know once you get Danny here you will not ship him off to prison?"

She sort of bit her lip before she answered that one, and then came out with what seemed honest enough, if not reassuring.

"You'll have to believe what I tell you, I suppose." And then after a moment's pause, "But I've done everything so far to keep the scandal from the public. I even went to your house—to—to—yes, to steal a paper which I thought contained—oh, I don't know what."

"How did you know I had such a paper?"

"From my uncle," she answered, quickly enough. "He received letters from Danny—threats—claims that my uncle was withholding money from him. He also wrote that he was giving into your trust, at the first opportunity, his will and a denouncement of my uncle. It was all like the wanderings of a disordered mind. Come!" she came to her feet—and I to mine, getting right in front of her. "Come!" she snapped it out again, "Haven't I done enough to hide the thing—haven't I spent thousands in buying off enemies who threaten to expose him and the Davidson name? He must leave the country—I shall pay him anything within reason—but I must have proof that he is my brother."

Fair enough, I thought. She didn't fit in with my idea of a young society girl, for she got out her words in a hard, determined sort of way. Just one more question, I thought. How did she account for her associates—how about Jake Minely beneath that window?

"That night at my house? The man beneath the window—who—" I started and stopped. She burst right in upon me.

"I shall show you the letters of the man who claims to be my brother. I have kept them all and— Wait here for me." She dashed across the room, flung open the door and slammed it behind her—and I heard feet racing along the hall and pattering on the heavy carpet of the stairs. Was she just trying to dodge my question—or was it time for the lad behind that curtain to do his stuff?

The curtains waved suddenly—heavy drapes they were too. And I had felt no draft from the hall when the door opened. I stepped to one side, jerked my gun into view and drawing a bead on the curtains, spoke.

"You may step out into the room." The curtains waved again. "And make it lively," I added. "Come!" I threw a hardness into my voice; I was curious to know who watched me and for what purpose, "I'll give you to the count of three—then—Miss Muriel will be needing a new pair of curtains.

"One—" I started in to count. "Two—" and I sort of hesitated. Not that I lacked the nerve, you understand—but would it be safe to startle the neighborhood with a shot? If— And I stepped forward quickly, skipped to one side and jerked back the curtains. There was a tiny alcove—two French windows—and emptiness. But the curtains waved now in the breeze from a tiny crack between the two windows. Some one had been there, and that some one had dropped from the window to the little side alley. Probably when the girl slammed the door. Or maybe no one had been there at all and the windows had blown open from the jar of the door. Maybe—I didn't look out. I pulled the windows tight, snapped over the brass bolt and dropped back the curtains as footsteps came upon the stairs.

It was possible that the windows had blown open—but the slamming of the door had nothing to do with the round pointed object which was now missing from the dainty folds of the curtain. I turned as the girl entered the room again.

"I didn't bring the letters." She looked up at me. "I can't—I don't dare trust any one." She walked straight over to the curtains and swung them back, letting in the light. "What do you say? Will you bring this—this man here?"

"I'll think it over," I told her. I didn't want to tip her the word that I didn't know where Danny was.

"I must know—now—to-night."

"Very well—" I stalled for time. "I'll call you to-night."

"No—" she shook her head. "I'll call you—at your house— seven o'clock."

"Good!" I nodded. That would be better—I could stall her off by not being home. She hadn't told me why Jake Minely was beneath that window—and I didn't ask her again. Perhaps Jake Minely himself would open up and talk loose.

The butler appeared suddenly and the interview was over. I sidled toward the door and out onto the sidewalk. Was the girl lying about the letters, or was it true that she didn't trust them in my hands? I couldn't blame her for that. If they were of a threatening nature and Danny proved hard to handle, they were weapons in her hand. And had Danny really written them? But he might have. He told me that he had threatened his uncle with the "truth."

I hadn't learned a whole lot. There was a feeling that I should have taken Barton Briskey's money and gone off for a good time. The will read that Danny was to get nothing. Briskey said he was to get nothing. Milly, the girl of the night, said he was to get nothing. His sister, Muriel Davidson, said he was to get nothing—and—and Danny himself was the only one who insisted he was due for money. What did he want the money for? For his sister, who already had it? That was the yarn he gave me. For a moment I paused there upon the sidewalk. Had this youth after all made monkeys out of me? If they hadn't tried to kill me—if they hadn't tried to kill me, maybe I'd drop the thing. But the earnestness of the desire to take my life was not simply a thirst for vengeance by the rats of the underworld, or the fear of the information

Danny might carry—and now I might carry.

Bigger things were in the world. Brains were behind it all. Money was behind it all. And some one who knew that once Race Williams puts his teeth into a thing, those same teeth stay there until he chews off his share.

27

Jake Minely Talks

I went straight home and waited for a call from Milly—but none came. Then I tried to get Inspector Coglin on the phone—but made no go of it. It was after dark when he finally called me.

"I've let Jake go," he said. "He'll talk to you."

"He will if I can find him," I snapped.

"You'll find him—in his room on Sixth Avenue." And he gave me the address. "Get to see him right away—for I've got a dozen or more plainclothes men guarding the block that should be back on regular duty. He can't get away—he's scared too and won't try. At first he hollered that it was sure death for him to open up—but we've got three convictions against him already, and there he was with a gun under your window. Thanks for the tip on the Baumes law; life imprisonment don't look so well to Jake."

"Did he tell you anything?"

"Not a word. He said he'd talk to you if I let him go. He went straight to the tenement he lives in and hasn't come out since. He's waiting there for you. If he talks interesting, he's to skip—if he don't, we'll drag him back in again. I'll meet you at Twenty-eighth Street and Sixth Avenue—make it snappy."

And I did. Jake would be the kind that would talk. Twenty minutes later I met Coglin.

"I had to let him out," Coglin said hurriedly. "He was blown hot and cold and Barton Briskey wanted to see him again. He needed the air—if he's in the same frame of mind he was, he'll open up to you."

"Briskey hasn't gone in to see him—or any one?"

"Not Briskey or any one we know of. Of course we didn't put a man on his door—that would wise up the gang and they'd beat it—but no one knows he's there and we've watched the dump pretty closely. Only those who belong have gone in and out. We've kept the closest watch we could without tipping off our hand."

We reached the tenement, and Coglin in his plain brown overcoat was not conspicuous as he turned in the doorway. On the third floor, by the front door, we paused. This was Jake Minely's hangout.

"You stay back there," I told Coglin, and kicking on the door I waited. Coglin walked slowly back into the darkness.

No sound from within the room. I tried the knob—turned it—and the door opened. Just blackness—I pulled my flash—backed up with a gasp—and Coglin was by my side.

"What's wrong?" he said in a hushed voice as he crowded into the room behind me. For answer I let my flash play upon the silent figure stretched there upon the floor and the six inches of steel that stuck into his chest.

"You over-played your hand, Coglin," I told him. "There's our answer to the questions we'd like to ask Jake Minely. It hasn't been done long either."

"No," said Coglin, "he hasn't been here long."

"And not a soul got in to him—even through the back." I tried to keep the irony out of my voice.

"People have come in and out." Coglin turned. "But none that we watched for. Who could know why I let him go?"

"They could guess it—and a guess is good enough when the stakes are high." I shook my head. But what was the good

172

of crying over spilt milk, or spilt blood if you must have it that way.

"He's alive yet." Coglin crashed to his knees. "Look—he breathes."

And he did—plainly the gasps came to me. Jake was slow about paying his debt to society.

"Grab yourself a doctor." I jerked Coglin to his feet. "I'll wait here."

Coglin was gone in an instant, leaving me alone with the dying man. I'm not a doctor—but I knew he was passing out just the same. You can't mistake it when a lad with a knife in his chest is going over. I didn't pull the knife out. I knelt down and pushed back the closed lids. Rat-like eyes blinked up at me. Lips moved, but no words came. Still, Jake was trying to talk.

I stepped to the sink in the corner and got him a drink of water; it ran all over his face and nearly choked him. But I was afraid to lift him. And—he was going to talk. I bent low.

"Barton Briskey did for me," he said.

"How, Jake?—he couldn't get in here."

"But one he sent did. You get Briskey and— It was my pal—my roommate, Ed Jackson—the one who held your attention the night The Beast followed you." And I knew that he meant the panhandler who had played the chauffeur and attacked Milly last night. Also Ed Jackson was the name given the dear boy who was supposed to be waiting for me when I left Briskey's office.

Jake's words were getting weaker and weaker. I'd never learn anything that way—only that Ed Jackson had more guts than I'd given him credit for—or perhaps it would be like him to shoot out of the darkness, as well as stab a pal.

"We'll get Briskey for you," I told him. "What's the game, Jake—what were you doing under my window—why kill me—and what of the girl there?"

"Hell—I was to get you and the girl. I—" he coughed—gurgled once—and then, "the girl—she knew too much—had to be kicked over—see Oliver Cronin; he's the old family lawyer."

"And you were to kill Muriel Davidson—why?"

"Not her." He raised a hand and clutched at his throat—then he began to laugh. "Kill Muriel Davidson? She's dying too damn fast now—that's the trouble—too damn fast. I—"

"But you were to shoot her—through the window—at my house—remember?" And more slowly, as his eyes got a faraway, vacant look to them, "Shoot—her—through—the window—Muriel Davidson."

"Not Muriel Davidson—the blonde, you fool—she knew too much, and Davidson didn't want to marry her. You see—you—" He jerked his head up suddenly and let it slam back on the floor. No, he wasn't dead—but he was near it.

He had done his best, so I slipped a coat under his head as steps echoed along the hall. Coglin was back with a doctor.

"Is he dead?" Coglin kept buzzing in the doctor's ear. And, "Can't you jazz him up so's he'll talk, Doc—just a word or two?"

As for me, I turned toward the door. Coglin put out a hand and stopped me.

"Did you learn anything—see anything?"

"I'm not that kind of a detective." I smiled. "There might be a hundred clews around and I'd miss them. I've got to have a target to shoot at. But—I have an appointment now—which may—I'll give you a ring."

"Do—" he said, and then turning to the doctor I heard him begging him to "jazz the lad up, Doc, and make him talk."

But just before I turned from the door the doctor came to his feet—and clearly I got the one word "dead."

The doctor was a young man, for there was feeling in his voice. As for Coglin—he was a wheel in a great machine—the death of Minely meant nothing to him. If the doctor had only "jazzed him up."

What had I learned? Anything Coglin should know—anything about The Beast? No. Anything that would lead to The

Beast? Maybe. But just what information had I received from the dying lips of Jake Minely? I mulled over his jumpy phrases and words—mainly he was thinking of vengeance on Barton Briskey.

Jake Minely was at that window to shoot down both the girl and me. Because she knew too much? Because Muriel Davidson knew too much? Or was he trying to tell me that the girl—the blonde who had entered my house and interviewed me at the Davidson house was not Muriel Davidson? Then who was she? "Some one who wanted to marry Davidson," Minely had said. Did that mean Danny—and certainly Danny didn't wish to marry her. But it would take a better man than I to think that one out. If this blonde wasn't Muriel Davidson—then where was Muriel Davidson? Had she been killed—murdered? But who would profit by that? Danny, her brother, if she hadn't made a will—and if she had— But certainly the finger of suspicion would point to the beneficiary under her will. No, I couldn't see murder.

And the blonde. After all she was nothing more than a hard boiled little doll—but so might Muriel Davidson be for all I knew. I tried to picture that night again, when she stood in my living room—her hand reaching for a gun—a gun that she would be willing to use. No novice this girl—no unsteady hand. She was an old timer at the game. Were Jake Minely's words after all the ramblings of a dying man?

A drug store, a blue sign of the telephone booth—and I stepped in. A hurriedly closed door, a nickel in the slot, and I had my number. The Davidson home on Riverside Drive. If this blonde was masquerading as Muriel Davidson—maybe just to me—Oscar Merrill Davidson must know about it. Now—

And it was the blonde's voice that came to me over the wire.

"I've learned a lot." I snapped into the subject. "And you've learned too much—far too much."

"Who—who is this?" She gasped, and the gasp was real.

"You can have three guesses. Now, Miss Davidson," and I

175

put a world of sarcasm into the name, "can any one hear what I say to you—will I speak out now or let you call me back? This is Race Williams."

A moment's hesitation—and then:

"Speak out—now!" She echoed my words.

"Good!" I gave her the whole show. "You wouldn't tell me why Jake Minely was under my window the other night because you didn't know why he was there. But I know—too much knowledge is a bad thing for a young girl—he was there to put a bullet in your head, and hang the killing of me on a dead woman."

"No—no." The words were very low, with a hissing sound to them, like frying eggs—but somehow I felt that she meant "yes."

"You were there—" I hurried on. How easy I seemed to explain the thing to her when a minute before I couldn't even explain it to myself. "You heard the auto horn that warned Minely of my coming—you knew that some one telephoned the police. It was a double crossing game all around—I'd be dead—you'd be dead—Minely would be caught by the police. Just why he had to be sacrificed too, I don't know; but—"

There was another period of silence—then a voice that broke with passion.

"Who told you this?"

"Jake Minely," I answered. "He died to-night—watch your step. If you want to come clean—why, I'll help you—that is, if you'll help me. Where is Muriel Davidson?"

Like Coglin, perhaps I had over-played my hand. In answer to my question there came a curse—a spontaneous flood of words that would put to shame a woman of the streets. But the tirade wasn't directed at me—peculiarly enough, the name of Oscar Davidson, Danny's uncle, came in for her little pleasantries. There was a jar and a crash—and silence. But certainly I couldn't kick. I had had five cents' worth of conversation and no mistake.

There was a feeling of satisfaction as I left the booth. Jake

Minely's message hadn't meant a whole lot to me, but it certainly had registered with the blonde dame. I've played the game a great many years, and dissension in the enemy's camp is one of the greatest assets in my profession. I had started the fireworks if Minely's story was true; and even if it wasn't true some one would have a good deal of explaining to do. And I thought that one would be Oscar Merrill Davidson. Here was an unknown quantity—a villain in the piece—an important actor perhaps. Yet, the show was well along and he hadn't made his appearance on the stage as yet.

28

A Bullet in the Back

Jake Minely hadn't done so bad for a starter. Now, what else was on his mind? Oliver Cronin, the family lawyer. I turned back from the drug store door, picked up the telephone book and let my finger drift down through the "Cs." Cronin stood out like a sore thumb—there it was: Cronin, Cronin & Cronin—Attorneys at Law. It looked like the business was going to stay in the family. I found Oliver Cronin, noted the address and decided to pay him a visit.

I changed my mind before I was fairly out on the sidewalk. I guess I'd hurry home. The blonde would have time to think things over—maybe she'd give me a ring and spill the works. So I jumped a taxi and drove home. An angry woman is a good thing for the other fellow.

And I had a visitor. A red light burned up in my attic window; Benny was home—and that light meant a visitor; a warning of one who'd stand watching. At least, Benny was doubtful of his character. I dismissed the cab, climbed up the steps and rang the bell. That would be better than using my key, for Benny could wise me up as to the caller. And he did.

"He's inside—in the library," Benny whispered in the vestibule. "Queer little runt—wouldn't give his name—said if

I didn't let him in, it would be worth my job—that you were anxious to see him."

"Gunman, Benny?" I questioned.

"Hardly—not a regular anyway—felt like frisking him, then thought he might be a real client. Acts peculiar—opened a window in the corner of the library and sits near it. All wrapped up like a mummy, he is and—"

I stepped by Benny, parted the library curtains—and pulled up sharp. There, sitting on the window ledge, was Barton Briskey. He smiled on the window over at me—both his slender, white hands folded across his knees.

"Dismiss your man and let me talk." Shrewd little eyes shot over my shoulder as Briskey got his words out, and one foot swung slightly over the sill as he saw my hand shoot to my pocket—but he never moved his hands—just kept them on his knees. He looked like a mummy all right. A dark scarf was wrapped around his head and under his chin, hiding most of his face—on his head was a tightly drawn cap.

I never took my eyes off him as I waved Benny aside—had him shut the large folding doors and stay in the hall. Then I walked toward Barton Briskey.

"Hold your distance," he snapped. "I don't expect you'd kill a man in your own house—but I don't trust you. You wanted to see me to-day—here I am—let me talk." And then as I came nearer to him, my eyes trying to read what was behind that queer expressionless little face, "I'll drop from the window—don't be a fool—let me get my say out. I have a gun—if you want it." His hand started toward his pocket when I spoke.

"Keep it, Barton." I moved to one side of that window, and sitting upon an arm of a chair crossed my legs, folded my hands and watched him. "If you want to draw that gun—you're welcome to it. You had your nerve, coming here—and you're taking a big chance."

"I know it." He nodded. "And I'm willing to take it. I've come to blow the game. I didn't know it was so deep—I won't stand for murder, not me. Now—if I put you in the

179

way of clearing up this Davidson affair will you give me free passage—set me right with the police—and if there's a million in it, see that I'm fixed?"

"What have I got to do with the police?" I lifted my shoulders.

He smiled knowingly.

"Lots, lately. Will you straighten me out with Coglin—at least, will you lay off'a me, tell Danny Davidson the part I play to-night—and let me horn in on the purse?"

"You don't want much," I sneered. "What's the game? Why are you here?"

"I like to be on the winning side." He shrugged his shoulders. But his easy air of indifference was feigned. He was a mighty scared man—the slender fingers biting into his palms showed that it took real will power to make his voice steady. There was a courage behind it all too. In the first place, he was willing to face me—in the second place, those itching fingers and snapping eyes that occasionally glanced hurriedly out into the night told of another fear—and the sudden, spasmodic twitching to his face at such times made the uncertainty of that fear greater than the fear he felt of me.

"If you've anything to say—say it. I make no promises."

He wet his lips before he spoke again.

"Suppose I save Danny's life for you—get him his money—all of it. Suppose I put things straight. Suppose I open up, and it is through me you reap your reward—get The Beast—save Danny—yes, and this girl—your girl."

"My girl!" That was a rich one.

"Sure—" he nodded. "I know—Milly. I offered her ten grand to sell you out—and she refused. She's run straight too and—"

I stopped him. "You are not here to tell me about the charms of a young lady I hardly know." Somehow I didn't want to hear him talk about Milly. I don't know why—so we'll let that ride.

"All right," he agreed. "Am I good for fifty grand and a chance to skip, if I can't beat any case the police have against me? Now—before you refuse to do business with me, understand my proposition. You are to be the sole judge—if I don't speak, Danny will die—to-night. For where one seeks money, the other seeks only vengeance—and the vengeance in man is stronger than the love of gold."

"I'll not stand in the way of your collecting, if you're worth anything. But I know much already and—"

"If you don't know more to-night—the boy dies—and the girl with him—and perhaps you too."

"Let's have the story."

"And you agree?"

"As much as I already have."

"So—" a hand stroked his chin, "I've got to take a chance." It was as if he thought aloud—then he turned those steely eyes on me. "I didn't know it was murder when I was dragged in. I had heard of The Beast—seen him once—and done business with him in Chicago, after he came over from England. A shrewd enough man—a killer by instinct and a craver for blood. And mark you this—don't belittle the underworld's belief that a bullet can't kill him. I stood beside him in a joint in Chicago when a drunken fool put a bullet in his chest. It took four men to pull The Beast off him, and if that bullet hurt him any— But that's not the point—I'll tell you about him later. It's the Davidsons that interest you.

"You've seen the father's will by now, and wonder why Danny must die that another may profit. It's because Danny's sister, Muriel, has never made a will. If she dies, Danny gets the money—but if there was no Danny, or if Danny was dead—Oscar Merrill Davidson, the uncle, takes the pot."

I don't know if he read anything in my face. He watched me closely enough, but I was playing poker—yet it was said that Briskey could look into a man's mind and read what was there. In a way he got my thoughts.

"Simple, isn't it?" He smiled. "Terribly complicated it seemed to you, eh? So you see—Danny must die; and since he has never yet appeared legally in the case, there won't be much trouble about Oscar Merrill Davidson collecting. Of course there is Danny's will and your entrance into the case. But if Danny dies first—he has nothing to will—so—"

"And then this Oscar Merrill Davidson will kill his own niece. Does he think he can get away with this double murder?"

"Kill her—" and Barton Briskey laughed—a strange, weird little laugh. "That's the humor in the whole tragedy. Oscar Merrill Davidson is doing all in his power to keep the girl alive."

"Where is she?"

He hesitated before he answered that—and then:

"In a private hospital here in the city. Her death will be natural enough. Oscar Davidson kept the fact that she had consumption from her until it was too far advanced for her to be taken to another climate. Now—he fears she'll die too soon. It's a matter of days—perhaps hours. He didn't foresee the long life of Danny—this Milly double crossed him. She suddenly stuck to the boy—hid him—worked to support him. It's strange what a woman'll do for a man—and the man she sent to prison too. Of course she didn't know or understand that there would be a gun fight that night. But, on the level, the boy isn't much good. We kept him quiet by letting him believe that his father left everything to him. They came to me after the killing and I arranged a second degree murder charge, and had Danny sent up under another name. So far, you see I was straight in the game."

Now, here was a story that rang true enough. Just one catch in the whole business. Why had Barton Briskey come to me? Why couldn't he stick it out with the crowd—certainly no one could suspect the extent of the plot to get the Davidson money. With Danny in jail, it was thought that his sister would make a will leaving all to her uncle—but she didn't; so the escape and the plans for his death.

"Why have you come to me?" I asked again.

"I never go as far as murder. I thought last night that I could buy you off—and then I had a real fear—Oscar Davidson had kept his name clear of these gunmen; not one of them

182

understands the interest he has in the death of Danny—in fact, he is in Washington on business, and will have an alibi. But who's to handle The Beast when things are over?"

"And The Beast—who is he?" But I thought that I knew.

"He is one who hates the name of Davidson. He married the divorced mother of Danny. Not for love, but in the hope of bleeding the Davidson fortune. And instead, D. Perry Davidson spent a part of his great fortune hounding the man who took his wife; searching his past record; disclosing his misdeeds to his wife—to the English police. He was a man bent on vengeance. Now, that vengeance has borne fruit to prey upon his children. This man they call The Beast would willingly sacrifice his life to hurt them. If the truth were told, Race Williams, I want to get out now that you are in. If you had refused to listen to me to-night I'd have gone straight to the police. Even yet I will. The Beast's quest for blood will not be denied. There are times when I believe that the man is mad—that his snarl is no longer a pretended thing, but real."

"Where does the blonde fit in?" I questioned.

Barton Briskey laughed.

"Just a weak link in a well forged chain. She's simply a moll that Oscar Merrill Davidson picked up—found that she could help him, and promised to marry her. I don't think she knew that murder was back of it. Now—he's got a woman in Washington. When that woman came in, it was time for me to get out. I can see the end of the whole thing—blood and murder, and a little green door."

"You say Danny's life is in danger. They can't find him if I—" But I didn't finish. Why tell Briskey that I didn't know where the boy was? "How will they find him?" I asked instead.

"The newspapers. Danny wrote that he would watch the personals in one of the threatening letters to his uncle. I've been watching the personals too. They'll get him to-night unless he senses a trap and gets in touch with you. Here!" Briskey was a careful, methodical man and did nothing to tempt my fire. He inserted two fingers into his pocket and produced a folded paper and pushed it over to me.

It was tough reading the tiny print and keeping an eye on Briskey at the same time—but I did. There wasn't much to it; nothing to excite suspicion.

"If D.D. will telephone 8874 he will receive word from his sister.

M.P.D."

"Here's another thought for you." Briskey bent forward so that his head was beneath the closed top of the window. "Danny made a will—and I have found the lawyer who drew it up—it was properly executed and witnessed. If Danny should die—you might inherit a great fortune."

"I—? But he couldn't leave the money to me."

"Not you. What was that?" Briskey straightened suddenly in the window. "It's my nerves, I guess." He laughed hoarsely. "Stick to me, Race—let us travel to big money with the law behind us. If Danny disappears—if that ad. fetched him—I'll tell you where to find him—but perhaps it would be best to wait. For they intend to kill him to-night—The Beast is to get him."

Now, what was he driving at? What did he mean that I'd come in for a pretty fortune if Danny died? Why, he had nothing to will until his sister had passed on and—

I saw the shadow and I heard Barton Briskey scream—and then I heard the crash as I whipped out my gun. There was an evil face, two glaring eyes, a snarling mouth—and the lifeless body of Briskey crashed to the floor, his skull crushed in as if it were an eggshell, and the heavy bit of lead pipe that had done the trick beside him. The open window, which was meant to protect him from me, had been his death.

I didn't fire for there was nothing to fire at; the face at the window was gone. I just lurched forward, placed my left hand on the window sill and vaulted into the court. Not three seconds had passed from the time that that evil face glared in at the window—and I was in the alley. And I saw my man as he dropped over the fence and into the yard of the vacant house next door. He had used that as a place of refuge before, but this time it wasn't the police who were on his trail. When the police came they could cart him away feet first.

I know my own yard; there's a little stone bench near the back. I made quickly for it, leaped upon it—and figuring that The Beast was bent on flight, took a chance and pushed my head over the fence. There he was just at the corner of the back of that house. Another second and he'd be behind the rear steps and out of sight.

We can't be over particular and if a lad won't take his lead facing you he's got to take it in the back. His head was crouched over too far to be sure of a bull's eye—and his legs wouldn't turn the trick. But his back! I just raised my gun and fired—a single shot in the night, as a car roared up the street, hiding the report. Did I miss? Did the bullet proof man turn and laugh? Not much, he didn't. There was a single curse and The Beast pitched forward on his face. To the story of his activities the police could write, "Finis." If this was the lad who executed the plans of Oscar Merrill Davidson—then Danny could breathe easy.

29

Police Protection

And that was that. Benny was crying frantically from the window. I dropped from the bench and slipped up to him.

"Was that a shot? I seen him like this," Benny nodded down at the floor beneath the window, "and you gone—Gawd!" But when he saw I wasn't dead, his whole body quivered—like a pleased dog. You couldn't beat Benny for real friendship.

"Drop out the window, Benny," I said, and as he joined me in the alley, "Barton Briskey's double-, triple-crossing days are over." But I felt that Barton had told me the truth, and The Beast had heard some of it. He had come there for me—or had followed Briskey—but it didn't matter now. His carcass was over in the yard next door. A pleasant sight for Inspector Coglin, that. I wished I had plugged him in the front of the body. But we can't always have everything we wish for. One thing was certain. I'd had a split second to aim before I fired. That bullet would be buried smack in his spine. Yep, day or night—I can mostly tell you where the bullet will be found. I'm a good shot if nothing else.

"Barton Briskey doesn't look so pleasant, eh, Benny?" I tried to cheer him up. "But I've a prettier sight for you. A lad who has really tried for my life and made no bones about it.

Come—we'll hop the fence and have a look. Keep close to the house—he might have friends. Benny, The Beast is dead."

So we jumped from the fence and, keeping in the shadow of the house, slid around the rear. I stepped past that back porch, looked down—and jarred erect. The body of the dead Beast was not there. It was gone. Gone—and there had not been time to cart the body away. I—I had missed then—missed a back of that size in less than ten yards. I—who can clip the spots out of a playing card at one hundred feet. Why—the thing was impossible. And this time I swallowed just a bit when I thought of my motto: ANYTHING IS POSSIBLE TO-DAY. A bullet proof body? No—that is a superstition of the ignorant. My years at the game, my knowledge of man, and lead too for that matter, denied such a preposterous idea. Yet, I'd rather believe it possible—a thousand times rather believe it than believe that I had missed—missed that broad back at that distance. But I wasn't blind. Didn't I see him plunge to the ground before the echo of my shot had died away?

I looked into the yard behind, even on the street beyond, and once again hurried about the yard. The Beast was not there. The doors of that vacant house were locked, the windows closed tight, the one The Beast had used the other night for his escape boarded up. Why look more—there was no place for him to go unless he jumped that rear fence and walked to the next street—yes, walked on his own legs.

A bell—distantly it came through the open window of my library. The phone? Would that be the blonde—Milly maybe—or Inspector Coglin? I jumped the fence, made my way along the alley, avoiding the window with the gruesome thing beneath it, and entering through the front door went straight to the downstairs telephone in the rear room. And the voice that came to me over the wire was neither the voice of the blonde, nor Milly, nor even Inspector Coglin. It was the wracked, whining voice of Danny. Unmistakable, those plaintive, cracked notes reached me.

"Mr. Williams—Race Williams—can you come to me—here in Spuyten Duyvil? I've found my sister—she's very sick—

but she knows me—and I never inherited my father's money—she has it—which is good and just and I'll be glad to— Bring my will—it will prove to her that I—"

"Easy does it." He was traveling a bit fast for me. That I didn't have the will with me and couldn't get it that time of night wasn't necessary to tell him. But he hadn't said where he was in Spuyten Duyvil, and his words were getting loose back in his throat. He sure was excited.

"Just where are you?" I asked.

"Spuyten Duyvil," he answered hurriedly. "Doctor Newcombe DeLancy's Sanitarium. Ask the policeman at the police booth there on Riverdale Avenue, after you turn off Broadway at Kingsbridge and reach the top of the hill. It's—"

"I know the police booth," I told him. "I'll be with you right away. You're sure that this is your sister and— Is she a blonde—well built?"

"No—dark and thin, and dying. There can't be a doubt— my father's lawyer, Oliver Cronin, is here—he looked me up and—"

"All right, Danny—I'll be right along up. Keep your face closed to outsiders—including Cronin, until you see me."

"And the will—you'll bring that?"

"I'm on my way—we'll talk then." I hung up the receiver and turned to Benny. "Get the car," I told him. "I'm going out—now. I'll get in touch with Coglin and leave you here— I'll explain when I get back." And as Benny disappeared I went to the phone. Coglin was on the job.

"No questions now, Inspector," I told him. "Get over to my house. I've got a surprise package for you. Bring the coroner along—it's The Beast's job." And I gave him a few particulars, without mentioning the story that Barton Briskey had told me. "If I'm not here, stick around for a message—I'll give you a ring. You'll find Benny waiting— and Briskey's a mess." With that I jammed on the receiver and, slipping into my hat and coat, turned back to the library. I'd have to frisk Barton Briskey before the police came. Not a pleasant job—but a necessary one just the same.

He might have something of interest in his clothes.

But he hadn't—not a thing that was worth finding—the old foreign make of gun, a few bills and a pocket handkerchief. Barton Briskey played the game well. Any information he may have had had died with him. So I turned to the door, and walking down the street met Benny at the corner and climbed into the car. Benny jumped out, and I was away. Occasionally I glanced back over my shoulder, but mostly I watched in the little mirror. I was not followed. That was good!

Barton Briskey was dead—that much was certain. And he had come to me first and told his story. Why? It wasn't like Barton Briskey to turn on his friends—unless the game was up and his own hide and his pocketbook made that move essential. Something had gone terribly wrong before he came to me—and just gone wrong too, for he had been instrumental in the killing of Jake Minely. What could have happened in the intervening time—a meeting with the crowd and a misunderstanding? Perhaps, but I thought not.

Then what could have happened? Something that told him there wasn't a chance to succeed; something that assured him beyond the shadow of a doubt that the money would be on my side of the fence. In other words, things had taken a sudden change, and Oscar Merrill Davidson's chance of getting the coin had blown up—not just doubtful. Somehow Briskey knew there wasn't a chance of collecting on the other side. So he faced death to come and see me—not only faced it but got it. None knew better than did Barton Briskey the chances he took—and yet he took them. Why? If I knew that, I felt that I'd be a pretty well informed young man.

Now, what of Danny? Had they trapped him as Barton Briskey said? Hardly that. I had only asked him one question or so—and it was a cinch the blonde was not playing little sister to him. Besides, this gang couldn't run up a sanitarium over night. My directions of how to get there knocked all ideas of a trap on the head. I could ask the cop about it—find out how long that sanitarium had been in existence—and if

Doctor DeLancy was an old hand at the business and when he started in to work at Spuyten Duyvil. Briskey had warned me of an attempt to trap Danny—well, we'd make sure they didn't trap me. And the girl Milly—was she with him—why didn't she talk? But I shrugged my shoulders as I twisted my head back down Broadway.

Spuyten Duyvil is in the city of New York all right—but you wouldn't know it except from the post office address. You might as well be up in the Adirondacks. It was a sweet place for a bit of murder, but it also was a first rate place for a sanitarium too.

I made good time the couple of miles from Broadway and up the steep hill at Riverdale Avenue, which led to the police booth at the top and the road that gave off Riverdale Avenue to Spuyten Duyvil.

I pulled up in the shadows across from the police booth and hopped out. A blue coated figure, buttoning his coat about his neck and swinging his club in his hand, stepped from the little wooden structure as I approached it. It sure was a lonely spot.

"Know where Doctor DeLancy's Sanitarium is, brother?" I asked the officer.

"Surest thing." He smiled. "A lonely, dismal place—good for the sick and bad for the well." He shivered slightly. "Down the road there—about half a mile, and"—peering over my shoulder and spotting the lights of my car, "I'll ride down with you, Buddy." He half turned toward the doorway of the booth. "Hey, George—here's a lift—half way to the station. George goes off duty," he explained. "Takes the train down—I've got to make the rounds."

Now, I hadn't figured on taking the cops day-day—but there couldn't be much danger in it. DeLancy's joint seemed to be O.K. with the police—but I'd put a few more questions to them on the way down.

Sociable boys they were—one climbed into the rear of the car; the other squatted beside me in the front.

"Got a friend sick?" the new arrival in the back questioned after his friend had explained the lift.

"Yep." I nodded. "Don't know much about this place though—this Dr. DeLancy, is he any good?"

"Don't know." The first cop shook his head. "Been in business here—well—seven years or more anyway—I used to be on duty there before. As to his being good—well, I ain't got much use for doctors—my wife, now—" And he was off on a long abuse of the medical fraternity in general and a certain specialist in particular. There I was with the two cops—both big men; the one in the rear given to weight and fidgety in the car as he kept changing his position.

"There's the dump." The cop in the rear poked his night stick out at a dark roadway. "You can't see the house but it's in there—we should have let you take us all the way down—it's a bit of a walk yet." He sort of growled as I pulled up the car by a little side road.

The fat lad behind came to his feet, half swung around, unbalanced slightly, swung back his club—and too late I knew—knew just the fraction of a second before the heavy night stick pounded down upon my head. I ducked slightly—saved myself a fracture of the skull, I guess. But that was the best I can say for myself. Things went reeling—the stars began to climb over one another and the barren trees to shoot up through the heavens to meet them—jumbling them up more than ever.

30

A Prisoner in the Shack

I never fully lost consciousness. At least I don't think I did. I knew that my guns were taken from me, and I knew too that they were looking for something else—for they were even ripping at the lining of my coat. The answer to that search was simple. Here were the pals of The Beast—the workers for Oscar Merrill Davidson, the villain of the piece, who had never appeared upon the stage. Would I see him now—now that it would do no good? Then I was lifted clear of the front seat and chucked upon the rear one.

They cursed considerably when their search for Danny's envelope proved useless. I half opened my eyes and tried to look ahead. Most of all I was angry—mad clean through. I had been taken in like a child. The simplicity of the thing! I'd given my confidence into the hands of the police, like any fool citizen. I didn't for a minute believe that these men were actually guardians of the law that had been bought over. I may knock the boys on the force—fight against them at times. But you can't buy them like this. No, all these boys had to connect them with New York's Finest was the blue uniform and the brass buttons—and perhaps the weighted night stick that had crashed on my head.

The tallest one was talking—half to me—half to his fat

friend. Certainly they were enjoying the party.

"If they'd let us handle it before, there wouldn't be all this fuss about the terrible, daring Race Williams."

"No," the other sneered, "he's a weak sister after all. Just likes to cuddle himself in with the cops and keep warm and safe. Give him an inspector of police and a half dozen flatties to lead the way, and he might even hunt for The Beast. Real brave he is—with them two toy cannons that he's willing to shoot down stairs with. A fine bird he is."

And I received a kick some place around the legs—since I was on the seat he couldn't kick my face. There was little pain with that kick—my feelings were somewhat numbed already. Dumb? Yes, I was all of that. And the boys went on talking as they saw my eyes open, and one of them climbed into the front seat and pulled the car into gear.

"It was very simple, Mr. Williams." The fat lad in the rear with me went on talking, mimicking a grown person speaking to a child. "We just had some one call the policeman out of the booth to look at a dead man down the road. And he wasn't disappointed either. He wouldn't report it as a fake message, for we had a drunk for him—a real first class drunk, that was imported from Forty-second Street. It wasn't hard to pick up a good one; give him a few more doses of liquor and drop him by the roadside." There was a ring of pride in his voice as he got it off, and altogether it wasn't half bad. If the policeman suspected the idea was to drag him off duty, those suspicions would be lulled by the identity of the drunk—an honest-to-goodness citizen who found life slightly boring. How clever the plan was didn't interest me then—it had all been clever enough to take me in—and that was enough.

Fake policemen—the sanitarium—the police booth—and the rest of it never could have been executed by a stranger though, or any one I could possibly be the least leary of. Danny had trapped me—he and he alone was responsible for my position. If I couldn't trust my own client, when I was working in his interest—then who could I trust—not many, I guess. And even Danny; I might have doubted him without the police booth and the story of how Doctor DeLancy had had his sanitarium in Spuyten Duyvil for years. Yes, Danny was responsible for the whole show.

Why? Had they caught him? Put the fear of The Beast in him? Promised him his life if he delivered me into their hands? Or was it Milly—did they have her too? Was Danny promised her freedom to get me? That was perhaps it—the girl's life depended on my capture. Danny had fallen for that "personal"; rung up the number and walked into the hands of the enemy. By now was he alive or dead? Alive maybe—until they were sure they had me. He was the meat with which they'd bait the trap to get me. If it didn't work the first time, then—but it did work, and there I was.

Damn the luck! And it wasn't that I trusted Danny—it was just the natural way things should go. The police—the police booth—a confidence in that. Yet, I should have taken it as a warning too—Danny would have little use for the police. Still, in that situation—where it would be hard to describe an exact place in that God-forsaken bit of old New York—it seemed natural enough. At least, at the time it did. And—

I tried to sit a little straighter. No use to think of the past now. It was the present—and most of all the future that concerned me. Would they just kill me or—? And I let it go at that. What a nice way to die! I'll never kick about dying, but I'd always expected that when the police picked up my body they'd hire a van to cart away the rest of the corpses—and here I was. As I sat the straighter I realized for the first time that my hands were bound behind me; that'll show you how far gone I was—and just how loud the little dickie birds were singing in my ears. I sort of felt for the ropes. And they weren't ropes—hard, cold, steel handcuffs were about my wrists.

The car bumped and jumped over a rough road; took another turn and bounced enough now to break the springs. We must have been traveling over a cow path. But there wasn't much of it; we jarred to a stop beside the dark outline of a shack—more like a barn. Far distant through the trees I saw a light; that couldn't be the street though. A house, I thought. Would the inmates of it hear a shot if the boys decided to do me in at once?

These fake cops must have thought that I did them wrong in my day, for they certainly weren't any too polite in helping me from the car. While one dragged me out, the fat lad pushed me from behind—and I sprawled in the road. A nasty fall with my hands behind me? Maybe. But I was thinking of other things. One, in particular, was the generous proportions of the fellow who knocked me out, and I wished that my hands were free and one of them held a gun. But wishing wouldn't help any. I gritted my teeth, staggered to my feet and let myself be shoved along to the old shack.

The tall leader kicked on the door—waited a few minutes and then rapped; four sharp raps—followed by another kick. In a stupid way they worked on signal.

The door opened and I was hurled in—tripped over the jamb and spread my length for the second time at the feet of another man. Was this The Beast—and I looked up as I came to my knees. No—it wasn't The Beast. It was my friend of the two previous nights—the panhandler who had tried to attract my attention when The Beast first followed me; the man in the chauffeur's uniform who had waylaid Milly and tried to steal her money; and also the man known as Ed Jackson, who was to shoot me down as I left Barton Briskey's office—the one who had waited at the foot of the stairs. Now he played another part—dressed up this time. A dark blue suit, blue tie with white dots and a diamond stickpin in the center of it. Yes, this was the costume player. Quite the gentleman now, if it wasn't for his face, and the nose that had been generously mussed about it.

"Beat it!" Ed Jackson spoke to the long cop—and to the other he said, "You stay here—not that I need you, but it's Raphael Dezzeia's orders." That was the first time I heard the name of Danny's stepfather spoken since the time

Danny himself mentioned it at our first meeting. Did it thrill me?—in a way, yes. It meant but one thing. I was not booked to leave that place alive.

I struggled to my feet and braced my back against the wall. I could expect no mercy now, nor would I ask for any. But they wanted something from me, else why bring me there— why let me live at all? Or was this Ed Jackson of the weaker type, one who gloried in the dramatic and whose weak little soul was satisfied with vengeance? I thought so. I had picked him as the weak link in the chain long ago. But now—he was bigger than I thought, with this gang. At least, he was boss there to-night.

"So, Race Williams." Jackson strutted up and down the room like a game cock; his eyes ever on me—a black gun dangling from his hand and an evil, gloating sneer on his lips, "My life was forfeited to you because I had attempted yours. A pretty thought that—and not a half bad one. If it works for you, why not let it work for me? You would have shot me down the other night—now it's my turn—eh?" The gun came half up—there was death in the man's eye, in his heart too, but mostly in the gun that he pointed at me. I don't think he could have resisted the temptation to press the trigger if it wasn't for the fat lad who was climbing out of his uniform in a corner of the old shack.

"Lay off that—and do your stuff," the fat man grunted. "Business first—pleasure later. I'm as anxious as you are to see him go out, and you can make it—"

"Shut your face!" Ed Jackson hissed fiercely. "I didn't intend to blow him over yet—not me—I got my orders." And then, waving the gun at me, "Get over there by the end of the table."

I took in the room as I stepped to the end of the long table that Jackson pointed out. A damp, cold place—just a single room, with an oil lantern hanging from the ceiling. There were no windows—at least, what windows there were were boarded up. There was one other door—a little one almost directly opposite from the one we had entered. Both doors were barred with a long section of wood slipped into wooden braces. Worn wood—shingled roof—a great beam and a half dozen thinner rafters stretched across the ceiling. The furniture consisted of a couple of old porch chairs, with big backs and wicker seats and huge arms. They had been rockers once—now the rockers were gone and they stood upon their short legs. Nothing else in the room but that long table, and the lantern swinging from the beam.

Ed Jackson sat at one end of the table, and at a motion from him I sat at the other end. The fat fellow who had removed his uniform and now wore a sweater and dark trousers stepped toward me.

"Snap off the cuffs." Jackson lifted his gun, set his elbow on the table and drew a steady bead on me. He was a vicious looking lad and no mistake. Calm, cold—steady. How differently he had acted when I held the gun—and now—yes, he was the typical underworld killer; a helpless man, or a shot from the dark into a man's back. Given a gun I bet I'd of had a chance to draw and shoot. This Ed Jackson was like the prize fighter who is a bearcat when he's winning, but goes to pieces at the first hard sock from his opponent. He had a yellow streak in him—but I wasn't likely to have the chance to draw it out. At least, though, my hands were to be free.

I saw Jackson wink as the fat lad stepped behind me—and I heard too the swish of the club and think that I saw its shadow cross the light. Certainly this blow was a good one—not so hard as the other maybe, but I had no chance to duck as the club swished through the air and caught me smack behind the ear. After that, darkness—deep heavy blackness, with a sinking feeling in the stomach. Funny things that come over you then. What did I think of? Death, and all that—and did the faces of dead gunmen bob up before me? No, just one thing shot through my mind. I skipped back to my childhood and seemed to be with Alice, of Alice in Wonderland fame, as she fell down the rabbit hole. Queer that—but true, just the same.

31

The Yellow Streak

Voices were buzzing; my head was throbbing, and dancing dots twisted before me though my eyes were closed.

"You hit him too hard, you fool." Ed Jackson was speaking, and I opened my eyes to hear him add, to another figure, "There was no need to send you over here. I'll get the paper if I have to cut his eyes out."

The room seemed to be miles and miles long. There at the end of the table which stretched off into the distance like a parade ground, was Ed Jackson—misty and small, with his head seemingly floating in the air; and far behind him in the corner my fat friend, wobbling and uncertain—with a long-barreled rifle in his hands. I blinked and tried to shake my head. Another figure was there. Twice I closed and opened my eyes before I was sure. But it was the blonde, all right—her misty blue eyes more hazy than ever. She was coming toward me—getting bigger and bigger—the blonde mop looking like a huge sponge from the Museum of Natural History.

"You might have caved him in." The blonde was talking as she crossed to me. "The dirty rat." And the words hissed through her teeth as she reached me, saw that my eyes were open—and pushing her hand under my chin, knocked it up with force enough to make me nearly bite my tongue off. But it served another purpose; sent the blood suddenly pounding up into my head. A dizzy feeling, a wobbling effect and a slow clearing of my brain—a warmness to hands that had been as cold as an open grave.

"The Beast telephoned he's on the way. Been ducking around the city," I heard her mutter. "This bozo tried to croak him—with lead too." And she laughed. "The cheap dick." And this time she leaned forward and struck me with her open palm—leaned close and spat straight into my face. I half raised my hand—but she knocked it down again—stumbled toward me. Her hands shot out to keep herself from falling; she muttered something about my feet—cursed loudly, and I felt her hand strike against my side.

Did she speak to me—whisper something in my ear as her hair brushed my cheek and the smell of perfume nearly put me under again? And if she had whispered something, what was it? A threat! A curse! Or—"pocket"—that was it. But I didn't get it—just saw the fat lad rush forward and the woman come to her feet—swing on me again—step back and laugh.

"Wanted to kiss me good-by." She laughed shrilly—harshly too, like there were two notes to it—a high one and a low one. Then she turned to the little side door.

"I'll leave him to you—The Beast will take care of the two up at the house. Don't be chicken hearted, Ed." And this in a rather loud voice as she looked over at me, "The girl Milly fell for the trap to save this Race Williams. Now—will he do anything for her—even if he has the chance?" I jerked up slightly. Was she sending a message to me?

Ed sneered over an answer to her and she crossed the room, flung open the little door in the rear and passed out. There was a blast of cool air that felt mighty good, the swish of a woman's skirt, and the slamming of the little wooden door. The blonde was gone—and Ed was speaking.

"A little hazy yet, eh?" He laughed. "Well, I would have it so. But clear enough to think—to see. Let me first call your attention to Brick, in the corner." He jerked his head back at the fat lad. "That thing in his hands is a rifle—and Brick got a medal for marksmanship. Besides, you will notice that my head is not between you and him—nor are there any curtains before him, like there were blocking my vision the other afternoon on Riverside Drive."

That was news, but what good would it do me now? I was lucky then, when I kept my hand on my gun and the blonde's head between those curtains and me. But Ed Jackson was still talking.

"The next thing I wish to call your attention to," and Jackson certainly liked to talk—be dramatic, "is my right elbow, that rests upon this table—too far away for you to jump forward and grab it. If you will run your eyes up that elbow to the hand you will see a Colt automatic—caliber forty-five. In the table drawer are your guns but I won't want them—won't need them."

And I saw the gun all right; the hand that held it and the elbow that rested upon the table. Jackson kept the gun trained on me—steady enough, and his eye ran along the barrel.

"After seeing all this, look upon the table before you," he went on. "There is pen and ink and a sheet of paper. You will take that pen and write an order on your bank—to deliver into the hands of"—he hesitated a moment, then wet his lips, "Oscar Merrill Davidson the envelope in your safe deposit box—the envelope that bears the name of Muriel P. Davidson. Simple!" His lips slipped back. "Who will have more right to that envelope than the uncle of the girl—shall we say the dead girl—for she will be dead when he receives it."

"How do you know? What makes you think that I have that envelope in a safe deposit box? And what bank? How do you know I didn't turn it over to some one who will produce it the moment anything happens to me?" My talk was loose—disjointed.

"Because you are a lone worker." He laughed. "And because you were followed to your bank and seen to go down stairs to the vaults—and because the envelope is not on your person. If you cannot remember the name of your bank I am perfectly willing to help you out."

Why I stalled for time I don't know. What chance did I have? But my head was clearing—I was trying to think. What had the blonde said to me—what did "pocket" mean? Was she trying to slip me a message—a warning? And through my mind rang the words: "Hell hath no fury like a woman scorned." But what—? I dropped my right hand from the arm of the chair, toward my pocket—nothing there—of course there wouldn't be. Queer thoughts in my brain—nothing more.

"You will keep both your hands where I can see them," Jackson went on. "And you'll write at once—now. Place your right hand on that pen, your left elbow on the arm of the chair with your arm raised and your hand high." And when I obeyed, "That is correct; now write."

"And if I write—what then?" I still stalled for time. The desire to live is strong in all of us, I guess. Time—nothing more—I just wanted time to gather my jumbled thoughts.

"We won't go into your future," he sneered. "Will you write?" The muzzle of his gun waved slightly.

"What will happen to me then?" I asked again.

Zip—his finger closed upon the trigger. There was a dart of flame, the roar of a bullet and a stab in my left arm. Not much pain—just a sudden jolt and my left hand fell to my side; warm blood rushed over the fingers.

"So we begin." Ed Jackson laughed. "I am going to enjoy myself, I see. Will you write now—or will I shoot you to ribbons? Shall we nick off that ear of yours—pretty shooting, but I'm willing to have a try at it. We only need the right hand, you know."

And the pain came from the bullet in my arm. My fingers moved spasmodically; clutched at my coat—at the pocket of my coat—felt something hard. Then my left hand shot into that pocket—and clutched a gun—the cold surface of a small revolver. "Pocket" and "Hell hath no fury like a woman

201

scorned" meant something now. The blonde had put it there—she wanted vengeance—and—she'd get it; at least, I hoped she'd get it.

"I will write," I said, as I picked up the pen with my right hand and started to drag the left from my pocket. Started to drag—and that was all. The muscles wouldn't respond to the orders from my brain; the muscles of the arm seemed dead. Funny that—for the fingers of my left hand were alive and strong, moved easily and folded nicely about the gun—my trigger finger already in place. But try as I would I couldn't raise that arm from my pocket. Tough? I don't know as I ever felt a situation quite so keenly. Here was the chance of freedom within my grasp and I couldn't take it.

I had fixed an eye upon the fat lad who held the rifle in the corner—and that rifle was resting on the floor. He was a cinch.

"I'll write," I said again. Perhaps the use of that arm would come back by the time I finished—at least I'd take my time about it. Maybe Jackson would be more interested in watching what I wrote than keeping that gun on me. But, no—he watched me; never took his eyes off me, though I was unarmed as far as he knew—he was sure of that. I wrote slowly, making my hand tremble—but no power came back to that left arm. God! but it was hard to die like that—with a gun in my hand—with my fingers wound about it—and yet without the power to use it. For I knew as soon as that paper was written, a bullet would speed on its way and I'd go out.

"I can write no more," I said suddenly, twitching my face up with pretended pain. "Don't shoot—let me lift my left hand onto the table—I can't move it—and the blood's going—fast. I—"

I guess my face was white enough. Anyway he fell; simply cocked his eye the harder along his own gun.

"Go ahead," he said, "pull it up—and no tricks. And I'll give you one minute to finish up that paper."

Very slowly I slipped my right hand to the left coat pocket—there beneath the table. I kept my eyes up and watched

Ed. There was no suspicion in his face; but was there suspicion in the eyes of the fat lad in the corner? I didn't know. I saw his glance toward the little door that the blonde had left—and I saw too that he raised the rifle and was slowly bringing it to draw a bead on me. Things weren't clear to him—just a hazy idea that something was wrong. And—he was going to voice those thoughts—even took a step forward as he opened his mouth.

So—my plans would have to change. The lad with the rifle would have to get his first, which would give Ed a chance to shoot me. Still—I'd die fighting. There was but one chance— but one hope. I must count on—gamble my life on the yellow streak in Ed Jackson. That he could give death but couldn't face it.

One step the man with the rifle took; one word he uttered and Ed half turned his head at the warning note in that single word. Oh, the fat lad meant to say more—but he didn't. He didn't fire either—he didn't have the chance. He twisted his gun upward—was caught with his foot half raised for another step when I swung up my right hand and fired. I didn't have to aim. I'd attended to all that before I ever felt the fingers of my right hand upon the butt of the gun. I aim with my eye, not my hands—nor the sight on the rod.

And as I fired I lurched forward on the table—shrieking straight into Ed Jackson's face.

"Death!" I hollered. Dramatic? Maybe—but it was to serve its purpose. It was to bring out the yellow streak in Ed. As for the fat lad—he took my first shot, smack below his heart. The rifle crashed to the floor; he spun like a top, threw up his hands like a moving picture actor going out, and spread his length upon the floor.

Ed gurgled in his throat before he fired. He was scared and his hand shook, and he fired where my face had been before I ducked forward upon the table. He didn't miss altogether. He couldn't very well, but he did little damage—just combed my hair as my finger closed again. Ed got only one shot. There isn't the man living who gets more when I'm clutching a gun.

Seven feet was all that separated us when I pressed the trigger. Ed's mouth was open—his eyes were staring at me—wide, frightened, glaring things. He knew before he died, I guess. If it had óf been my own forty-four, Ed would have turned a back somersault—as it was I couldn't complain. His right hand slowly dropped to the table, still clutching the gun in lifeless fingers. There was a tiny black hole in his forehead, that was quickly turning to a vivid blue sort of red.

The glare just snapped out of his eyes as the life went. If ever a soul went crashing the gates of hell, that was the soul of Ed Jackson. Just a snap, like you'd turned off the electric light. His lips dropped, the pasty yellow of fear left his face—a stony white face, from which glassy eyes looked vacantly at me. A second or two he sat so. It's peculiar how death acts—then he pitched forward on the table—dead! I guess they don't come much deader than Ed. No moving picture business for him; and no message to the boys in jail.

32

The Scream of a Woman

I staggered to my feet. Mainly, I have said, I am a man of action. Well, I'd had plenty of it for that night—yet there was more to come—much more. Not that I owed anything to Danny Davidson—he had betrayed me into the hands of the enemy. But Milly? From what had been said she was caught—trapped—in an effort to save me. What else had the blonde said? That The Beast was expected at the house any minute.

Hastily I made a tourniquet and bandaged up my left wrist. The blood stopped—that would help. Then I pushed Jackson away from the table and shot open the drawer; my guns were there. I broke them open—all set—bullets ready. I looked for water but could not find any. I stepped to the fat fellow upon the floor—he laid on his face. Was he dead? I didn't know. I'm not a doctor, nor a coroner either—but I don't go to put bullets in a lad that's stretched out like that. However, I saw the handcuffs on the table and snapped them onto his wrists. Then I picked up my partly written order on the bank, tore it into bits, kicked the rifle across the room, staggered toward the little door, lifted the bolt and reeled into the night.

Things were not so good by Race Williams, yet I couldn't

complain. So far I'd given a mighty good account of myself. The bleeding of my wrist had stopped, but when I dabbed at my forehead with a handkerchief I found that the bullet that parted my hair had also worn a tiny groove across my scalp.

The air was bracing—yet I reeled. Funny that! I couldn't be sure why I was there. For Milly? Yes, I knew about her. The Beast too—and the house. But it was all a sad jumble. There was the light in the house—in fact, several lights. The whole house seemed to be lighted up, as if there were a party there. Strange that! Murder was to be done out there in the wilderness—yes, the wilderness, on the very edge of New York City. But the lights! I closed one eye and looked. The lights snapped suddenly out—that is, all but one light. I opened both eyes again—and again the illumination.

So that was explained. Not so good! There was one light in the house and the rest in my head—my reeling head. But it didn't ache any—or if it did I was not conscious of it. One thing was sure: I was needed at that house—one light or a hundred lights made no difference. Milly, the girl of the night—the girl who had been trapped to save me—the girl who had given me that childish embrace there by the station—was waiting for The Beast; or was already a victim of The Beast. But some one was still there.

I raised my right hand to my forehead—no blood this time. That was a good sign. Or was it? Had the cold of the winter night stilled the flow? But no matter. It wouldn't trickle into my eyes when the time came to meet The Beast and place a bullet in him. A bullet? I thought that out as I plodded along. I had placed a bullet in him before, and what good did it do me? None at all, from the later events. How about this time? After my escape from almost certain death, was I now going to a surer end? Maybe—but I was going just the same. I clutched my gun in my right hand and stumbled forward.

If there were guards watching that house they had better shoot first and holler "who goes there?" afterward. I had asked no quarter this night—and from now on I'd give none. In quick action lay the life of a girl—a girl with a hard little face—that had softened—that had buried itself upon my shoulder, with lips that had— But enough; she had been trapped for me. I owed something to her—and it wouldn't be said that Race Williams didn't pay his debt. I clenched my fingers about that gun. Milly would be the living proof of that—Ed Jackson was already the dead proof of it.

Things sort of cleared up as I went along—the lights got less and less, until finally just the single light in the second-story window shone out. Nothing needed now but to get rid of that feeling that I was tramping lightly from cloud to cloud. Pretty rough clouds too. Twice I pitched to my knees, and it was the last time up that the old brain cleared; and with the clearing of that brain came the need of caution. So far I had tramped through the woods like a regiment of soldiers—cavalry, more like. I guess I made nearly as much noise as an army bringing up the heavy artillery.

The moon was fairly brilliant, the trees barren of all foliage; and a moving object could probably be seen from a fair distance. So I slipped along from tree to tree as the huge, bleak house loomed up under the moon. I guess my eyes weren't any too good, for I was less than fifty yards away when I spotted the car—a long low powerful affair, drawn up in the shadow of the huge pillars before the front porch of the house. And I mightn't have seen it at that if it hadn't of been for the moving figures—three of them were milling about there on the steps. I shut one eye—there were still three. Were they entering the house or leaving it? What sort of a thing had I gotten myself in for? Would I have to battle with a whole gang?

What did I do when I saw the strength of the enemy? Did I turn and run back through the night? Not me. I just slipped to my knees and crawled forward. There are times when I run— but I run forward and not backward. Just one thought—the girl of the night a prisoner there; just one wish—that my left hand was as good as my right at that moment. That would even up things and even give me an advantage over the bunch at that. Conceited? Maybe. But it's the truth just the same, and exactly the way I felt. One thing was sure as death and taxes—I'd see the thing through now.

I snaked close enough to that party to get a shot at them; the last twenty or thirty feet I crawled on my stomach. Not pleasant going either, with a bullet in my left arm and the track of one across the top of my head.

A tall lad was talking to the others and getting a laugh too. A low nervous chuckle that lacked mirth—that slight reaction that comes after a murder, even with the most hardened criminals. I wasn't sure of the tall lad—but I thought I knew him and what he spoke about. It was of the trapping of me—and my death. So the nervous chuckle—each one felt that my blood was on his hands. Not a guilty conscience, you understand—but a fear of the stomach, that is accentuated by the thought of one word—RETRIBUTION. I've always contended that the gunmen of the underworld—even those who often go in for murder—are the greatest cowards at last. And I'm alive yet to prove it.

It mightn't have been bad policy to scatter a bit of lead into these boys—but I hesitated. Shots in the night now might mean the death of the two inside; the girl, Milly, if she hadn't already been done for. It might mean also the escape of The Beast.

Planted there on my stomach close to the house, I was safe enough. There wasn't a doubt that I could get the three of them before they even knew where I was—and don't get the idea that my sense of fair play prevented such a slaughter. I won't pose as any milk and water hero with high ideals. I haven't any. I'd of plugged them in a moment if I had only myself to think of. But there was Milly—so I lowered my gun and waited. No luck—they didn't talk loud enough for me to hear what was said.

Two minutes passed—maybe three—and I was glad that I withheld my fire. Two more men stepped from the house onto the porch—walked quickly down the steps and jumped into the waiting car. Then a voice came from the darkness of the doorway—a gruff voice; but it made my head shoot up and my spine tingle. There was a sneer in that voice; a whine in it; and I thought too that there was a snarl in it. The Beast was already there— The Beast, whom I had shot less than two hours before. What of Milly? I gripped my gun tightly. Would I after all have to be content with vengeance?

"Beat it, all of you." The man in the door fairly snarled the words this time. "And you, Billings; on the door where you belong. I'll go upstairs, with the meat."

Two of the three standing by the porch slunk into the car. The third—the tall one, called Billings, moved slowly toward the front steps—walked warily up them, ducked suddenly, and followed by a curse disappeared in the darkness of the house. So—The Beast after all wasn't a half mad creature. He was able to give orders, and what's more able to see that those orders were carried out—for Billings had passed into the house and the high powered car was slipping into the darkness, picking its way cautiously over the rough road without a light—nothing but its black hulk that finally was lost in the night.

For a minute or more The Beast stood in the doorway. I could hear him sucking in the cool night air, and I thought that I caught a low scraping noise as he rubbed his great hairy hands together. After all, he wasn't some abnormal monster who had to be guarded. Just a killer—whose brutal strength and wicked snarl made him a leader of the human wolves that prey on society.

"You stay at the door," he cautioned Billings again. "Remember always that the reward will be big—and remember too that the retribution will be just as big. You and each of the others are just as guilty of murder to-night as if you pulled the trigger of the gun—or twisted the knife which soon will be buried to the hilt in the whelp of a Davidson." The snarl in the final word "Davidson" was real—and I knew too that Danny was still alive. But what of the girl—Milly?

Were there others in that house? I thought not. Should I jump forward and fire? But no—that wouldn't work out. I couldn't see either of the men from where I lay, and The Beast had already passed within. It would be foolhardy to hunt him in the darkness of the house. Yet, if he got above—and murder took place while I waited— And I decided to move as heavy feet echoed on carpetless stairs.

I crawled to the rear corner of the porch. There was a curve between the front door and where I climbed over the railing. The cold boards bit through my socks, for I slipped off my shoes. I didn't wait now—I didn't dare. And once I passed around that curve on the porch I was within the vision of Billings if he were looking out of that doorway. That he was still there I knew, for I could hear his feet scrape nervously.

It was necessary to stand erect as I shoved my body along close to the house, then by a window—and so, nearer that front door. Billings might have looked from that doorway and not seen me if I had snaked toward him on my stomach—but the danger was too great. If he saw me, then I'd have to shoot from an awkward position—and besides, I'd have to climb to my feet and dash in the doorway and up those stairs. I didn't need to be told that the first shot would mean the death of Danny and the girl. Nothing short of this Beast's death would save the boy and the girl from him now. I licked dry lips and slid along.

I reached the doorway—just to the side of it—without the head of Billings once coming into view. I held my gun forward, and waited. The seconds went like hours—but no head appeared; just the unsteady shuffling of feet. And I waited— waited without knowing what took place on the floor above.

Somewhere far off in the darkness of that dismal house there came a scream—the scream of a woman. Milly! Was it the shriek of fear or pain—and I felt that it was pain—physical pain too.

33

Face to Face

I could wait no longer. The feet scraped inside the doorway and I stepped forward—jammed my gun against soft flesh and spoke.

"A single word—a single cry—and they'll bury you beside Ed Jackson."

Luck was with me this time, for Billings had evidently turned at that cry and now his back was to me. He didn't speak—didn't cry out—just sort of made a gurgling sound deep in his throat.

"Your gun, Billings—slip it behind you. So—" I took the gun from his nervous fingers before he dropped it. Like his kind, Billings didn't have the guts when the show-down came. He knew who was behind him—knew my voice, I guess—and he knew how quickly I'd shoot too. I wasn't bluffing—one peep out of Billings and I'd of shot him through the back. Make no mistake about that.

"Don't kill me," he muttered, "don't, Williams. I give you my word I won't holler a warning—won't run away—if you—don't kill me. I give you my word of honor."

"That's fine, Billings," I whispered close to his ear. "And don't talk any more. Your word is your bond with me—just kneel so, at my feet—while I bind your hands. There—" He knelt without a murmur—just sunk to his knees on the worn old mat before the door as I whispered on. "It will never be said that I didn't trust to the word of an honorable gentleman like you—so—" Maybe the rest of it isn't pretty to write. More of the brute to it and less of the man, you think. I wasn't thinking of my own life when I struck Billings—I was thinking of the girl upstairs—and the cry I had just heard. But I won't apologize. I laid Billings out with a crack behind the ear, with the barrel of my forty-four. Just one blow, and without even a groan he spread himself out upon the mat. If he bothered any one again that night I'd be very much surprised. When I club a man I can tell you within an hour when he's going to sit up and ask who else was on the wrecked train. Billings would be a peaceful citizen for a good five hours.

I was in the house now; no light to guide me—nothing but a mumbled, jumbled sound that might have come from above, and might have come from my own throbbing head. However, I found the stairs and made my way up them toward that jumble. I should have gathered up my flash when I left the shack—but I didn't and that was all of that. I wasn't exactly in a position to have a messenger go back for it.

The girl screamed again. I half stumbled and regained my balance as Danny began to beg for his life. I could hear his cracked voice echoing from behind a closed door, and I caught too the laugh of The Beast—a high-pitched, hysterical note in it. And I found the door—turned the knob—backed my shoulder against it for the final rush—and it opened. A scream from Danny drowned the creak of the door, and I stepped into the dark room. Dark, but for a single stretch of light that came from curtains that were not tightly enough drawn, separating this room from an adjoining one.

The voice of The Beast came to me now—thick with passion—yet high with fulfilled passion, I guess you might call it.

212

"So—my Pretty," he was saying, "we go out for one scream and we fetch two—what a remarkably sharp knife it must be. But I am sorry for you—yet, it is through you that I bring the agony into a Davidson—I'm afraid, my dear, you'll have to die first. And Danny shall watch and see—"

The girl cut in as I reached the curtain—and her voice was remarkably steady, even if her words did race a bit onto each other. It was as if she talked against time.

"Listen, Raphael Dezzeia," she hurried on, "you told me that by coming here I could save this Race Williams. Why not go through with it—why not take this money—Danny's money? He'll get it when his sister dies, and you say yourself she can't live but a few days. Come—his life—my life—and Race Williams' life for this vast wealth. Think—Oscar Merrill Davidson is to inherit it all. Is it likely that he'll give you so much—half so much; isn't it just possible he may give you nothing? You trapped Race Williams through Danny, promising Danny his life if he got him here. As for me—I'd of bitten out my tongue before I put Race Williams in your hands."

The Beast laughed and I looked through the curtains. Danny was there—white and straight—propped up in a chair, to which his arms and legs were bound. But more attention had been given to the tying of the girl. Her hands were bound behind her—and a rope was even wound about her neck, holding her head straight. A few flecks of blood were on her cheek. The man known as The Beast was partly sideways to me. There were the puffed cheeks and the eerie, colorless green eyes—the thick lips and the great mass of hair, for he wore no hat. In his hand he held a sharp pointed knife—almost like a stiletto, but a bit thicker.

"I shall have it all." The huge shoulders of The Beast came up, rolling the back of his neck into great animal like folds. "This uncle is a Davidson—after we bleed him we'll let the truth come out. For others must be paid—it is a great organization that works for me, and they must have their bonus. Though most of them were glad to work for nothing where

213

the life of Race Williams was involved."

"Why kill him?" the girl cut in. "He has nothing to do with us—with Danny—with your hatred of the Davidsons. Let him go—and I— Don't—" she shrieked suddenly. "Not that again—kill me if you must, but not that—that knife."

The Beast laughed before he spoke.

"A bit louder, my Pretty—Danny does not hear so well. Come! once more. She died hard, did Danny's mother—and not a cent from his father to even bury her. There—I'll drag the knife—so."

And Danny's shriek of horror drowned out the roar of my gun.

But The Beast knew. The hand that held the knife dropped to his side and the knife itself rang upon the floor. He didn't turn at once, but swung slowly—a bewildered, surprised look in those colorless eyes—but eyes that glared from beneath shaggy brows just the same—eyes that glared with animal like ferocity.

"'Race Williams' is right." I smiled over at him as I stepped into the room. "Don't act as though you didn't expect me. You see, I'm bullet proof too. Here—hold your ground," I shouted, for he had suddenly bent forward, and clutching up that knife hurled himself toward me—the knife raised in his left hand, his blood stained right held before his face. And I fired again—the bullet must have torn a hole somewhere just above the third button of his vest.

I didn't think about his being bullet proof then and neither did he, I guess. He went down like a thousand tons of brick— dropping in his tracks and crashing against the wall. I shrugged my shoulders slightly as I looked at his huge crum- pled carcass. But as he fell I thought I heard the click of a key—or the rattle of a chain. I stood silently listening, half turned to the door—but the great house gave up nothing but a deadly silence, the jumping breath of Danny, and the quick gasping sob of Milly, as black eyes spoke what trembling lips couldn't utter.

With just a glance at that silent form on the floor, I crossed to the girl—noted that she was bound with rope, not chains—and turning quickly, knelt at The Beast's side and jerked the knife from his fingers. My head began to feel hot as I hacked at the rope that held Milly's throat erect. A mist obscured my vision—a mist that was real and soft and warm. I raised my hand to my head; it was wet—and I knew. The heat of the room had started the blood again. I brushed it from my eyes, freed the girl's hands, and bent toward her feet when she spoke.

"Race—and I thought you were dead. Now—" The knife fell from my grasp and I staggered to my feet, clutching at my gun—for the girl had cried out a warning.

And I saw him before he fired. The Beast was on his feet, his back braced against the wall—a gun in his left hand, and that gun was trained on me.

We fired together. He missed and I hit. But he didn't go down this time—he sort of jarred himself up against the wall and clutched at his side, where the bullet had struck.

I got in three quick shots to his next one. The blood got in my eyes; things were foggy and blurred—but I hit him all right—and what's more important, he hit me. "An eye for an eye" business was going strong, only it should have been "a side for a side," for his bullet cut like a knife above my hip. I'm no bullet proof man either. I knew that I was hit—that it hurt—that if it had been much higher I'd of gone down and not gotten up.

My eyes popped, I guess, when my bullets didn't lay The Beast out. I fired wildly and missed more than once. I could use my left hand again but it wasn't good for sporting a gun—and I found myself with two bullets left, and The Beast still on his feet. He was getting ready to finish me too. It was surprising how bad his aim had been, but it was his own fault. He shot with his left hand and held his right arm up before his face. It was an ugly enough map, but why try and hide it at a time like this. Now he was taking careful aim—his eyes glaring over his arm—just two slits—narrow, mean, piercing, as his broad chest heaved up and down.

My own marksmanship was nothing to blow about. My whole body seemed to tremble, my gun hand wobbled, and the blood trickling from my forehead down into my eyes made the man appear hazy—in sections—as if I looked at him through waving, red beaded curtains.

You can understand how bad I was when I took a shot at his glaring eyes and cracked the gun he was aiming so carefully. Then in sheer weariness my right hand dropped to my side.

The Beast misunderstood that action. He thought it was my last shot, I guess—and he lunged forward, both his hands outstretched—huge hairy things that were reaching for my throat as he staggered across to me. Those hands came nearer—held high—half hiding his face; the left hand a whitish yellow, and hairy—the right, just red. Through blood I looked at blood.

I was tired—about to drop. I braced myself for his coming—ready to throw my gun at him and fight it out with bare hands. Man to man, or beast to beast—more likely, man to beast though. Not much chance for me there. He staggered and lurched, to be sure—while I did neither. If the truth were told I didn't have a good stagger left in me. All my efforts were bent on standing erect and keeping the floor from coming up and slapping me in the face.

On he came! The impossible—the bullet proof man who— And as those hands reached out for my throat I saw it—the glitter of it—the torn vest and the twisted steel beneath. I know now what that clink of chain came from, and also why his arm constantly guarded his face.

Two hands reached for my throat—and my right hand came up. Thick lips snarled, great teeth parted—and his mouth opened for the shout of triumph as those hands felt for

216

my neck. And I fired my last shot—not into that generous bulk that had tempted me before, but straight into that red, yawning mouth. We'd see how his digestive system worked. The secret of the bullet proof body was out; he wore a shirt of steel chain.

34

A Last Stand

He died funny. Yep, I got a laugh out of it; a weird, gurgling sort of a laugh. His mouth seemed to close upon the bullet, as if he tried the taste of it—and his arms still stretched toward me. Then those twitching fingers closed on the empty air; the great head with the matted hair ducked down upon his chest.

He died on his feet, but unless you looked straight into those sightless eyes you wouldn't have known it. His feet gave slowly and doubled up beneath him. He slipped to his knees, knelt so a moment—as if in prayer—then pitched forward on his face. Dead? He was as cold as an old maid's smile.

I stood there and looked down at him; this bullet proof business cleared up. Of course that steel vest or shirt, or chain mail—or whatever you call it—had saved his life before. And he didn't pitch to the ground to fool me—not much he didn't; forty-fours may not get through good steel— but if you're hit with one it'll knock you; and The Beast was feeling those shots when they landed square—just the glancing ones that shied off had no effect on him. So he held his body sort of twisted and protected his face— yet, I'd lay a nice bet that a couple of my bullets had left dents in him big enough to stick your hand in. It was the simplicity of the thing that helped him put it over.

I didn't look down long—the effect was bad; like looking from a great height. How Milly got to me I'm not sure. I guess she untied her own feet. Anyway there she was—dabbing at my forehead. She was a remarkable little woman—another would be fainting now. And that thought was hardly out when Milly started to do her stuff—sort of crumple up against me.

"Lay off, Kid," I muttered. And then as a queer sort of groan came from Danny, "There's Danny—he needs you."

It braced her. She did a straight up, turned and went to the boy. I saw her bending over him—not much nerve, had Danny; he was grunting like a stuffed pig.

Bang! Maybe it was the wind, but certainly a door down-stairs had slammed. Footsteps too—no mistake about that—many of them; on the porch—in the hall below—on the stairs. Were the gang in the car coming back? That must be it. They'd find Billings, and guess at the rest. I thought I saw it all. They had stopped at the shack—seen the dead Ed Jackson and hurried back.

"Come here, Kid," I called hoarsely across to the girl. For the life of me I was afraid to move; but I could see fairly well and my brain was not so bad.

"Quick!" I told the girl when she reached my side. "Much depends on you now—maybe, Danny's life. Lead me to that table—there. Not so fast." Damn my knees; was I going to cave in now? But she got me to the flat table that faced the curtains of the room beyond, and I flopped into the chair, took a quick breath and coughed out my orders.

"My other gun—left coat pocket—that's it." She tugged it out and slipped it into my right hand. Six shots now. I propped my elbow on the table, half leaned back in the high stiff chair, and watched those curtains that led to the anteroom. "Now—that handkerchief—around my head, so—mustn't have the blood in my eyes. The boys are coming back."

"Beat it, Kid," I told her, when she had bound up my head.

"It looks like curtains—I'll stick it out. But one more shot—"

"You think it's death?" She was crying now—snuffling like.

"Beat it—" I waved my hand; then decided I wouldn't try that little experiment again—it sent my head rocking like a boat. "Steady, boy—" I told myself. After all, it was going to be one glorious end—five of them—six shots; if they didn't knock me over first! But perhaps I could make it a round half dozen of us. It was hard though, holding the gun steady like that. I began to wish they'd come—I couldn't keep my arm up much longer. Would they crowd in the door or come one at a time?

There was a weight on my shoulders; something pressing me down. I tried to shake it off but it wasn't mental this time—the thing was physical and real. It was the girl. She hadn't gone yet—and the feet were on the stairs; cautious, creeping feet—but I heard them.

Arms went around my neck—a wet cheek brushed mine.

"I love you, Race," Milly was saying. "Very, very much. I want you to know—to take it—away with you—in the thing beyond—we may have trouble finding—I—finding you—and—"

"You'll find me all right—I'll be sitting with the old boy himself." And some one laughed—shrilly—a hoarse, weird laugh like—like— and I jerked up my slumping body. That laugh was mine—and Milly loved me—she was telling me so.

"There's the boy, Danny." I thought aloud. The Kid had a duty, you know.

"Danny—" a bit of sob, and then, "he's dead—just—just his heart, I guess."

I nodded at that—I remembered that heart. It had skipped over a beat at last, and missed on the pick up. And Milly loved me. When I spoke again my voice seemed to come out of my chest.

"The dead so soon grow cold." Funny that I got that off. It was years since I had read Oscar Wilde or any of his wise cracks. But it fitted in at last—I hadn't seen much sense to it then. Now—

"You must understand." She was talking fast. "It was pity for him—remorse for the deed I had unknowingly done—and if he'd lived I'd of married him if he wanted me and gone through with it—but it's you I love. There's no way to explain—I wouldn't ever tell you if—but I even threatened Briskey with the police to get that thousand to help Danny. I—"

And the feet were in the hall—many feet—louder—by the door—I heard them plainly.

"Beat it, Kid," I said again. "By the window—I'm—"

"I'm going to stick," I heard her mutter as the feet crossed the room.

Somehow I pushed her off. I couldn't sit like that. Not me—not Race Williams. I'd go out on my feet. It took all I had to come erect but I did it, and was standing there when the curtains parted.

"Come in, boys." I just bellowed out the words. "It's Race Williams—hell ain't filled up yet—not yet—not yet." And I couldn't make the gun work—and I couldn't lift my hands and I— But I saw them—many of them—the blue of the uniform—the slouch hat and the racing cigar of Inspector Coglin. And I laughed. Somehow I couldn't help it. He looked funny—wild eyed—surprised; and the cigar got stuck and wouldn't travel any further. And—the floor did its stuff at last; just came up and slapped me in the face. Rough that? No, I can't say that it was. It felt kind of good—and restful.

The cops made a lot of fuss—tramped around above and below and raised particular. Coglin talked; and I—a question kept buzzing in my head. "Why had Barton Briskey come to me?" It just obscured everything else and wouldn't let me think clearly. If I knew that I could have died in peace.

From a long way off the voice of Inspector Coglin buzzed.

"The Beast is dead—and the boy too—I wonder when the boy died—that's important—he's warm and—" He turned to me. "This thing they called The Beast was a notorious English criminal. He was this boy's stepfather—Raphael Dezzeia."

"Why bother?" I laid back against the pillows that had somehow slipped into the chair. "He's dead and that's the ticket; you can straighten that out with the authorities—and another lad or two. But— Who put you wise to this joint?"

"A lady—a very temperamental and abusive lady, who telephoned me at your house. She gave us a tip that picked up a pretty bunch of five men, who were speeding back to the city. She told me something else too."

"What else? Did she tell you why Barton Briskey visited me?" You see, the thing was still there.

"No—but she told me everything else. About the plot of Oscar Merrill Davidson—the vengeance of Raphael Dezzeia—referred me to this gentleman here whom we brought along. Mr. Oliver Cronin."

And a little old man stepped into the room.

"A most distressing affair." He addressed me, Coglin, and the slumped figure of Danny in the chair. "Very sad, Mr. Williams. But I think that the dead boy here is entitled to the money. I have had charge of the trusts for years. Coglin has spoken well of you; now, I have heard and seen for myself. If I have anything to say in the matter I shall see that your fee is paid—in full." That last line of the little lawyer went right to my heart. He knew his groceries all right—a calm little runt as he leaned upon his cane and looked down at the bloated face of The Beast, whom one of the policemen had turned over on his back.

"Ah—yes." Mr. Cronin tightened his glasses upon the bridge of his long nose. "Raphael Dezzeia—the man who first brought strife into the Davidson home. A sad affair—but if a house be divided against itself that house cannot stand."

"How come Danny got the—would have gotten the money?" It was hard for me to get out the words—but I licked my dry lips and did.

"Why—he's just died, you know—and his sister died at six o'clock this afternoon—at Dr. DeLancy's Sanitarium on Sev-

222

enty-fourth Street. She'd been sick for some time; each day Oscar Merrill Davidson called up from Washington—he seemed so interested that she live."

He went on talking but I didn't hear him. I was thinking, thinking hard. Barton Briskey had come to me—he knew of the girl's death then.

"Barton Briskey—" I gulped it out. "He knew of her death—the death of Muriel Davidson?"

"Yes, yes, he did." And with real feeling in his voice, "The crooked little shyster was leaving the hospital just as I went in."

"Did her uncle know?" I asked.

"No." Cronin shook his head. "He called up from Washington less than an hour before she died. They reported her condition the same as usual. After that came the sudden turn."

But I didn't listen to any more. I had the answer to my question. I knew why Barton Briskey had come to me. With the death of the girl the money had gone into Danny's hands. Briskey at once jumped with the money; came to me and tried to make the best deal that he could. But Danny wasn't dead then—and Briskey didn't know that Danny had told me he was leaving the money to his sister. So—why it would come back to Oscar Merrill Davidson again. But I didn't bother to think any more.

I heard Coglin telling me that he had telephoned the police at Washington to arrest Oscar Merrill Davidson on the strength of the blonde's story—for it was she who had called him on the phone.

"You won't arrest—Milly?" I put the question to Coglin as they carried me from the house and into the waiting car. "She came here to help me." And when he didn't answer at once, "Come clean, Coglin—what do you intend to do with her?"

"Technically, you're both under observation." Coglin had the cigar working again now. "But things will break all right. A good night's work—I'll stick to you, Race."

"And the Kid?" Words were beginning to stick in my

223

throat and Inspector Coglin began to float around a bit—an airy-fairy sort of drifting movement that wasn't in tune with the dominant chin, the hard eyes, and the thick black cigar. I was slipping and I felt pretty cheap not to be able to stick it out now.

"And the Kid?" I tried again—and although I shouted the words only a whisper came back to me. "She's a good Kid."

But he heard me all right, for he answered,

"And the Kid, Race."

I smiled and nodded—felt the little hand that crept into mine—wondered that Coglin's mit could be so soft and tiny—and—some one pulled down the curtain, shutting off the light.

35

Bon Voyage!

There was a ride—a woman or a girl crying—a man talking—
and something biting at my arm, tearing at my head and
chewing at my side. Somehow I was in a thick forest and The
Beast was there. I fired wildly and he fell, and I laughed and
up he jumped—then another and another, until I was shooting in a circle; but they were on me—a dozen or a hundred
snarling animals. Down I went in the struggling mass—
clutched at a hairy arm, felt teeth sink into my hip and—I
opened my eyes.

A white coat—a white sheet—a white clad woman—white
walls—and the black head of a girl who leaned against a door
and a big man who held her. Then a face and a cigar—and I
knew. I was in a hospital.

"He'll do nicely now." A face jumped out of the white coat,
spun around—and the white coat drifted across the room,
pinched at the cheeks of the girl in the doorway, and laughed
softly before it spoke.

"Bless your heart, there's nothing to cry about. Another
week or ten days and we'll need to tie him in bed. Go talk to
him if you wish—his head'll swim, but—" And I heard no
more.

It was Coglin who came to the bed and leaned over it.

"I suppose I shouldn't get this off—but if I were laid out and a case bothered me, I'd like to know the breaks. We've been in touch with Washington. A girl had called Oscar Merrill Davidson on the telephone before the police reached his hotel. Who she was or what she said can only be guessed at—but Davidson has put a bullet behind his ear. What do you say to that?"

So died the unseen actor in the tragedy; the last of the Davidsons went out by his own hand.

"Hell hath no fury like a woman scorned," I muttered. "Their love and their vengeance is hard to understand."

"Their love—yes," Coglin muttered. And I saw him glance back over his shoulder at the little figure that still stood in the doorway.

"Can you sign a bit of paper? Cronin would like a look at that will of Danny's, I guess."

"There isn't much you don't know." I looked at him.

"Not much." Coglin nodded. "That woman said a lot in a short time—but I haven't peeped—to Cronin even."

"Have a representative from the bank bring that envelope to me here in the morning—Cronin can show up too—but there'll be no monkey business."

"You'd better see the Kid." Coglin jerked a thumb over his shoulder, and when I said nothing, "She's a good Kid." He mimicked my former words. So I waved a hand for him to beat it, and another toward the girl in the doorway.

"Oh, Race," was all she said as she came and sat upon the bed—but she didn't need to say more. As Coglin said—she was a good Kid.

One talks foolish at times—and I did—and she did—and Coglin and the nurse had no right to leave us alone—but I was young and she was young—and I wasn't very strong. Besides, some one went and shut the door.

The next day Cronin read that will in the little hospital room. There were Milly and Coglin, and they had propped me up a bit. It left most everything to Danny's sister, if she was still alive. But in the case of her death, Danny left all to "Mildred Ferris."

I looked at Milly and she nodded, but she couldn't speak. After all, names don't count for much.

"There is no one to contest the will." Cronin smiled at his rich client. "It's a great fortune—I'm sure this young lady will do a great deal of good with it."

"I don't want it." Milly set her lips tightly as she looked at me. "I couldn't touch it—let it go to charity."

But Cronin shook his head.

"It isn't that kind of an inheritance," he told her. "It's mostly interest on trust funds, the principals of which won't fall due for some time. It's easier to shirk one's responsibilities than to accept them. With this money and a little labor on your part you can do a greater good than—"

Milly started in to speak again—but I cut in.

"You take it, Kid," I told her. "Then if you owe any debts, pay them."

"Any debts—" she started and stopped. "Yes—perhaps I do—perhaps there are many others who have sunk as low as I have and—"

"Not risen so high." I shut her up. After all, it's bad to talk for an audience.

Milly, rich, was another thing. Yet, I couldn't get away from her. They kept me in that hospital, and she was there—always there. I pretended even to myself I didn't want her—but I did.

"You told me you cared," she kept saying over and over. "That first night here, before the will—now—I'll give up the money before I'll give you up; unless of course you don't—don't care." And she had a way of getting that off that made my blood run hot and fast.

It was a lot of money—still, each conversation ended with the slip of a girl's head down on my chest. What a woman I had thought her—and what a child she really was! Given half the chance—but why keep writing this? It was real and wonderful and hardly believable to me—but mush to the outsider. It all depends upon whose chest the head is on, I guess.

Is there more to tell? I don't know. I got Milly shipped off to Europe; she must get away from old associates for a time. Somehow her wealth leaked out, and scum of the underworld suddenly remembered their undying devotion to her, to say nothing of blackmail. When I got on my feet I'd put a stop to that—even now, when Coglin came in and the nurses were out I got to cleaning my guns.

The Kid was gone and I was out. We both had time to think—she was to write me from Europe if she still thought the same of me. And I was to come if I still thought the same of her—or the same as she thought I thought of her, if you can make anything out of that. Did she write? Only once a day, with cables in between.

Did I go? I don't know—so you don't know. The old proverb still rang in my ears. "He travels farthest who travels alone." But does he get any place? Is it like a trip on a merry-go-round? Of course I've always said that I'm not a marrying man, but I have also said ANYTHING IS POSSIBLE TO-DAY.

We'll let it go at that—except perhaps to say—that I got in a row last night about an outside stateroom on one of the fastest ships sailing to England. About money! It may seem hard boiled but I put in my bill against the Davidson Estate and got paid in jig time too. We mustn't get sloppy over business matters you know. Besides I don't think any one will deny I earned the money and since Coglin and I had split the price on The Beast's head I was dough heavy.

So—bon voyage! I'd always thought of taking a trip to Europe anyway.